Rachel Augusta Whiting

Golden Memories of an Earnest Life

A Biography of A.B. Whiting

Rachel Augusta Whiting

Golden Memories of an Earnest Life
A Biography of A.B. Whiting

ISBN/EAN: 9783337074647

Printed in Europe, USA, Canada, Australia, Japan

Cover: Foto ©Andreas Hilbeck / pixelio.de

More available books at **www.hansebooks.com**

GOLDEN MEMORIES

OF

AN EARNEST LIFE.

A BIOGRAPHY OF A. B. WHITING:

TOGETHER WITH SELECTIONS FROM

HIS POETICAL COMPOSITIONS AND PROSE WRITINGS.

COMPILED BY HIS SISTER,

R. AUGUSTA WHITING.

INTRODUCTION

By REV. J. M. PEEBLES.

His years, 'tis true, were few;
His *life* was long.

We live in deeds, not years;
In thoughts, not breaths.

BOSTON:
WILLIAM WHITE AND COMPANY,
" BANNER OF LIGHT" OFFICE,
No. 158 Washington Street.
1872.

Stereotyped at the Boston Stereotype Foundry,
19 Spring Lane.

TO THE

SPIRITUALISTS OF AMERICA,

WHOSE CAUSE HE SERVED THROUGH LIFE AND WITH HIS LATEST
STRENGTH; TO THE *MUSIC-LOVING WORLD* THAT CLAIMED
HIS FELLOWSHIP; TO THE *FRIENDS* WHO LOVED
HIM; AND TO THE *LOVERS OF FREE*
THOUGHT AND FREE SPEECH
EVERYWHERE,

This Brief Memorial-Record,

THE LIFE-STORY OF A FIRM AND CONSISTENT ADVOCATE OF THE
SCIENCE, PHILOSOPHY, AND RELIGION OF SPIRITUALISM;
A TUNEFUL SOUL, A FAITHFUL FRIEND, AND
RESOLUTE DEFENDER OF PRINCIPLE
UNDER ALL CIRCUMSTANCES,

IS MOST RESPECTFULLY DEDICATED

BY THE AUTHOR.

PREFACE.

DESPITE well-established custom, I would willingly waive the privilege of delaying the reader with prefatory remarks, were it not that I desire to acknowledge courtesies received, and state a few explanatory facts, for which there seems no other suitable place.

Soon after the close of my brother's earth-life, I began to be urged by friends — visible and invisible — to undertake the task of preparing for the press a *résumé* of his life and labors. I was assured, by those who best knew him and the world, that a record of his career and peculiar experiences could not fail to be of interest, not only to the many who knew him in his public capacity, but to a large class of minds who seek to learn concerning unusual phases of life and mental phenomena. Circumstances had rendered me the most — if not the only — suitable person to perform this labor. While, therefore, I felt keenly the responsibility of the undertaking, I felt equally that which would rest upon me should I withhold aught that might tend in the slightest degree to benefit the world or more deeply enshrine his memory.

I accepted the task, and arranged my material as time would permit, but was not able to enter upon the work until January, 1872. Simultaneously occurred my entrance upon the rostrum; but, for the succeeding four months, the most of my time was given to this work, and also the intervals between lectures since that time.

My material has been ample, — consisting of a journal

5

extending from 1852 to 1862, and complete files of letters from the latter date down. To this is added my own perfect knowledge of his life during later years, and copious data furnished by other parties, whom it would be impossible to mention in detail, but to all of whom I desire to offer my sincere thanks.

I have abridged as much as possible, and generally preferred to relate facts without note or comment. Of course a sketch of this kind can contain but a very small portion of *all* the events of a life, and the selection of those most prominent is no easy task when so much must remain untold. I have endeavored, as far as possible, to confine myself to the principal events of his public life, giving only those of a private character which had a molding influence upon his public career. For the rest, — the rich joys and deep sorrows of the inner life, which words are too poor to hold, — they belong to those who loved him, to the friends who knew him true, and any attempt at their portrayal would not only be vain, but needlessly expose to public gaze matters sacred to private life.

For the frequent mention of myself in the course of the narrative I have no apology to offer; for, from that far-off day when he took me in *his* arms and soothed my baby grief, to that other day when *mine* sustained his failing strength, the fibers of our lives have been so intertwined, that it is impossible to entirely separate the closely-woven threads. The faint outline contained in Chapter II. will perhaps explain this as well as I am able to do. It is for this reason that I have chosen not to attempt to conceal my personality, lest in so doing I should be guilty of a mere refinement of egotism, and have only claimed the reportorial privilege of alluding to myself in the third person in relating those events which occurred previous to my own remembrance.

As the major part of the narrative was written at our home (Albion, Mich.), I have maintained that stand-point throughout, — although a portion has been compiled else-where, — during a lecture engagement at Albany, N. Y., a visit to the town of our birth, and a stay of some weeks in this city.

I wish to add a few words in reference to the contents of Part Second. The poems are not presented as models of metrical composition, but as purely improvisations. They were, without exception, written entirely impromptu, and as rapidly as hand could move a pencil, and were never either corrected or copied by him. I have chosen, however, to present them entirely unchanged, with the exception of supplying obvious omissions. I do not consider them equal in literary merit to his usual spoken improvisa-tions; nor did he, but always complained of the impos-sibility of writing fast enough to catch the lines as they traversed his thought, and consequent blunders in tran-scription. It was partly for this reason that of late years he had almost abandoned the attempt to write anything save the words of his songs. Those were, for the most part, as I have stated elsewhere, composed simultaneously with the music, while sitting at the instrument, and written down from memory afterward.

Those comprised under the heading "Published Songs" are included here by permission of the several publishers. They are issued in sheet music form, as follows : —

Groups I. and II., by J. L. Peters, New York, N. Y.
Groups III. and IV., by Whittemore, Swan & Stephens, Detroit, Mich.
Group V., by C. J. Whitney & Co., Detroit, Mich.
Group VI., by J. S. White & Co., Marshall, Mich.
Group VII. will be found in the "Spiritual Harp."

I have hesitated whether I should include here the words of two songs which were not entirely his composition, but have decided to do so, with this explanation, in order that the list may be complete. I allude to the piece entitled " O, tell me not of Fields of Glory," which was written by me at his request, after he had composed the music, and that called " The Outcast," the substance of which was furnished him by a lady friend, and by him adapted to music, with the addition of the refrain and the name, Evyrr Allynn.

Under the head of " Unpublished Songs," I have gathered a few poems, the music for which was never completed, or has been lost. Besides these, he has left a number of complete compositions, which I contemplate arranging for publication uniform with his other music, as soon as time will permit, and which, therefore, are not included here for obvious reasons.

As I take leave of my completed task, it is with the earnest hope that the result may not wholly disappoint the expectations of those by whose solicitation and encouragement it was undertaken, however much it may fall short of my ideal of what might be compiled in the way of an interesting and instructive narrative — a worthy tribute to his memory.

It may fail to command any general attention, any marked recognition at the hands of the public ; yet I dare dream that, at least, many will gladly welcome it for the sake of the pleasant memories it evokes, and, so dreaming, am content.

R. Augusta Whiting.

Boston, July 16, 1872.

CONTENTS.

CHAPTER XIV.

CHAPTER XV.

CHAPTER XVI.

CHAPTER XVII.

CHAPTER XVIII.

PART SECOND.

EARLY POEMS.

WRITTEN IMPROVISATIONS.
1855–1857.

FRAGMENTARY POEMS.

UNPUBLISHED SONGS.

PUBLISHED SONGS.
GROUP I. " THREE HEART OFFERINGS."

ABSTRACT OF LECTURE

INTRODUCTION.

"Presumptuous skepticism, which rejects facts without examination of their truth, is in some respects more injurious than unquestioning credulity." — *Baron Humboldt.*

"Before experience itself can be used with advantage, there is one preliminary step to make, which depends wholly on ourselves: it is the absolute dismissal and clearing the mind of all prejudice, from whatever source arising, and the determination to stand and fall by the result of a direct appeal to facts in the first instance, and a strict logical deduction from them afterward."—*Sir John Herschel.*

"Spiritualism is at once a science and a religion, based upon tangible *facts.*" — *Prof. S. B. Brittan.*

"Behold how they loved him." — *Gospel of John.*

HUMAN life is twofold, — physical existence and spiritual consciousness, — and history is its story.

In the University of Strasburg there flourished in the early part of this century a worthy student of nature, who, during thirty years of toil, collected and classified a museum of *facts.* The industry was admirable; continental scholars were grateful; but this gathering, this numbering of items, these labeled skeletons, strung with nicest precision,

15

did not constitute history. The inspiration of living genius was wanting.

Facts are as paints and brushes to artists. They symbolize ideal truths, and, if rightly applied, picture real life. Instead of being considered as isolated phenomena, facts must be studied in connection with their causes. They must be resolved into groups, and put in relational order. Then, master minds, tracing the consequences that uniformly follow, may reach and announce logical conclusions. This is properly the method of inductive study, and relates to those physical manifestations connected with the science of Spiritism.

Traversing in thought the mystical river of time, it is clearly seen that humanity is but an aggregate of individuals, and that biography, though a record of personal motive and action, is fraught with almost infinite consequences.

Seeing is knowing. Eulogy and invective are equally blind. To fully measure, to really profit by the life of another, we must grasp the hand, hear the voice, feel the heart beat, watch the ebb and flow of fortune, suffer the stings of partial defeat ; and, considering the rapid march of the truth mutually loved, join with fellow-pilgrims also in peans of gladness.

Intimacy of this kind not only conduces to happiness and fraternal sympathy, but, giving opportunities for genuine insight into the mysterious currents of being, it unrolls the life-leaves of character and reveals the *man*.

These were just the privileges granted us by our neighbor,

friend, and co-worker in the cause of Spiritualism, A. B. Whiting, while a resident of Michigan.

Each individual is not only a radiating center of force, but a spirit — a conscious spirit, *now* existing in harmony with the lyrical principles of the universe, though encased in a mortal body. And it is a proposition too plain to require proof, that wherever the spirit or mind can reach, there it can observe ; and wherever it can observe, there it can induct ; and wherever it can induct, there it can discover. This Baconian train of reasoning, made practical, bridged the two worlds, — the to-day and the to-morrow of existence, — leaving the gates of immortality ajar. Longfellow, aflame with the inspiration of spirit communion, sings that

> " From the *world of spirits* there descends
> A bridge of light connecting it with this."

As Protestantism in Luther's time was a protest against Roman Catholicism, so Spiritualism is a protest against this puritanical Protestantism, that constructs creeds, cramps the intellect, crushes the soul's aspirations, and throws a vail of doubt over a future conscious existence, by denying the reality of present converse with the world of spirits.

Protestant theology, though voiced from thousand pulpits, has proved to be the barren fig tree of the eighteenth and nineteenth centuries. Angels and advanced souls in the heavens, seeing the utter failure, initiated the spiritual dispensation. The opening cycle, recognizing the message, the cradle, the manger-home, was in Hydesville, N. Y., a place of more note than Nazareth, in Syria.

If " holy women of Palestine," mediumistic and intuitive, were the first to announce, "*He is not here, but risen,*" good and true women in the morning hour of this spiritual era were the first to devise the method for translating these telegraphic tickings into readable language, revealing the progress and conscious blessedness that obtain in the love-lands of the angels !

Modern Spiritualism, complementing, differs from that of Jesus and John only in the superior number of its manifestations, in the increasing variety of its marvels, the better understanding of its philosophy, the general concession of its naturalness, and its wider dissemination through the different grades of society.

The rapid diffusion of the divine principles involved in Spiritualism has astonished conservatives.   Heaven-born and angel-guarded, it already occupies an enviable position.   The march of the movement has been marvelous ; it is cosmopolitan ; its banner floats beneath all skies, and its sun of inspiration illumines the most distant islands of earth.   English thinkers have admitted it into the fold of the sciences.   Professor William Crookes, an eminent chemist, Fellow of the Royal Society, and editor of the " London Quarterly Journal of Science," has, in a recent issue, an extensive review of Robert Dale Owen's " Debatable Land," under the heading, "*Notices of Scientific Works.*"   The distinguished English naturalist and writer upon the Darwinian philosophy, . A. R. Wallace, treating of the

"Spiritualism" in the "Debatable Land," says, "It is certainly, as Mr. Owen maintains, a science of itself; a *new science*, and one of the most overwhelming importance in its bearings upon philosophy, history and religion." These and other admissions of learned men on both continents mark an era in our progress, putting "Spiritualism" squarely before the world as a *science!*

> "The promise still outruns the deed —
> The tower, but not the spire, we build."

Among the faithful, energetic workmen, who, early entering the vineyard, aided to bring about this recognition of Spiritualism as a science, this public acknowledgment of its moral worth and beauty as a mighty redemptive power in the world, was A. B. Whiting, now risen and robed in the vestures of immortality. The blood of a noble ancestry flowed in his veins. He was born a seer. In the sunny years of childhood he was considered strange, because he saw angels and conversed with the gods. This juvenile clairvoyance had much to do in shaping his future. It was to him a light from heaven. Immortal teachers, in lute-like words of promise, prophesied a career before him of great usefulness. While the flush of early youth was upon his cheek, few fully comprehended him. Mystics given to glimpsing visions delight to be alone. In a higher sense, media, as stars in constellations, are never alone. Converse with celestial visitants bears but little relation to solitude.

Commencing his public labors as a trance-speaker some-

time during the year 1855, he continued in the field, under
the inspiration of his efficient spirit guides till his translation to the Better Land, winning laurels and golden
opinions as an improvisatore, speaker, public debater, and
poet. The songs that gave such zest to his services were
original words and music.

As a lecturer upon the rise and fall of civilizations, and
upon ecclesiastical history, touching its relations to religious persecution on the one hand, and Spiritualism upon
the other, he had no equal upon the rostrum. Sentences
dropped from his lips like pearls, chaining and charming
the multitude. His controlling intelligence when speaking
was GIOVANNI FARÍNI, an Italian poet and cardinal, flourishing early in the seventeenth century. Another of his
ministering spirits was an ancient wise man of the East, or,
as he termed himself, "*the old man of the mountains,*" —
AB-DEL-MURETT-EL-ZULEKE. When under the direct influence of this eccentric sage, who passed to the higher existence early in the twelfth century, Mr. Whiting was truly
a prophet, changed and transfigured. This is the nature of
positive spirit influence ; it affects, fashions, *molds* media,
more or less, into the image of those who pour upon them
currents of baptismal magnetism. Conscious of this, aware
of the fountain from whence flowed his spiritual strength
and inspiration, our noble co-laborer awarded the honor,
like a true man, to his attending guides.

For the monument of Thermopylæ, where fell the brave
three hundred, Leonidas wrote this epitaph : " Stranger, go
and tell in Lacedæmon that we fell here in defense of her

laws." With cause for greater gratitude, let us tell to future time the story of our media and comrade's deeds in lecture-fields, with a monument that shall say, "*Pilgrims journeying to that bourn beyond the crystal river, go and proclaim through the limits of the land, that we, soldiers of truth, — we, media for the manifestations, — by over-work, sacrificed our lives, and found premature graves, in the defense of the principles of the spiritual philosophy.*"

What matters it though no flinty obelisk point to heaven; though no broken column symbolize a fading mortality; though no sculptured rose, drooping on its shattered stem, or gorgeous pile, indicate the place of the changing dust? There are hallowed memories and blissful recollections of our loved, that necessarily live and bloom in perpetual loveliness, live when marble pillars have crumbled to their primitive atoms. Representative men, and the principles they elucidate, are on earth immortal.

With a thinking public, A. B. Whiting was a favorite; with intimate friends, he was cordially beloved. Besides his mediumship and his music, he had many qualities to win esteem. Charitable, candid, and honorable, his history is full of instruction and encouragement to others. With him friendship was a principle, and honor the true badge of loyalty. Deeply do we sympathize with the mother, the sister, and the extensive circle of friends and admirers. But the Spiritualism of which he was an able and eloquent exponent gives us positive assurance that

we shall meet him, know him, and love him in the upper
kingdoms of eternity!

> " O, pale grew the robing that folded the mountain,
>   And wrapped its grieved face in a sorrowing spray,
> Exhaled the last heart-drop from Poesy's fountain,
>   When he sang with angels, at breaking of day.
>
>   .   .   .   .   .
>
> " Be his in Valhalla the throne-room of glory,
>   The scepter of poets, the crown he has won,
> The purple of spirits; and ours be the story,
>   The sweet rhythmed life which at morning was done."

J. M. PEEBLES.

HAMMONTEN, NEW JERSEY.

PART I.

BIOGRAPHY.

BIOGRAPHY.

CHAPTER I.

BIRTH AND LINEAGE. — DOES BLOOD TELL?

THE month of December, 1835, was a time long remembered in the annals of New England as the cold December. On the 12th of the month a heavy snowstorm had fallen, making the roads impassable in many places until the labor of men and teams had cut away the huge drifts. The cold was intense, and had been so continuous that it is chronicled (*vide* "Hill's Meteorological Index") as an unusual circumstance that "on the 14th it thawed a little in the sun." On the morning of that 14th of December, in the village of East Abington, Mass., the subject of this biography made his entrance into a cold world in the most literal sense. But a warm welcome awaited the little stranger in the home he came to gladden, a home of which he was the sunshine and joy all his days, and over whose desolate hearth his loving spirit still watches from the eternal hills.

The town of Abington, which is situated upon the Old Colony Railway, midway between Boston and Plymouth, was also the birthplace of both his parents. His father, Albert Whiting, was born in 1803, and during his youth and early manhood saw something of travel and adventure, both by sea and land, acquiring thereby broader views of life than were common in his time. He was a man of few words, but a close thinker; and when he did speak, his words, few and well chosen, always carried weight. Pre-eminently calm and gentle in all the relations of life, few persons ever saw him moved to anger; yet this not on account of any lack of sensitiveness, but from a natural, inherent power of self-control, which is a strongly-marked trait in all the members of his family. Indeed, this peculiar power, together with accurate and scholarly habits of thought, is clearly traceable through successive generations back even to that remote German ancestor, who, seeking in the then wilds of Virginia an asylum for free thought, brought with him all the lore and culture of a great German university, while leaving behind his baronial title as so much dross. The mother of Albert Whiting was a woman of superior mental endowments; and from *her* family he inherited the musical talent which he, in turn, transmitted to his children.

Of her, further mention will be made in the course of this narrative, as she lived to an advanced age, and formed a prominent feature in the early mental landscape of her grandson.

Albert Whiting was the eldest of five children, of whom the other four, two brothers and two sisters, survive him and still reside in Eastern Massachusetts. On March 9, 1835, he was united in marriage to Miss Rachel Bennet, then of East Bridgewater, she having removed from her native town on her mother's contracting a second marriage, with Mr. David French, of East Bridgewater. This lady, the mother of the subject of this biography, was of English descent, and of a family allied by blood and affinity to many of the noblest names of English history; noble, not alone in rank and title, but in the true nobility of intellect and culture.

Such names as Marlborough, Witherell, North, Guil-
ford, and Dudley, need no prefix to render them illustri-
ous, least of all that brave old Dudley, who, himself accused of sorcery on account of his great learning and
spiritual gifts, not only signally discomfited his ac-
cusers in his own case, but, although then advanced in
years, took a long and tedious journey, traveling night
and day, in order to defend certain persons who were
on trial for the alleged crime of witchcraft, causing their
triumphant acquittal, and by his eloquence producing
such an effect that *that* was the last trial for witchcraft
that ever disgraced the soil of England.

Rachel Bennet was born in 1801, and was the fourth
of six children, of whom she is now the sole survivor,
although her brothers and sisters, with one exception,
attained to an age beyond the average of human life.
Indeed, her mother's family, the Gardners, were remarkable for longevity, her mother reaching her ninetieth
year, and her maternal grandfather his ninety-second.
Her paternal grandmother also lived to an advanced
age, a fair and stately lady, a little proud withal, and
devoted to the memory of the husband who, in the
prime of manhood, laid his life upon his country's altar
during the dark days of the revolution. Her eldest son,
George, the father of Rachel Bennet, also died in middle
life, having served through the war of 1812, and returned home only to battle a few years with consump-
tion, and then pass tranquilly on to that future life
which none of his race ever feared or dreaded, and of
which many of them were able to catch faint glimpses
while yet dwelling in the flesh. His daughter Rachel,
who was about twenty years of age at the time of his
death, had inherited to a great extent his mental organ-

ism and acute spiritual perceptions; and it was feared that she would also develope the same consumptive tendency. She had been slender from childhood, and now, worn out with watching and anxiety, her symptoms become so alarming to her friends that it was thought imperatively necessary to remove her from the keen air of the seaboard for a time. Accordingly she was sent to reside with an uncle in the western part of the state, a long journey in those days of stage-coaches, about equal to a trip across the continent now. There she remained two years, growing well and strong among the hills of Hampshire, and returned to Abington rejoicing in a bodily vigor which she had never known before. Three years later, on her mother's second marriage, as before mentioned, she accompanied her to her new home in East Bridgewater. Seven years passed on, and, though more than one good and honorable man would gladly have shared with her his home and name, she hearkened to the inward voice, which bade her be true to her own soul, and kept on the even tenor of her way, untroubled by that silly dread of the title of "old maid," which drives so many girls to loveless wedlock.

It was during a visit to her oldest brother, then residing in Abington, that she made the acquaintance of Albert Whiting. Both were in the prime of life; both of that noble and engaging presence, which, springing not from mere physical beauty, but from something within and beyond, seldom fails to attract attention and win regard. Their fathers had been friends in youth; each found in the mind of the other many points of sympathy and mental kinship; and the mutual interest thus awakened grew and strengthened into a firm and enduring affection, that true conjugal love which neither

time, nor sorrow, nor the chill waves of the shadowy
river, can change or dim. They were married on the
9th of March, 1835, and their oldest child, the subject
of this biography, was born the December following.
He was named ALBERT BENNET WHITING, but in the
family was usually called by his second name alone.

Born of such lineage, and of parents so truly wedded,
is it wonderful that he should have possessed a massive
intellect, a refined spiritual nature, a warm and loving
heart? *Does* blood tell? Not in that narrow sense in
which the blue blood of royalty has been quoted to sustain the divine right of kings, but in the broad philosophical sense which seeks for each result a cause.
Can a stream rise higher than its fountain? and, if the
source be muddy, will not the stream be, to a certain
extent, impure also? We know that in the career of
nations, races, and civilizations, history constantly repeats itself. Does it not also repeat itself in families,
in the reproduction of certain well-marked traits, characteristics, and capacities, even to the remotest generations? Is there not, therefore, a philosophical reason
for the existence in the human mind of a certain pride
in and respect for honorable ancestry, entirely apart
from and independent of the merely adventitious circumstances of rank and fortune? We have been taught
that pride of birth is a sign of weakness and folly, and I
grant with truth, if it be founded upon mere outward
distinctions; but I believe there is in every soul an in-
born feeling of respect for the memory of one's ancestors. This is by the Chinese exaggerated into worship,
and in many European countries is little less. As
Americans, we have gone to the opposite extreme, and
attempted, in our boasted equality, to make every per-

son look upon his own ancestors in exactly the same light as another's; which is no more natural, or possible, than for us to look upon other people's brothers and sisters as we do upon our own; nor does the fact, that we do not and can not, detract aught from their worth. While, therefore, we concede to all an equal weight in the broad scale of humanity, we can not be blind, either to those real differences that exist, or to those ideal ones which are no less natural; and we may, without shame, confess to that pride of birth, which, being both natural and reasonable, is rather to be commended than rebuked, and which I, for one, will never disown.

CHAPTER II.

CHILDHOOD.—NATURAL SPIRITUAL SIGHT.—BROTHER AND SISTER.—FIRST BEREAVEMENT.—THE MYSTIC TIE.

FOR seven years Albert Bennet remained an only child, his brother Willie being born in 1842, and his only sister two years later. It was fortunate for him that it was so, for he required the most unremitting care and watchfulness of both parents to keep his large and active brain from wearing out his frail body. He early exhibited a wonderful memory, and startled his mother by learning to point out certain letters on the heading of a newspaper before he could speak their names. But, more alarming than all, he saw people and scenes not visible to other eyes. As soon as he could speak he talked about " the people," as he called them, and continued to see these spiritual beings all through his childhood. Sometimes, at night especially, his room would seem full of them, and he could hear them converse with each other about him, and on various subjects. Of course, when he spoke of these things he was told to *hush*, that there was "*no one there*," that it was vapors, or something the matter with his eyes or brain. His mother, more patient with his oddities than others, would say, "Never mind the people ; you will get over such sights when you get older. I used to see just such things when I was a child." This was small consolation, for he loved his ethereal friends, and never feared them, and firmly refused to disbelieve in their identity, having the same consciousness of, and faith in, their care and protection as he felt toward that of his parents. His extreme delicacy of physical constitution caused his parents great anxiety, and the best physicians gave it as their opinion that he could live but a few years, on account of his immense head and slim body. One eccentric old doctor said that he " would like to have him live, to see what he would make," but that it was "impossible for him to see his twelfth year."

When the child would overhear such remarks, the persons making them not supposing he would understand their purport, it made him very angry, and he would say, "I *will* live, for *the people* say so." One instance I will relate : He had just been examined by a celebrated physician, who proceeded to tell his parents, in the usual dogmatic way, that the child " could not possibly live to grow up, and was liable to drop off at any time," when he startled the wise M. D. by exclaiming, " Dr. ——, I will live to visit your grave, for the man in the gray cloak [a spirit] says so, and he knows." (This physician died about fifteen years later, and the prophecy was fulfilled.) This is only one of many similar incidents which attended his early childhood.

He was seldom well enough to be sent to school, but learned at home, with ease and rapidity, everything that was placed before him ; so that, although no effort whatever had been made to hasten his advancement, but rather the contrary, yet when he did enter school he was far in advance of those of his own age. This fact, together with his old manners, made him generally disliked by other children, and so increased his isolation from them. Upon his little brother he lavished the most unbounded affection, and when, as if in answer to his oft-repeated wish, a sister, too, was given him, he was perfectly content. Devoted to their service, he would spend hours amusing "the babies," watching their every motion with all the solicitude of a fond grandmother.

This absorbing employment was of great benefit in diverting his mind from books, for which he already manifested an undue fondness, and fixing it more upon things suitable to his childish years. But soon his little brother Willie sickened and died; and his mind, thus early brought face to face with the great mystery of death, struggled — as many an older mind has done — with all its puny strength, to comprehend the wherefore, the great unsolved problem of the ages. Yet, though his loving heart was almost broken by the loss of his cherished playmate, he did not mourn with the noisy demonstrativeness usual to childhood, but with a silent, repressed grief, which seemed exceeding pitiful to those who understood him, while casual observers said, " He is not old enough to realize his loss." He realized more than would have seemed possible to them. With a tact and thoughtfulness far beyond his years, he strove to divert and console his stricken parents, and when the baby sister called in vain for her vanished playfellow *he* was her surest comforter.

In this fellowship of sorrow there first began to be developed between the two children that peculiar and mysterious bond of sympathy, which, though probably inherent in their mental constitutions, became more strikingly noticeable in later years — a sort of mystic sixth sense, by which the one was enabled to understand the thoughts and feelings of the other when the causes of those thoughts and feelings were beyond cognizance by any ordinary method, and by which any strong emotion or desire of the *one* was inevitably transmitted to the *other*, even at a distance. It is proper to observe, that a tie in some respects similar also existed between the children and their mother, as regards the transmission of any extraordinary mental agitation. I do not pretend to explain or furnish a reason for these singular facts. Such instances have been known to exist in the case of twins, and have furnished much food for speculation, with, I believe, little definite result. We can call it mental telegraphy ; we can say that the similarity of mental structure, which subsists between minds under certain circumstances, may link them together by an ethereal wire, across which may flash messages from soul to soul ; yet the mysterious laws which govern the existence, or non-existence, of this intercommunion are a sealed book, and the angel who shall break the seals hath not yet appeared.

3

Suffice it to say, that the mental relationship between this brother and sister was doubtless the same in kind as that alluded to as sometimes existing between twins, and traceable to the same unknown law; for, despite the nine years' difference in age, the resemblance in mental organization was in most points complete and minute, becoming, however, more strikingly apparent, even to themselves, as added years made the disparity of age less noticeable. This correspondence grew to be so exact, that, when both had arrived at years of maturity, each could count with the utmost certainty upon the opinions and feelings of the other upon any given subject, knowing that, the same data being furnished, they invariably reached identical conclusions. It should not be understood, however, that, with all this generally minute resemblance, there were *no* points of difference to determine for each mind a separate and distinct individuality. These differences, though few, were well defined, and seemed so arranged that the aptitudes which were lacking in one were possessed by the other in unusual degree; thus making, in these respects, the one mind the complement of the other, and increasing their mutual dependence.

That between two thus bound by the very law of their being there should exist the most unreserved confidence, the most unquestioning faith, is natural, and in the nature of things inevitable; for, while perfect *love* casteth out all fear, perfect KNOWLEDGE destroys the possibility of doubt, distrust, or misunderstanding.

I have thought best to give this explanation here, and in this general way, rather than more particularly, and in the order of time in which we came to understand these things, for this reason — that, while the peculiar relationship described as existing between my brother and myself necessarily exerted a powerful influence, permeating the lives of both, yet this influence was so subtle in its character as to defy any attempt to measure its extent or define its limits. Hence only generalization is possible.

As children, we, of course, did not know that there was anything exceptional in the perfect sympathy which we instinctively realized, but supposed the same to exist equally between all brothers and sisters. In this view *I* regarded with most sincere pity those little girls who were not blessed with a " big brother," while *he* looked no less compassionately upon those unfortunate boys who had no " little sister." When observation taught us the fallacy of this belief, we concluded, next, that it was because we were only two that we loved each other more ; but when, to our astonishment and horror, we learned that there was not invariably harmony even between two, — that *this* was not the bond of peace, — we were puzzled indeed.

We were told that " good little children should *always* agree," and in the light of that teaching were forced to conclude that " good little children " were not so plenty as they might be, and, I dare say, regarded that fact as highly complimentary to ourselves. Yet we could not but see that those who made the most constant effort to be kind and forbearing, if not always successful, were more worthy of praise than were we, to whom no effort was necessary. Thus the unsolved problem still haunted us, and would not be dismissed, until time and investigation, throwing light into the dark recesses of mental science, had shown us that our unanimity, and the inharmony we saw, rested alike upon inexorable law, and, consequently, was neither creditable nor discreditable to either. We could only rejoice that we had been so blessed.

As years rolled on, and we comprehended, more and more, that the experiences which were so familiar to us were in some respects unique, and belonged to a class of unexplained phenomena, occurring only in rare and exceptional instances, we devoted much mutual thought to the endeavor to unvail, if possible, the hidden workings of the mysterious law that united us; to discover what was the force which caused and regulated the transmission of thought and its method of operation.

Without attempting to enter into a critical disquisition on the subject, I will briefly state the principal facts that we were able to glean. In the first place we discovered that it was not so often the isolated thought or emotion that was conveyed, as that the mental state of the one was reflected, or photographed, upon the mind of the other, from which the causes of that mental state were readily inferred, and with almost invariable accuracy. We next sought to decide whether the power of transmitting these impressions was due to, or dependent upon, an effort of the will; and found that, while the exertion of the will might deepen the effect, and in the case of others might be indispensable, that, as between ourselves, the message was transmitted, not only without any volition on our part, but sometimes *in spite of* our will to the contrary (as when one would wish to withhold from the other the knowledge of trouble or sickness); and that the vividness of the impression sent would be in exact proportion to the strength of the cause in the mind of the involuntary sender. But we also discovered that two causes might

interfere to modify the vividness of the impression received: first, any unusual pre-occupation or agitation
on the part of the receiver; and, second, the intervention of a powerful supra-mundane will. In the first
case the impression received was liable to be confused
and indistinct, and in the second case it might be diminished in strength to such a degree as to be almost im-
perceptible, but *never* totally interrupted or destroyed.
These facts, ascertained by repeated experiment, place
these peculiar phenomena so evidently within the dominion of law, albeit a law not fully understood, that
it were folly to question their existence, or ascribe them
to coincidence or fancy. On the contrary, their actuality has been so abundantly proven to my mental consciousness,—so fully realized,—that, were all other
proofs of immortality swept away, I could fearlessly
rest my hope — my knowledge — of continued life and
love beyond the grave on this: that, from beyond the
shadowy vail that divides the visible from the invisible
world, the twin-soul still responds to mine as clearly
and unmistakably as of old. Thus the mystic bond,
which triumphed over distance and outward circumstances here, is still our solace, and, unchanged by death,
reveals at once its own eternal nature and the soul's immortal life.

CHAPTER III.

SCHOOL-DAYS. — TEMPORARY WITHDRAWAL OF THE
CLAIRVOYANT GIFT. — CONSEQUENT SKEPTICISM.

UP to the age of twelve, Albert Bennet continued to
see and converse with the ethereal beings spoken of in
the last chapter, though he learned to keep his own
counsel, and ceased to try to convince others of their
reality. Soon after reaching his twelfth year he was
prostrated by an attack of lung fever, with threatened
congestion ; and all the wise ones said, "Lo! the time
has come which we foretold." The struggle was long
and desperate, but life and destiny conquered at last,
and, after well nigh passing the limits of the shadowy
valley, he awoke on earth ; but the strange gifts of his
childhood had departed. Of his sensations at this time
and subsequently I shall quote his own words in describing them to a friend. He said, "An indefinable
loneliness came over me, and in time I grew to look
upon the past second-sight as a delusion, pleasant, but
gone forever. I thought I saw the correctness of my
friends' assertion, — that it was a shadow on the eye or
mind, — and I seemed to myself to have grown immeasurably older by its removal. For six years to a
day, I saw nothing of a spiritual character ; for that six
years I believed death to be an eternal sleep, and
thought of it only with a shudder." Those six years
brought some change in outward circumstances and

surroundings. He grew rapidly toward manhood, and a portrait in oil taken at the age of fifteen shows a youth slender and spiritual in appearance, but with a maturity of expression in excess of his years. He is taken as a student, book in hand, and looks the character to the life. He was at that time attending school at East Bridgewater Academy, an institution of little classical pretensions, but where higher English branches and modern languages were taught in a thorough and systematic manner. During the two years that he remained there, his studies were frequently interrupted by ill health, and his eyes, naturally short-sighted, became so weak from the strain of continuous study as to compel the wearing of glasses, thus gaining for him the playful *sobriquet* of "The Professor." Yet, under all these disadvantages his progress was rapid; he enjoyed his school-life immensely, and was always foremost in all those little enterprises which abound among students, such as the publication of a paper, amateur theatricals, &c. In these pursuits he developed not only considerable literary and histrionic talent, but a genius for depicting the ludicrous, which nobody would have suspected from his staid and sober demeanor. He was peculiarly happy in burlesque, when the mood was on him, and delighted to show up sham pretensions and inconsistencies, whether existing in the small world of the school or the great world without. Some of the articles written by him at that time abound in hits at the popular vices and follies of society, and, stripped of certain local allusions, would read well now; but they are chiefly valuable as serving to show how instinctive was his study of human nature, and how clear his insight into human motives. Bigotry and intolerance he caricatured remorselessly; for he was ever the champion of free thought, and hated tyranny as earnestly as he despised hypocrisy. Among his favorite subjects in serious writing were Reform, Free Speech, and kindred topics.

His religious views at this time were decidedly heterodox. He rejected utterly the Christian dogma of an angry God, — who would punish the wicked forever and ever, — and regarded immortality as not proven. It seemed to him much more reasonable to suppose that death was the end — as birth the beginning — of life, a dreamless sleep, than to accuse a just God of creating beings, endowed with immortal life, only to doom them to eternal torment. How strong his feelings were upon this subject, and how prophetic of the spiritual awakening which was coming, will be best shown by the following extract from his journal, under date East Bridgewater, June 11, 1851: —

" Most of the people here are a hundred years behind the times. Why, some of the older people call me a blasphemer, because I dare to speak the truth. They uphold the doctrine of everlasting punishment and eternal damnation! O, vile misrepresentation of Almighty God!

" Why, if their description is true, God is an unjust and cruel being, a villain of the deepest dye. *God is love, all love!* and the miscreant who would stand up in the pulpit, and with solemn look misrepresent his Creator, deserves to have his lips sealed forever. He is a deceiver of mankind and a traitor to his God. . . .

" They talk about the Bible being the Word of God. What nonsense! I believe it to be a history — nothing more. The time will come when people will wonder that ever a race of beings existed who worshiped a book.

I hope whoever reads this journal in after years, when I am gone to the spirit land, will say with truth, 'He had a faint idea of the right.' "

Twenty-one years have elapsed since those lines were penned, and, in the light those years have brought, I doubt not many will fulfill his modest wish, seeing in this passage, though crude and harsh in expression, a foreshowing not only of the present, but of the future yet to be.

Soon after the date above given, he was obliged to leave school permanently, on account of continued ill health. He regretted this much; for, aside from his love of study, he highly prized the friendships and pleasant associations there formed, and kept them in tender recollection all his life. About this time — 1851-2 — his attention was first directed to the subject of spiritual manifestations, so called. A year or two previous he had attended a course of lectures given by the celebrated Dr. Dodds, on Mesmerism and Psychology. He was very desirous of being mesmerized, under the idea that it might benefit his health, but could not be affected in the least by this most powerful and learned of psychologists (nor by any other whom he ever met); but, strange to say, found himself to be a powerful operator. He took private instructions from Dr. Dodds, and studied the subject a great deal; and when, soon after, the phenomena of Spiritualism was brought to his notice, he did not call it a humbug, but a new and different form of biologic development. "But," said he, "it can't be spirits, for there are no spirits. They are vapors of the mind." His grandmother Whiting, for whose superior intellect he had the utmost reverence, was among the first to investigate the "rappings," and become convinced of their spiritual origin. His own mother was thereby induced to inquire, and with the same result; but he was still positive in his skepticism, saying to them, "I used to see ghosts when I was little, and you told me it was a delusion; now you are crazier than I *ever* was. Nothing short of seeing the spirits will convince me that there are any." That this absolute proof was not long delayed will be seen in due time as our narrative progresses.

CHAPTER IV.

REMOVAL TO THE WEST. — RETURN OF THE OPENED
VISION. — INTRODUCTION TO SPIRITUALISM. — WON-
DERFUL MEDIUMISTIC EXPERIENCES. — DEBUT AS A
PUBLIC LECTURER AT THE AGE OF EIGHTEEN.

IN the fall of 1852, the subject of removal to the west was first seriously considered in the family, in the hope that change of climate would be beneficial to the health, not only of the son, but the mother, who was again suffering from the consumptive tendencies of her early days. Our father, accordingly, took an extended tour of observation through the west, and was so well pleased with the country — and with Michigan in particular — that, in the ensuing spring, he removed his family thither, choosing for their home a small farm adjoining the village of Brooklyn, Jackson County.

That a youth of seventeen should enjoy a journey of this kind, and enter with keen relish into all the little amusing and interesting incidents of travel, is natural. The spirit of adventure found plenty of excitement, nor was the piquant seasoning of danger lacking, for crossing Lake Erie in the month of April, with the ice just breaking up, and a furious storm raging, was no joke at the time, though the occasion of many humorous anecdotes and reminiscences afterward.

The village of Brooklyn was, in 1853, quite insignificant in size, although it had been settled some twenty years, and hence the surrounding country was well improved, and by no means a wilderness. It lies about fifteen miles south from Jackson, which was its nearest railway station until 1855, when the building of a branch from Adrian to Jackson created a station at Napoleon, only four miles distant. The farm before mentioned lay to the west of the village, the house being not more than a quarter of a mile from the main street, while the fields belonging stretched back about the same distance to the beautiful River Raisin, which formed its western, and, by a bend, a part also of its southern boundary. The house faced the east, and was a neat frame building, containing in the main part two large rooms on the ground floor, with the same above, to which was added a wing on the north, comprising bedroom, kitchen, pantry, &c. The front, or east, chamber was the room occupied by my brother, the stairway lying between that and the western (my own) room. I am thus particular in description to render clearer the events soon to be narrated.

The summer of 1853 was marked by no important event. The time passed swiftly in out-door employments and sports, which seemed to produce something of the beneficial effect hoped for, and as the people were very kind and friendly, the feeling of strangeness soon wore away. In the early fall, a lady, who had called several times, broached the subject of spiritual circles, said there was one in the place of which she was a member, and invited our father and mother to attend. The latter excused herself on the ground of ill health. The lady thereupon stated that at a recent meeting of their circle, a lady medium present, while under control, had told them that there was a medium in our family. She was informed that it was a mistake, but still urged attendance upon the circle, "just to see what would come of it," and finally asked if, as mother was unable to go out, it would be agreeable to have the circle held *there* at some time. To this mother consented readily, as the members, few in number, were most of them known to her as persons of unexceptionable character and standing in society. The appointed evening came, and with it the party, as arranged. The medium above spoken of — an elderly lady, and a fine healing and test medium, as was afterward proved — was among the first to arrive. She was a total stranger to all the family, but no sooner had she entered the house than she walked directly up-to my brother, and laying her hand upon his shoulder, said, "This is the one of whom I spoke." She then went on in the most explicit language to predict his future career, which prediction, both as regards the phases of his mediumship and his public life, has been literally verified; although, I think, not one of the persons present really believed it at the time, including the medium herself. He, certainly, was anything but credulous, and never spoke of the matter afterward, except to laugh at it, and think the "prophetess" a queer person. Nothing occurred to change his skepticism until the following January, when, suddenly and without warning, the spirit-sight, the lost gift of his childhood, returned to him. Of the manner and circumstances of this return I shall give his own account, as preserved in his journal.

"On the night of the 21st of January, 1854, I was suddenly awakened by four persons, bearing the appearance of Indians, who stood before me as distinctly as any persons I ever saw in my life. My room was brilliantly illuminated, although the night was very dark; I rubbed my eyes and half arose, to be sure I was awake; but there they stood, until I had time to look at each one in detail, and compare and note the points of difference in their appearance and accouterments. At length one of them — a chief of gigantic stature — approached my bedside, and addressed me as follows: —

"'Child of earth, take back the inheritance of your ancestors, the gifts of your childhood! We are spirits; we will give you health, and a knowledge of spiritual life and intercourse. Other spirits will make you an instrument in their hands to proclaim this knowledge to the world. Tell what you have seen.'

"The speaker then returned to his place with the other three, and they all departed together, taking with them the light they had brought.

"The solitude and darkness of a winter's night was again around me, and, as if to render the scene more impressive, an old wooden clock — which is older than I am — struck twelve three times, at intervals of a few minutes. I disobeyed their injunction, and told no one what I had seen. They came again the next night, and the next, and for ten consecutive nights, the same four always, and the same one of the four acting as spokesman. Still I told no one. It had become a source of annoyance to me, for I feared I was really becoming insane. Finally, the tenth night, I said to them, somewhat pettishly, —

" ' If you *are* spirits, why can't you bring some one whom I will know, instead of Indians altogether ? '

" ' It shall be as you desire,' was the reply.

" The next night, when they came, to my surprise and gratification, my little brother, who had been dead, as I thought, for several years, appeared plainly before me, and spoke to me, saying, —

" ' It is indeed true that spirits exist and communicate. It is my pleasure to return, giving my testimony to sustain what has been told you. I live, and am happy ; your brother still in love, truth, and reality.'

" He also charged me, as had the others, to tell what I had seen ; but, when morning came, I could not make up my mind to do so. The next night my visitors did not appear, nor the next, and so on for several nights, until I had begun to think perhaps it was a delusion after all, and rejoice that I had not exposed myself to ridicule by telling of it. About two weeks after these appearances ceased, one night about sunset, as I was walking out with my father, I saw what I supposed to be a genuine Indian, of flesh and blood, standing by the fence at the roadside. The idea that it was a spirit, or one of the same apparitions I had seen in my room, did not occur to me, as they had only appeared in the night-time, and had so long ceased altogether. So I innocently remarked to father, —

" ' See that Indian ! What can he be doing there ? '

" He looked. ' Why,' said he, ' what do you mean ? There is nobody there.'

" ' There is ! ' I replied, positively.

" So we both walked toward the place where he stood ; but, as we approached, my Indian rose into the air and vanished, laughing as he went. They had adopted this ruse to bring me out, and make me tell what I had seen, for, of course, I had to explain to father, and tell him what I had witnessed before.

" ' Well,' said he, ' it is very strange ! Come back into the house, and request them to come again when we are all present.'

" As soon as we had seated ourselves, a spirit appeared whom I did not know. I saw him, though none of the rest did, which was a great mystery to me. I described him, and as soon as I had done so, my father said, —

" ' That is your grandfather Whiting — my father.'

" Now, I had never seen my grandfather on earth, nor was there a portrait of him extant. I also saw at that time several others that I knew, and ever since have seen them more or less every day. I can say that I *know* spirits exist; and in their existence and communion I behold the glorious fact, the soul-stirring realization, that I, too, am to live eternally. They tell me that this opened vision will never wholly leave me again, and that the changes through which I was passing — mentally and physically — made it necessary that it should be withdrawn during those six years."

After that, the Indians came to him every night, and would throw him into a kind of semi-conscious trance, and make him exercise for the benefit of his health, putting him through many singular forms of exercise. When it became warm weather, in the ensuing May and June, they would sometimes make him get up and go out of doors in the middle of the night. I will quote from the journal one incident of many.

"Last night they put me in an unconscious trance, and took me to the river. The first I knew, I found myself in father's large row-boat, out in the middle of the stream. I was astonished, thought it must be a dream, until one of my Indian friends appeared, and said,—

"'I brought you here; reach out and pluck a lily; put it in your pocket.' I did as directed. 'Now,' said he, 'row the boat ashore.'

"'I can't,' said I, 'I never rowed a bit in my life.'

"'I'll help you,' said he.

"So I made the attempt; succeeded very well. When I had got the boat ashore I again lost consciousness, and when I awoke it was morning, and I was in bed as usual. 'Well,' thought I, rubbing my eyes, 'I have had a queer dream.' Then I remembered the lily, and going to my pocket drew it out still wet."

His health gradually improved, and finding that these Indian spirits were doing for him what no earthly power could do, he gave himself up to their treatment. After a time other spirits controlled him, some to speak, some to write, others to sing; giving a great variety of tests.

When he wrote it was wholly mechanical, with one hand as well as the other, and sometimes both at once. Frequently, too, the writing would be upside down to him, or reversed, so that it was necessary to hold it before a glass to read it. He preserved in one small blank book upward of twenty different handwritings, and seven different languages, and carried it with him after he began to travel, until all the languages had been tested by persons capable of deciding as to their genuineness. He understood, at that time, only three languages, and one of those imperfectly. (This writing gift wholly left him soon after he began to lecture.) He was sometimes quite violently controlled, lifted in the air and moved from one part of the house to another, but never injured in the least. At one time, I remember, he was taken up from a reclining position on a lounge, carried across two rooms, and deposited upon another lounge, without once touching the floor, a distance of at least thirty-five feet. This was in broad daylight, in presence of our mother and myself. It was done very quickly, — quicker, I think, than he could have run the distance. It was also entirely unsought and unexpected, as were all the manifestations of a similar character that ever took place with him. Indeed, they seldom happened at all, unless to assist him in difficulty, or remove him from danger; but *power* was never lacking in such time of need.

Of course the report of his remarkable gifts drew crowds of visitors, some of whom were actuated by curiosity, and some driven by the natural longing of bereft hearts for tidings from the other side. To many of both classes the most satisfactory tests were given, so that it often happened that those who came to laugh remained to pray for more light from the beautiful beyond. To multiply instances would be tedious and unprofitable. Thousands of similar ones are taking place all over the country to-day, though then comparatively rare. The test was generally threefold. Where the person inquiring was a total stranger, and not introduced by name, the spirit, or spirits, who appeared with him, would call him by name, state their own names and relationship, and give some reminiscence of their life

4

or death to confirm their identity. To this was sometimes added a few words of advice concerning private
business, or an allusion to circumstances known only
to the person addressed, or to facts *not known* to him or
her at the time, but afterward ascertained. He continued to give such tests up to the time of his advent
as a public lecturer; but after that, though he saw just
the same, he rarely got any communication direct, except from his own circle and personal friends.

About six months after he first saw the Indians, he
was first controlled by the Italian spirit, Farini, who
caused him to speak and sing in Italian as well as English. His development and physical training went on
for a year longer, at the expiration of which time his
health was firmly established. He had spoken some to
public audiences in places near home, where an interest
had sprung up; but now came his definite entrance upon
public labors.

Extract from Journal, July, 1855.

" The other night Farini appeared to me, saying,
' On the 15th day of August approaching, you must
begin your work.' I pondered upon it. What can it
mean ? thought I. Last night he came again.

" ' Prepare to fulfill your destiny ! ' were his words.

" ' Let me know my destiny,' said I in return.

" Then he lifted the vail that obscured the future,
revealing to me my future as a public lecturer, the day
I should start, the mode of traveling, the direction
necessary for me to take, and many other particulars.
Feeling that the power which had restored me to health
was at least entitled to respect, I signified my willing-

ness to obey his directions.   He then addressed himself
to me in these words : —

" ' Go, child of earth ! Fame, honor, and glory await
you in this world, and in that heavenly clime where
I live to be your guiding star.   Be faithful to your
trust ! Be true to yourself ! We will be true to you.
Many, calling themselves friends, will try to turn you
from your course ! Heed them not, but pass on in your
allotted pathway ! Enemies will oppose you ; the opposing world will frown ; fear them not, for truth is
more powerful than error, and must prevail.   Although
foes may be as thorns in your path, we will cover them
with the fair roses of spiritual love, and the love of
earth shall respond, more than counterbalancing the
hate and scorn it opposes.' "

Extract from Journal, October 1, 1855.

" On the 15th day of August, I left home with the
firm determination of fulfilling the wishes of my spirit
guide.   He told me on starting, —

" ' The compact shall be for two years, during which
time you shall lecture as I direct.   At the expiration of
that time, you shall be at liberty to decide whether you
will remain longer under my guidance and instruction.'

" To this I assented, and started with my horse and
buggy, as directed.   Stopped the first night at the
house of a friend, and the following day went on to
Albion, — a town on the M. C. R. R., — twenty miles
west of Jackson.   Arrived there about dark ; called at
the house of Mr. John Phipps, — a fine, whole-souled
man, an Englishman by birth, and a strong spiritualist.
He received me cordially, and introduced me to several
others.   .   .   .   .

" They desired me to lecture the following Sunday. I did so, and the interest was all I could desire. The poetic element in my lectures, the faculty of composing poetry impromptu, was new and interesting. At night Farini came to me, and said, ' This is only the beginning. Before the two years shall have rolled away, you shall lecture in most of the principal cities of the country, and not only improvise poetry, as now, but upon any subject given at the time by the audience.' This seems a rather large promise, but all that he has hitherto foretold has been verified; so I can not well doubt this."

He continued westward, speaking at Marengo and Marshall, two evenings each, Ceresco one evening, Battle Creek two evenings, thence northward to Bellevue, where he also spoke twice. While there he made the acquaintance of Mrs. Sprague, — afterward Mrs. Tuttle, — a trance speaker, well known and well beloved, who, unable to endure the vicissitudes of public life, has long since passed on to her reward. He spoke again at Marshall, on his return, the audience consisting, as before, entirely of skeptics, and also another Sunday at Albion, returning home after an absence of four weeks. On this, the first trip of our spiritual Quixote, he made no charge for his services; nor did he for some time subsequently, but accepted whatever remuneration the people were disposed to give. Later, perceiving that this course of procedure worked injustice, not only to himself and other workers, but to the public, inasmuch as places and persons the *least* able often gave the *most* liberally, he adopted a different and more impartial method.

Of his second trip I shall quote the account from the journal.

Extract.

" I heard that there was to be a convention of Progressive Friends — a so-called Free Meeting for the discussion of all reforms — at a place called Livonia, fifty miles from my home. I was impressed to go ; could not see the object then, but can now. I went ; found a motley collection of people, black and white ; some cursing the churches, some raving against the Union, some making long speeches against war, but no room for anything spiritual ; so I left for Detroit. As I was on my road thither, Farini addressed me, saying, —

" ' I brought you here to teach you not to look to any class of reformers, so called, many of whom are fanatics in reality, to sustain you. Spiritualism must stand by itself, unhampered by any of the ' one-idea-isms ' of the day. It is for the poor and lowly, also for the rich and great ; for the southern slaveholder as well as for the northern abolitionist. Keep yourself aloof from all side issues.'

" I remained two days in Detroit, attending the state fair, and finding a friend in a namesake of mine, Dr. L. C. Whiting, and then returned home, having learned a valuable lesson."

He made one more trip with horse and buggy, visiting again the places mentioned above, viz., Albion, Marshall, Battle Creek, &c. While at the latter place he went out to Harmonia, six miles distant, where there was a school, founded upon liberal principles, which seemed to give good hope of future usefulness, but for some reason was soon after abandoned.

It was now into November, and leaving his horse and carriage, he took his fourth trip on the cars, going first to Adrian, thence to Munroe, then westward to Jonesville, Coldwater, Sturgis, Constantine, South Bend, and Laporte; at each of which places he lectured from two to six times, making many friends, whose names are recorded in his journal with the kindest expressions of regard. Among these was Hon. S. C. Coffinbury, of Constantine, who, twelve years later, again stood by his side in defense of another principle, the sacred right of free speech. He next lectured in Waukegan, Ill., and Racine and Milwaukee, Wis., meeting at the latter place Mr. S. J. Finney, then a lecturer upon the Harmonial Philosophy. Returning again to Waukegan, he was accompanied thence to Chicago by a party of friends, among whom was that remarkable medium, Mrs. Seymour, since gone home to the spirit world. The phase of her mediumship that attracted most attention was the appearance of writing upon the arm, often the name of some spirit entirely unknown to her. This test was given by her in public during his lectures in Chicago, the letters remaining plain and distinct until nearly all the large audience had time to pass by and examine them. After delivering six lectures he retraced his route, and next went northward to Ionia and Grand Rapids, Mich. By this time the winter was far spent, and he returned home to rest and recuperate.

CHAPTER V.

FIRST EASTERN TOUR AND TRIPS THROUGH THE
WEST. — INCIDENTS. — MEDIA MET WITH. — CLOSE
OF FIRST YEAR OF PUBLIC LIFE. — THE COMPACT.

On the 11th of March, 1856, he started upon his
first eastern tour; lectured at Adrian, and went from
there to Cleveland; called at the office of the " Universe," — a spiritual paper then published, — and, by
invitation of the editor, lectured on the following Sunday afternoon, Mr. Pardee speaking in the evening.
He there met, for the first time, Mr. J. B. Conklin, of
New York, — the great ballot-test medium, — of whom
he says, —

" His manner of giving tests is as follows: The
investigator writes upon slips of paper the names of
several of his spirit friends, folds them up separately,
without showing them to Mr. C., then lifts them up one
at a time, asking, ' Is this one here? ' When the right
one is taken, the table tips, or Mr. C.'s hand writes the
answer. Other questions are answered in the same
way." From Cleveland to Painesville and to Buffalo,
where he spoke two Sundays, occupying the desk of
Mr. Forster, who was absent. Buffalo was, at that date,
a great center of spiritual light. The " Age of Progress " was published there. Thomas Gales Forster occupied the rostrum, Miss Cora Scott — then a slender girl
of fifteen — already gave promise of eloquence and

future usefulness, while the array of physical media
was such as we rarely find in the limits of a single city.
Among this number were the since famous Davenport
Brothers, whose wonderful mediumship has created so
much excitement and controversy, both in this country
and Europe. It may not be uninteresting to give his
brief account of what he witnessed at their *séances;*
showing, as it does, that though they were mere boys,
and hence could not possibly have had "years of practice to enable them to perform their feats," as is sometimes alleged, yet the demonstrations in their presence
were no less satisfactory and convincing than at the
present day. He says, —

"Several musical instruments were played upon at
the same time; a spirit calling himself John King spoke
through the trumpet; at times spirit hands appeared,
which all could see and feel. The boys were tied and
untied without mortal aid, and once, when Ira was tied
with a stout bed-cord, his coat was taken off and the
ropes not disturbed at all. These demonstrations were
given under conditions which precluded the possibility
of deception, even had there existed any disposition to
deceive."

Another of the Buffalo mediums was a Miss Brooks,
in whose presence the piano was played upon without
visible hands, the instrument being turned with the
keys toward the wall. Not only were accompaniments
given to anything sung by the company, but sometimes original compositions of no small merit. One
of these, called "The Shipwreck," was especially fine,
— the roaring of the waves, the rushing of the wind,
the creaking of timbers, the final crash, and even the
shrieks of the dying, being plainly distinguishable.

I subjoin one other account of phenomena witnessed by him in Buffalo, some of which then seemed almost too marvelous for belief even to an eye-witness, but which will easily find credence now, as parallel cases have become in some degree common, and are well attested.

" There was in Buffalo a Miss Judah, who lay sick, and whom the physicians had given up to die. Indeed, she was so low as to be unable to turn herself in bed, but lay in a kind of stupor, apparently unconscious of anything that took place around her. In her presence some of the most wonderful manifestations took place that I ever saw or read of, either in ancient or modern times. These consisted of speaking and singing in audible voices, without mortal agency; some coarse and boisterous talkings, others more refined; men's voices and women's voices, sometimes two or three at the same time. The principal speaker was a coarse-voiced woman, who called herself Frank, and seemed to be very powerful; another voice was that of a young man who sang beautifully, accompanying himself upon the guitar. Sometimes Frank would interrupt him, — tell him to stop, for she wanted to talk, &c. Spirit hands opened and shut doors, and were visible to all. This Frank seemed to have a particular spite against the doctor, would throw sticks of wood at him, and order him out of the house every time he came. She would call every one by name. The first time I went there she addressed me by my whole name, which was known to no person in Buffalo; informed me that she liked me ; had been to hear me lecture, and should go again ; told me the dates upon several pieces of money in my

pocket, and then asked me if I would like to have the
'young man' sing for me. I said, 'Yes.'
"'Well,' she rejoined, 'he shall sing for you. What
piece will you have?'
"'O,' replied I, laughing, 'have him sing my favorite.' Thereupon the guitar was taken and tuned, and
the voice sang the Scotch song, 'Annie Laurie,' in the
most unexceptionable and expressive manner. When
he had concluded, Frank said, —
"'There! you didn't think I knew what your favorite song was — did you? You know better now.' I
admitted that she was right.

"I went there several times, and on each occasion
the talkings came in a similar manner. On my last
visit Frank said, 'Albert, I am going to write you a
letter;' and sure enough, just before I left, from the
half open door of the room where the sick girl lay, a
large hand and arm was reached forth, the hand holding a letter, which, on taking and opening, I found to
contain several lines coarsely written with a pencil, and
a small velvet flower."

From Buffalo he continued eastward toward New
York, lecturing on the way at Rochester, Syracuse,
Homer, Courtland, and Binghamton, arriving in New
York the 21st of April. There he found a true
friend in A. J. Davis, and also made the acquaintance
of Messrs. Partridge and Brittan, who were then publishing the "Spiritual Telegraph." He spoke, the following Sunday afternoon, at the Stuyvesant Institute,
where the Spiritualists were then holding meetings,
and in the evening in Brooklyn. On Monday left
for Hartford, Conn., where he met Mrs. Mettler, the
clairvoyant healer, and lectured once only, as he had

an engagement in Boston for the first two Sundays of May.

Not being entirely devoid of that traditional reverence for the " Hub " which is supposed to be inherent in the constitution of every child of New England, he felt that here was the turning-point in his career, and that if he could succeed in the " Athens of America," he had nothing more to fear. On Sunday, May 4, he occupied the desk at Music Hall for the first time, and again the following Sunday. His success exceeded his most sanguine expectations. The " New England Spiritualist," A. E. Newton editor, gave him most kind and flattering notice, and the Rubicon was passed. It was during his stay in Boston that he first improvised from a subject presented by the audience, the first trial being made in the presence of some friends, at the residence of Mr. Tenny. This feat, the fulfillment of a prophecy made nearly a year previous, was afterward repeated in public, and became a prominent feature in his public efforts. A list of the different subjects so given, and upon which poems were pronounced, would of itself fill a good-sized volume. He once kept an account of the different themes so presented in two months, and the result was forty-two; and this might be considered a fair average during at least ten years.

After speaking one Sunday at Lowell, he next went to Portland, giving there six lectures, which drew large audiences, and were highly praised by the daily press. Two weeks later he gave a second series of lectures there, and also went to Brunswick, Maine, — the location of Bowdoin College, — lecturing, Sunday evening, in the Unitarian Church. When a theme for a poem

was called for, a smart young student gave the subject
of "Humbug," which, to his surprise, was accepted
without hesitation, and he received more than he bar-
gained for, in the way of a lesson on the subject proposed.

The time intervening between the two Portland
engagements was spent in visiting his old home, East
Abington, from which he had been absent over three
years, during which time he had so changed in appearance, by reason of his improved health, that hardly one
of his relatives recognized him at first sight. While
there he delivered a course of lectures and attended a
large mass grove meeting of Spiritualists, at the celebrated Island Grove, which had been a favorite resort
of his boyhood, and where he now addressed an audience of about two thousand people. What were his
emotions that day, as he looked back over the changes
of three years, and realized that he had entered upon
another "Act" in the grand "Drama of Life," can
never be told.

He enjoyed on this occasion a visit with his grandmother Whiting, whom he found as great a spiritualist
as ever, — her intellect undimmed by age, — and from
whom he received an intelligent appreciation and earnest sympathy, which he highly prized.

It was now into July, and he started homeward,
stopping one Sunday at Rochester, and going thence to
Buffalo, with the intention of taking the steamer
Northern Indiana to Toledo. Here occurred a remarkable instance of foresight on the part of his spirit guide,
which he relates as follows : —

"As I was going on board the steamer, Farini appeared to me, and said, —

" 'Do not go upon that boat; go over and take the steamer Mississippi, by way of Detroit.' I did so. In the night he again came to me, saying, —

" 'The reason I told you to come by this boat is this: The "Northern Indiana" will be burned to-morrow.' The next day, about ten o'clock, the two boats being about seven miles apart, the 'Northern Indiana' was discovered to be on fire. I was the first to see it, for I was expecting it, relying upon the information I had received. About fifty lives were lost, the balance being rescued by our boat. The scene was heart-rending in the extreme. Thus was my life preserved from the most imminent danger by a spirit, and I arrived home in safety on the 17th of July, after an absence of four months."

The ensuing fall and winter he spent in the west, visiting most of the principal towns of Illinois, several in Wisconsin, and also St. Louis, Mo., averaging five lectures a week during the entire time, and meeting with the most gratifying success. In many of these places he delivered the first public lectures on Spiritualism to which their people had ever listened. Of course he did not escape the abuse of enemies, nor, in all cases, the misconception and ill-judged zeal of friends; but he had the rich satisfaction of triumphing over all difficulties, and reaping not only the reward of an approving conscience, but also of generous appreciation at the hands of the public. At Mendota he, for the first time, conducted a funeral service — an office he was often thereafter called upon to fill. He spent his twenty-first birthday in St. Louis, being on that occasion most hospitably entertained by a good friend, Mr. A. Miltenberger.

The beauty of some of these western towns was highly gratifying to his æsthetic taste. With Rockford and Bloomington, Ill., he was particularly pleased; also Madison, Wis., of which he says,—

" It is the *prettiest* city I ever saw. It is situated on a slight elevation of land, sloping gradually on either side to beautiful lakes. In the center, upon the top of the eminence, is the public square, containing fourteen acres of land, covered with oak trees in a state of nature, although the grounds are laid out in elegant style. On this square are the Capitol buildings, built of cream-colored stone,—of which also most of the buildings in the city are composed,—presenting a most beautiful combination of nature and art."

At Rockford an incident occurred which he records as follows: "I was sent for to visit a man who was about to be executed for murder. I went and talked with him about an hour; gave him my views of the future life; told him many things; so that I trust, when he awoke in the spirit land, he was not entirely a stranger to its realities. Of the barbarity of this killing a man according to law I said nothing then, nor of the murder which he had committed, for I consider the former the most brutal of the two. I can not look upon it as right to kill a man in cold blood because he has killed another, so long as we have secure prisons in which to confine him. That interview was a source of instruction to me as well as to him."

May 1, 1857, after a brief rest at home, he set out for Philadelphia, lecturing by the way at Cleveland and several other points in Ohio. This was his first visit to the Quaker City, and he found it "different from any other city" he had seen, but was very favorably impressed with the people. The venerable Samuel Barry, who kept a spiritual bookstore and periodical depot, took a great interest in his welfare, and on parting, presented him with a letter which might be considered a model specimen of apt and affectionate advice from age to youth.

He also had the pleasure of making the acquaintance of Professor Hare, Dr. Child, and many other noble workers in the spiritualistic ranks. He returned home through Central New York, spending the month of July at Syracuse and Saratoga, and remained until after the 15th of August, at which time the two years of his contract with his spirit guide expired. He naturally awaited the dawning of that day with some curiosity, particularly as, for the two weeks intervening between his last lecture at Syracuse and that date, that constant friend seemed to have departed, and left him to his own reflections.

Extract from Journal.

" With the day came Farini. He said, —

" ' The time has expired. Are you satisfied with your success ? '

" ' I am more than satisfied,' I replied.

" ' You now believe in the power of a spirit to guard and protect — do you not ? '

" ' Yes ; I am fully convinced of their ability to guide those whom they choose as their instruments.'

" ' Do you wish to continue under my guidance ? '

" ' I do.'

" ' I anticipated your answer. It shall be so. I will again be a light in your pathway, supplying you with knowledge, fit food for humanity. The time shall be

unlimited. You have fulfilled your portion of the contract; mine I voluntarily continue; and you, of your
own free will and pleasure, accept my proffered aid.
Still will I o'ershadow you with such mantles as I
deem adapted to your mental constitution and the
wants of those to whom you minister. Go forth again
upon your mission.'

"I had many invitations to lecture on hand, but had
replied to none, wishing first to consult him to whom I
am indebted for so much help, in whose presence I feel
myself but a child. After receiving these words of
encouragement, I at once made arrangements for the
fall and winter."

CHAPTER VI.

SECOND APPEARANCE IN BOSTON. — THE HARVARD
PROFESSORS. — PROFESSOR FELTON SELECTS SUB-
JECTS FOR IMPROVISATION. — EXTRACTS FROM THE
BOSTON PRESS. — FIRST TRIP TO THE FAR SOUTH. —
RETURN HOME IN APRIL, 1858.

HIS first engagement was in Providence, R. I., the
Sundays of September. During the month he spoke
week evenings at Norwich, Conn., Greenwich, Pawtucket, and Newport, R. I., and also enjoyed sundry ex-
cursions to Rocky Point and other places of interest in the
vicinity; saw some powerful physical demonstrations at
the residence of Judge Manchester, through the mediumship of his daughter. One evening he was there to

tea; the table was spread for twelve, the tea poured out, when the table began to rise slowly, and, with no person touching it, remained an instant suspended at a hight of about two feet from the floor, and then gently descended, without breaking or displacing a dish or spilling a drop of liquid. From Providence to Portland, Me., for a month, and thence to Boston, beginning there Sunday, November 22, to a good audience, which was increased the next Sunday. The week following he spoke in Cambridge, and there met the renowned Harvard professors, who became sufficiently interested in his lectures and improvisations to induce them to attend his lectures in Boston the ensuing Thursday evening, December 3, and also the two Sunday evenings following.

As, several years after, there arose some controversy with regard to the discussions which took place at this time, particularly with reference to the language used by the learned Greek scholar, Professor Felton, which was only settled by recourse to the full reports given by the Boston press at the time, I shall give a more extended account of the matter than I might otherwise deem necessary.

Besides the brief account contained in his journal, and the general recollection of living witnesses, I have before me files of several newspapers published in Boston at the time, among them the "New England Spiritualist," "Banner of Light," and also the sheet which was at that time considered the organ, *par excellence*, of old fogyism, viz., the "Boston Courier." From these papers, holding such widely different religious views, yet agreeing in their reports in all material respects, I shall give some extracts.

5

From the New England Spiritualist, December 12, 1857.

A. B. WHITING AT THE MEIONAON.—TWO PROFESS-
ORS IN THE FIELD.

Mr. A. B. Whiting lectured at the Meionaon on
Thursday evening of last week, taking as a text
"Man, know thyself." He spoke of man as a trinity
— soul, spirit, and matter combined — the image of God
— the fairest of his works. Man should search into
the depths of his own mental and spiritual nature. He
can thus learn more than by studying the outward
world; for man is an epitome of the universe. As he
learns the laws of his own being is he better prepared
to understand the nature of spirit life. Everything
that gives us a knowledge of the soul is of use. Therefore, if no other benefit were to be derived from spirit
manifestations, they are useful in causing us to investigate the laws of mind, and in teaching man to know
himself. As lofty minds are led to examine this subject,
though they may form diverse opinions upon it, yet will
they help to expand our knowledge of human nature.

As spirit communion becomes more common, minds
will become more unfolded, and men will receive
higher lessons of truth. Their greatest knowledge
will be to know that knowledge will never cease. When
the time should arrive that there was nothing more for
man to learn, it would be well for him to become another creature, for his existence would cease to have
any interest. It is a rule in nature, that nothing can
understand that which is above it; we can fully comprehend only that which is on a level with or below us.
Men understand the past better than the present. No

age is appreciated in the present; but when it becomes the past, its merits and its virtues are looked back upon and acknowledged. So will it be with the present age and its spiritual developments. The future that now is will look back upon them and assign them their true worth. Man will never understand the present in which he lives until he becomes more intuitively developed.

He then went on to speak of the wonderful faculties of the human mind, and the desirability of developing them to that state where they will be in harmony with all God's works. Men were drawn nearer the spirit world by spirit communion, and the more a man knows of that world the better for him, intellectually, religiously, spiritually. The earth was made that man might exist; man was made to give birth to a spirit bright and beautiful, to live a holy and happy life. Man was made in the image of God — not physically, as some say, but spiritually. He contains within himself the germ of wisdom, love, and truth. When man shall learn better the faculties of the mind, he will learn better the laws by which the universe is governed, God being the soul of the universe, as the soul of man is the animative power of the body. "Man, know thyself."

At the close of the lecture Professor Felton, as chairman of a committee appointed at the opening of the meeting to select a subject for improvisation, read a list of topics, remarking that they were not designed or expected to test the medium's claims to spirit influence, but as affording subjects to improvise upon. The medium chose from the list as read the following selection from Schiller: —

"On the mountain is freedom! the breath of decay
Never sullies the fresh-flowing air;
O, nature is perfect wherever we stray;
'Tis man that deforms it with care."

An extempore poetic composition of some fifteen minutes in length was then delivered with too great rapidity for a reporter's pencil to follow. As to its merits, the reader will form his conclusion after reading what here follows: —

Dr. Gardner, at the conclusion of the poem, said that remarks would be in order from any person in the audience; whereupon Professor Horsford arose and made the inquiry, " Though this performance is not put forth as a test of spirit influence, is it not to be taken as such by the audience? Is it not expected that it will be received as proof of the presence and power of spirits from another world?"

Dr. G. replied that he expected each individual to judge for himself. For his own part he did not consider trance-speaking, by itself, as conclusive proof. His belief in spirit manifestations rested mainly upon other evidences.

Professor Horsford remarked that improvisation is a common thing in some parts of the world. In Western New York he had heard Methodist exhorters who spoke in a surprising manner — quite equal to Mr. Whiting. Improvising poems is quite common in Italy, where numerous persons can be found who for a small coin will recite poems on any subject named. He knows a child six years old who will repeat rhymes by the hour together. He is acquainted with several young ladies who have practiced the same thing successfully. A poem was once given Coleridge in a dream, which so impressed his memory that he wrote it out in full upon waking. This gift is not a remarkable one, and should not be regarded as evidence of a spirit acting upon men. [Here follows a rejoinder by Dr. Gardner, to the effect that if a man performs in the trance that which he could not in the normal state, he could not account for it except upon the supposition that there was an assisting power above and beyond him.]

Professor Felton then rose and said that he must bear evidence to the truth. He claimed to be a Spiritualist, a devout believer in the existence of spirits in a better world. He had listened with pleasure, and not without admiration, to the improvisation of Mr. Whiting, and with nine tenths of what had been advanced he did not differ, but he saw no evidence in it of the truth of Spiritualism. His belief in spirit existence was drawn from the study of human nature, from the writings of philosophers, and from the Scriptures. He did not differ from Dr. G. or the speaker, except where they have assumed what is unproved — that these things come from spirits. Like Professor Horsford he looked upon improvisation as nothing extraordinary or wonderful. In Greece, the land of poetry, there are hundreds who can not read or write who have a remarkable faculty of improvisation. He gave the medium credit for the talent displayed, and admitted there were many poetical expressions in the poem, and this power was proof of the presence in its possessor of a very *bright* spirit, be it embodied or disembodied.

But there were imperfections in the production, as might be expected. Only a poet of the very highest genius could have improvised a faultless poem. The speech, as is the case with all mediums, was characteristic of the individual. He thought it, therefore, rational to suppose that it all came from the medium. It required longer legs than he had ever seen to make a logical step to the conclusion that it came from a disembodied spirit.

Dr. Gardner thought that the fact of the communications, partaking in some measure of the peculiarities of the medium, did not militate against their spiritual origin. He illustrated by comparison: A stream of pure water, when made to run through pine logs, became impregnated with the quality of the wood, so as to taste differently from what it would if taken fresh from the spring; but it was the same water, nevertheless, and came from the spring. Scripture furnishes analogous examples. The inspirations of Moses and Jesus are widely different; they partake of their general characteristics.

[The discussion, having thus become general, was continued to some length, but having no further personal reference, is omitted.]

Repetitions are tedious; therefore I shall only quote one paragraph from the "Courier" report, viz.: the first remarks of Professor Felton, which will be seen to coincide almost exactly with the report given above.

From the Boston Courier, December 4, 1857.

Professor Felton then rose and said, that he claimed to be a Spiritualist, a devout believer in the existence of spirits in a better world; but he had not seen any evidence to sustain what is called modern Spiritualism. He had listened with pleasure, and not without admiration, to the improvisation by Mr. Whiting. But he must consider it as nothing extraordinary or wonderful.

Among the nations of Southern Europe improvisation is a common practice. In Greece, the land of poetry and poets, men and women who are not even able to read or write possess the power of improvisation to a remarkable extent. That power was proof of the presence of a very *bright* spirit, be it embodied or disembodied.

The following Sunday — Dec. 6th — the poem on the subject of "Belshazzar's Feast" — a fragment of which will be found in another part of this book — was improvised, and in the evening Professor Felton was again at the head of the committee, as will be seen by the subjoining extract.

From the Banner of Light, December 12, 1857.

At the close of the singing, Mr. Whiting took his stand in the desk, and the subject of the discourse was announced as follows : " The Religious Nature of Man, and its Application to Modes of Worship," upon which an exceedingly interesting and instructive discourse was given, commanding the earnest attention of the audience, not even excepting the learned gentlemen from Harvard.

After the close of the discourse, the subject for a poem was announced by Professor Felton, and was as follows: " The Duty of the Living to the Memory of the Dead." Several subjects had been prepared by the committee, but on the first and second being read, the controlling intelligence announced its preference for the first ; and, after a moment's delay, the medium commenced the *improvisation*, which occupied near a quarter of an hour, showing the " duties of the living to the memory of the (so-called) dead ; " teaching

us that our duty to those who have left the form, and
passed to a higher life, is to live lives of *purity, love,*
and *kindness* to our *fellow-man,* and thus show our
appreciation of the GREAT SOURCE of our being —
teaching us that we should understand the great truth,
that those friends who have left the form, and passed
to the spirit world, are *not dead,* but that they are only
born to a more beautiful state of existence, with the
ability to return to us, whom they loved when with us,
and cheer and encourage us onward in our efforts.

I will only add the report of the proceedings upon
the succeeding and closing Sunday of this engagement, from the columns of the "New England Spiritualist," of December 19.

"Mr. A. B. Whiting closed his series of lectures at
the Melodeon, on Sunday last, in a manner to add to
his already high reputation as a medium. In the afternoon he spoke on the 'Harmonies of the Universe,'
after which an improvisation was given — subject,
'The Transfiguration of Christ on the Mount.' The
evening discourse was on the Golden Age, and was,
without question, the best that has been given by the
speaker in this city. For an improvisation he chose,
from a list of topics presented by a committee, the
theme 'Knowledge cometh by Suffering.'

"After the close of the evening services on the part
of Mr. Whiting, Professor Felton rose and expressed
his opinion of the discourse. He admired the ability
displayed, thought the style was elegant, and the language appropriate, and the sentiments exalted. He
approved of it unqualifiedly in these respects ; but he
saw no evidence that it came from a spirit, and he

must protest against any such conclusion. The ideas advanced were not new; they were the same as had been advanced by Socrates and Plato centuries ago, and by many intelligent minds since. He himself had entertained similar views for years; but no disembodied spirit had ever come to him. It required no spirit from another world to tell us that a righteous life is the way to happiness. . . .

"Dr. Gardner thanked the professor for his high compliments to the medium, and said he thought it would be foolish in a person like Mr. Whiting to attribute such excellent discourses to other minds, when, if they were his own, he might receive the individual honor which he now disclaimed. As to the idea that it required no spirit to come and inculcate these doctrines of virtue, he thought, on the same principle, that God did not need to embody himself in humanity, and come down to earth to teach men to love one another.

"As Professor Felton had made allusion to Socrates, he was asked to explain what Socrates meant by speaking of his familiar spirit?

"The professor, after some circumlocution, said he probably meant the *voice of conscience.*

"The inquiry was then made: Could the professor explain how it was that, three days before he took the poison, Socrates predicted that a certain vessel which was expected to arrive would not arrive till after his death?

"Professor Felton thought it too difficult a question, involving too many abstruse points, to enter upon the merits of at that time and place.

"'But,' returned the questioner, 'did not Socrates himself say that he obtained his information from a demon or spirit?'

" The professor replied that Socrates did claim to be under the guidance of a '*daimonion;*' but he did not think he meant a disembodied spirit. He was then asked to give the plain English of *daimonion.* He said that according to some authorities it meant one of a *certain order of spiritual beings.* As this concession created some sensation in the audience, the professor repeated that he did not understand it to mean the disembodied spirit of a human being.

" The learned gentleman was then appealed to for an explanation of what Plato meant when he said, 'Good men's souls are made demons of honor.'

" The professor replied with politeness and a good many words, but failed to touch satisfactorily the point at issue. He was then requested to explain the difference between the influence of this 'demon' upon Socrates, and that spoken of by mediums as spirit influence.

" If any one obtained from his answer a correct idea of the difference, this reporter did not; and therefore our readers must remain in ignorance.

" His questioner then wished to know if a communication was not once made to Socrates through the oracle at Delphi?

" *Professor Felton.* 'Yes; he was declared the "wisest man;" but it required no oracle or spirit to say that.'

" ' But the point is, did not Socrates himself receive the Delphic communications as coming from something higher than the Pythoness, who was the medium?'

" *Professor Felton.* 'I cannot speak with positiveness on that point; but if Socrates accepted the belief, I do not.'

"The discussion was kept up with considerable earnestness on both sides, until Professor Horsford rose and turned the current into another channel. Professor Horsford said that illusions of the senses were very frequent in certain states of health. We often see and hear what does not exist. Nicolai, of Berlin, often saw figures before him, and heard them talk. On one occasion he saw the figure of his wife, who had been dead some time, and, rushing to meet her, was stopped by running against a door, and thus brought to his senses. The phenomena always occurred when his digestive organs were in a certain state. But his case was submitted to the doctors, and on his being thoroughly bled, the phenomena entirely ceased. Persons in typhoid fever often used expressions like ' *We* are thirsty,' ' Give *us* some drink ' — adopting the plural form, like Mr. Whiting and other mediums ; but physicians understood this to be the result of disease ; and thus is the foundation of these assumptions of spirit influence knocked away, and the whole shown to be a fallacy.

"Dr. Gardner wished to know of the professor whether the apostles did really see Moses and Elias on the Mount of Transfiguration, as is asserted ; or was it an illusion of the senses proceeding from their state of health at the time ; and would an operation in phlebotomy have removed the conviction from their minds that they really saw those spirits, and thus proved it all a fallacy.

"The professor denied that there was any analogy between the cases — thought that the Bible instances were entirely out of the question — a separate and distinct affair.

" Professor Grimes, ' the Phreno-Geologist,' thought it more extraordinary to suppose that the young man had composed the poem delivered that evening *im-promptu*, than to believe it came from a spirit. Here was something wonderful, if it were really true that Mr. Whiting had no knowledge beforehand of the subject matter. He questioned the originality of the poem. Professor Felton said he would do Mr. Whiting the justice to say that the production was entirely original." The professor himself selected the subject; so there could be no collusion about it.

" After a session of over two hours and a half, which engaged the constant and earnest attention of the large audience, the meeting adjourned."

So much for his public labors in Boston at this time. He made many new acquaintances during his stay, among whom may be mentioned two or three well-known laborers in the spiritualistic ranks ; Frederick L. H. Willis, whose expulsion from Harvard College was then a quite recent event; Thomas Gales Forster, who was one of the editors of the " Banner " at that time ; and Mrs. Henderson, a trance speaker. Of the latter he says, —

" I heard her at a funeral; was much pleased. O, how much more beautiful on such occasions are the consolations of a spiritual gospel than it is to hear preached the old philosophy of an eternal or temporary sleep and final resurrection ! How much more consoling to realize that the dear departed one still hovers near to guard, guide, and instruct, still bringing to the souls of earth garlands of beauty plucked in bowers of affection. How appropriate upon such occasions to hear one speak, who, having tasted death, is consequently prepared to give an explanation of its realities, telling what lies beyond the valley as none other can ! ''

The last of December he left Boston for Providence to fulfill a second engagement of four Sundays. At the expiration of that time he went to Baltimore for the first time, and thence west to St. Louis, and down the river to Memphis, Tenn., and other southern towns and cities. This was his first trip south of St. Louis, and he enjoyed it very much. He says, —

" I spent the time pleasantly and profitably to myself, and I trust to them and the cause of truth also."

Educated in the shadow of Faneuil Hall and the " Boston Liberator," where, by most people, slavery was regarded as the " sum of all villainies," and the slaveholder as a sort of half-human monster, he was naturally on the lookout for some of those horrors which he had heard so often and graphically depicted. The result of his observations on the subject he records as follows : —

" During this trip I had a chance to see more of slavery than I ever saw before; find it is quite a different thing from what it is described to be in the " Liberator " and " Tribune." The negroes are generally well treated and cared for, and contented with their condition. The negroes of Memphis, in particular, are a fine-looking set; would contrast favorably with free negroes anywhere. One day, seeing an advertisement which said that there would be a public sale of slaves that morning, I dropped in to see for myself what has been so often described by others, some giving one view, others differing widely. Of the number sold none seemed to care anything about it. I heard no shrieks, saw no tears, nothing terrible, save the idea of selling men. The slaves generally were a jovial set, and the auction was a very different affair in reality from what it is described to be by those who have never seen for themselves."

April 1st he was obliged to turn his reluctant feet northward to fill engagements at Attica and Delphi, Ind. He would gladly have tarried longer in the Sunny South, whose climate was so delightful to him, but he was always scrupulously exact in keeping appointments, even at great sacrifice of personal comfort. He was somewhat compensated, however, in this instance, for physical discomfort, in the good appreciation of his labors at the above-mentioned places, and returned home in May, well satisfied with the work of the past eight months. In his retrospective glance over his stay in the "land of cotton and sweet potatoes" he says, —

"Farewell, home of magnolias and mocking-birds, of lovely ladies and whole-souled men. Farewell to 'Old Tennessee.' I hope *not* 'forever;' but, however that may be, in memory will still a place be found for each loved friend north and south. There they will repose with no sectional differences to divide; for all good friends are dear to me in proportion to the amount of real mental affinity existing, not depending upon the place where they were born or the peculiar political views they may entertain. . . .

"The past is past: regret or exultation are alike unavailing. Man is controlled by a law which he can neither evade nor alter. Many things, which we mourn as evils at the time they occur, we recognize in after years as blessings. Thus it has been with myself as regards many events in the past; so I trust it will be in the future.

"Man is subject to the same great law that controls all other forms of life. Each person fills his own place — is a part of the great whole. There is a fatality that governs the life and destiny of every human being; but we also have a freedom to investigate and search for knowledge. My prayer is, that I may be led into truth. I have not a single opinion which I would not willingly exchange for a better."

CHAPTER VII.

IN NEW ENGLAND AGAIN. — SIGNS OF PROGRESS. — RECALL HOME IN JANUARY, 1859. — SICKNESS AND DEATH OF HIS FATHER. — SORROW AND CONSOLATION.

ON the 1st of June, 1858, he again returned to New England, speaking first in Boston, and spending the balance of the summer in that vicinity. He found that much progress had been made during six months toward organized effort. In twenty-five places, within a radius of as many miles of Boston, regular meetings had been established, and were flourishing. The demands upon his time were far greater than he could meet, and he only took time for two weeks' rest at home in September, and resumed his labors in Providence in October. It was during this engagement there that he first had the pleasure of listening to Emma Hardinge, who then, as now, ranked among the ablest and most

eloquent exponents of the Spiritual Philosophy. It is
one of the unavoidable deprivations of a lecturer's life
that he can so seldom listen to the public efforts of his
friends and co-laborers. Many of his life-long friends
he may perhaps never hear more than once or twice, if
at all. Such was the case with my brother, as with
many more, doubtless, whose whole time was given
to the public. His engagements from this time until
the ensuing January included Portland, Me., Boston, New Bedford, and Waltham, Mass., Providence,
Newport, and Westerly, R. I., and Willimantic,
Conn. Near the latter place he saw some remark-
ably powerful physical demonstrations through the
mediumship of a little girl, of which he says, "She
placed her hands on a large stove, which I could not
lift. It bounded to and fro in answer to questions,
lifted up, and finally, as we were about to depart, the
front part of it rose at our request, and shook hands with
all present — a very wonderful proof of the power of spirit
over inert matter." At New Bedford he also witnessed
an unique musical manifestation. A harp fastened under
a table was made to play most beautiful music without
the aid of mortal hands — a fact that could not be questioned, as the room was brilliantly lighted, so that the
concurrent testimony of the senses of sight and hearing
was available.

He had intended, on closing his labors in New England, to go thence to Baltimore, and spend the winter
in the South; but across the mystic "mental telegraph"
flashed the urgent message, "Come home!" and, though
he had received no outward intimation that all was not
well, he obeyed the summons. He found on his arrival
that a letter had just been dispatched recalling him on

account of the illness of our father, who was again suffering from a cancer, which had been operated upon the preceding summer, and, as was supposed, cured, but had broken out in more malignant form. From this time — January 12, 1859 — he devoted himself to the care of our suffering parent, speaking, a portion of the Sabbaths, at places within a day's journey of home, — Albion, Jackson, &c., — until May 1, and after that remaining at home entirely, until, on the 24th, death came to relieve the sufferer. Our father's last days were illumined by spirit presence and recognition; and it was a source of great pleasure to him, that his son could also see those who waited to receive his freed spirit.

Extract from Journal, June 1, 1859.

" In our bereavement we find in the Spiritual Philosophy a holy and real consolation. How much more beautiful than the cold materialism of the world, or the superstition of the church, come the sweet tones of the angel band, to cheer the earthly mourner when death takes the loved ones from our outer vision. I have been blessed with seeing my father! O, the deep, soulthrilling joy of spirit vision! For years it has been dear to my soul; but it is immeasurably dearer now that I have this new tie to bind me to the higher life. When music's soft notes fill the air, angel voices mingle with the song and prolong the sweet melody. By day and night, in sorrow and in joy, I feel the presence of spirits immortal, among whom now stands my beloved father. O that all might behold with me the reality of spirit presence and communion! Although the form my father once wore is in its mother earth, I *know* the immortal spirit still lives; that, though death may prostrate

6

the body, and time cause it to mingle with its kindred
elements, the soul, the real man, eternal in its essence,
shall exist eternally, and not only live, but love and
grow in knowledge, power, and happiness through un-
ending progress."

The above allusion to angel voices refers not only to
the general fact, that he often heard them, but also to
the particular circumstance, that, on the evening when
we last sang together beside our father's bed, the voices
of unseen singers blended with ours and were distinctly
audible to us all.

Desiring to remain with us as much as possible, and
still continue his public labors, my brother gave no time
to idle sorrow, or even to needed rest of mind and body,
but, June 1, entered upon a three months' engagement at
Lyons, Mich., which place was at that time the residence
of Colonel D. M. Fox, in whose family he was hospitably
entertained. The only event of account that occurred
there was a correspondence with a Methodist minister,
the Rev. R. Sapp, which arose from an anonymous letter
of the latter to the "Ionia Gazette," in which paper
the reply and consequent rejoinders were also published.

CHAPTER VIII.

A TRIP BEGUN WITH STRANGE EXPERIENCES, AND
PREMATURELY ENDED. — THE REVENGE OF OUT-
RAGED NATURE. — THE DEATH-TRANCE AND WEARY
JOURNEY HOME. — CONVALESCENCE. — DEBUT AS AN
AUTHOR.

ON the last of September, he started out on what he
intended should be a long tour, as he had engagements
in the East and South reaching to the following spring.
That this expectation was not fulfilled will appear in
due time. The very outset of his journey was marked
by a curious adventure, of which the following is a
brief account: —

Journal.

"I started from home late in the afternoon to walk
to the station — nearly five miles distant — in time for
the evening train. It had been a beautiful day, but
when I had gone about half the distance, heavy clouds
suddenly gathered in the sky. It began to rain, and
grew dark as pitch. I was obliged to go entirely by
sense of feeling, until there arose before me — out of
the ground apparently — a pale blue light, about the
size of a common lantern. It lighted a place large
enough for me to walk, and kept the same distance in
advance till I got to Napoleon Village, then burst and
disappeared. I was still half a mile from the station.
'What shall I do?' thought I, 'without my spirit lan-

tern.' A voice answered, 'You will see in due time.'
The next I knew, I was standing on the railroad, about
two rods from the depot door. I went in, and discovered, to my astonishment, that I was *not wet*, except
the outside of my boots and bottoms of my pants, and
that I had traversed the entire distance in five minutes
less than an hour. I did not feel any inconvenience
from weariness, and took no cold."

His first point was Willimantic, Conn. He filled his
engagements there and at Providence, speaking also,
week evenings, at Pawtucket and Spragueville. But
the trials and fatigues of the last few months had worn
upon him heavily, and a cold taken in Providence
opened the way for disease to attack the feebly garri-
soned citadel of life. Still he struggled to keep up,
and entered upon an engagement at Putnam, Conn.,
the first Sunday of November. On the succeeding
Tuesday he was taken very sick with congestion of the
lungs, and the following night, to all appearance, died.
Until almost morning he lay in a death-like trance, but
not unconscious, as it seemed. Of his sensations he
says, —

Journal.

"I was a spirit with immortal beings. I could see
my body as it lay upon the bed, cold and lifeless. I
thought of my mother and sister at home, dependent
upon me ; of their deep sorrow when they should hear
of my departure. The spirits around me were conversing together. Some said, 'Let him stay with us!'
Others said, 'No! let him go back to earth and fulfill
his destiny.' Then my guardian spirit said, 'He shall
return to earth.' I recognized, among those around,

the tall Indian chief, — one of the first four spirits
who appeared to me, — and a number of others whom
I knew; but soon one approached whom I had never
seen, — a man of venerable and majestic aspect. He
was attended by a numerous company of spirits, and
eagerly greeted, as if expected, with the request, 'Aid
us to restore to earth this wandering mortal.' I saw a
green and yellow light fall upon my dead body, and I
knew no more till I awoke in the form. I was cold
and stiff, and could not move for a long time; but
gradually warmth and feeling returned, and the next
day I arose and told the astonished friends that I was
going home. They said I could not possibly live to get
there, and, indeed, gave me no hope of recovery if I
remained. I knew I *must* go; so I coolly replied,
'Well, I won't die here,' and started on Thursday
morning. I arrived at Niagara Falls Friday, where I
found my old friend, Judge Manchester, — formerly of
Providence, — and in his excellent family rested until
Monday. Then, though even more feeble, and against
the wishes of my kind host, I continued my journey,
and reached home the Tuesday following, more dead
than alive."

For weeks life and death hung trembling in the balance, and when at length the crisis was passed, and he
began to recover, the most sanguine of our mundane
physicians foreboded that he would never be able to
resume his public labors. But his angel guides said,
"Hope for the best;" and, thanks to their care and
advice, that hope was fulfilled.

During the winter, while still confined to the house,
he prepared for publication a pamphlet of about one

hundred pages, entitled "Religion and Morality: a Criticism upon the Character of the Jewish Jehovah, the Patriarchs, Prophets, Early Church Fathers, Popes, Cardinals, Priests, and Leading Men of Catholic and Protestant Churches, with a Defense of Spiritualism;" and, as the title indicates, was an *exposé* of the absurdity and weakness of the wholesale charges of immorality preferred against Spiritualists and mediums, — and ascribed to their belief, — by the representatives of the popular theology, which reverences men as particularly chosen of God, whose practices would be considered, in any other persons, as highly immoral and reprehensible. It showed from statistics that there was less crime among the Spiritualists than any denomination, in proportion to numbers, and that their teachings necessarily inculcate and foster the highest morality by declaring that virtue is the only path to happiness here or hereafter, that vice brings its inevitable penalty. It admonished certain reverend claimants of extra morality, that if the derelictions of individuals were to be charged upon the form of religion which they advocated, the result would be far more damaging to *their* claims than to those upon whom they sought to throw disgrace and opprobrium. The work had a large sale at the time, but has now been out of print some time. He intended to have prepared a revised and enlarged edition for republication; but other occupations prevented him from carrying out that intention, though he had carefully collected data for the purpose.

CHAPTER IX.

THE NEW SPIRIT GUIDE. — THE TWO PORTRAITS. —
REMOVAL TO ALBION. — EARLY ACQUAINTANCE WITH
DR. SLADE. — DEBATE WITH REV. JOSEPH JONES AT
DECATUR, MICH. — KENTUCKY IN WAR TIME (SEP-
TEMBER, 1861). — LEGALLY ORDAINED, JULY, 1862.

THE book was published in March, 1860, and he
began gradually to resume lecturing, speaking only
Sundays, and in places within easy distance of home;
Port Huron, Jackson, Albion, Kalamazoo, &c. In April,
having disposed of the Brooklyn homestead, he removed with mother and sister to a pleasant place in
Albion, which was his home for the remainder of his
earth life.

The venerable spirit, spoken of in the preceding
chapter as first seen by him on the night of his death
trance at Putnam, Conn., continued to visit him, and
at times would control him to tell perfect strangers
their history past and present, and to a great extent
the future also, giving sometimes important advice,
which, when followed, invariably accomplished the result foretold. Many whom his clear sight has relieved
from danger or difficulty, in different parts of the
country, during the last twelve years, will remember
with gratitude the "Old Man." This was the name
by which he was known, at his own request, as, his real
name was difficult of pronunciation. He was an Egyp-

tian by birth, educated in Persia in all the learning of
the Magi, was versed in the mysteries of spirit communion, and hence called by the church a magician, and
on one of his visits to Rome was imprisoned by the
command of the reigning pope, and doomed to the
flames, for dealing in magic and forbidden arts. But
the powerful spirits that surrounded him opened his
prison doors, and he escaped to Persia, where he departed this life at the age of one hundred and twenty.
He is known to history as " The Old Man of the Mountain " — the last chief of that title; but his history is
little known, and what has been preserved is distorted
by the pens of his enemies — the church historians.
He lived on earth in the twelfth century and beginning
of the thirteenth. He spoke and wrote, not only Egyptian and Persian, but Arabic, Greek, Latin, and Old
French. He spoke English quite imperfectly at first,
and always with a peculiar guttural accent, and never
wrote it. He often made himself visible, not only to
mediums, but to those who never saw any other spirit.
Of his power of reading persons, he said, " I can read
their past and present like an open book, and from the
tendencies and circumstances there revealed, the character of the person, and other data and relations, I can
forecast the future much as you would calculate and
solve a mathematical problem, and with the same accuracy. I do not claim infallibility. An error may occur
in the figures of the most practiced mathematician; so
there may in mine, but with about the same infrequen-
cy. I never say anything positively of which I am not
as certain as I am that ' figures cannot lie.' "

The preceding year my brother had obtained, through
the mediumship of W. P. Anderson, the spirit artist, a

finely-executed portrait of his Italian guide, Farini. It was drawn in the city of Jackson, and completed in two hours, though the work is elaborate, and includes considerable vine-work, aside from the head, and has won merited admiration from all classes of people, including artists and connoisseurs of no mean pretensions.

Now he desired greatly to obtain also a picture of the "Old Man;" and the latter said, "I will go and sit for my portrait on such a day." My brother accordingly wrote to Mr. Anderson, that on a certain day, a spirit (not saying who) was to sit for a portrait for him, and to forward the result, if any were obtained. Mr. Anderson was then at La Salle, Ill. The appointed day passed, and the spirit reported that the sitting *had taken place*, and a good likeness was obtained, but not so nicely finished as Farini's. In due course of mail the picture came, and was exactly as described.

About the time of our removal to Albion, a literary association there was debating the subject of the Origin of Man and Unity of the Races, and considerable interest had been aroused in the community by the participation of several of the college faculty and other well-read men. My brother was induced to take part in the discussion, which continued several evenings, and evoked much thought upon subjects usually not much regarded by the masses. In the month of April he returned to Chicago to lecture, after an interval of nearly three years, dedicated a new hall for the society, and spoke five Sundays, and, consequently, was in the city during the session of the Republican Convention, which he looked in upon, and chanced to be present when the name of Abraham Lincoln was put in nomination for the presidency. He spent the month of

June in Port Huron, St. Clair, and Kalamazoo, and on
his return home met, for the first time, Mr. J. G. Fish,
formerly a Baptist clergyman, but then a Spiritualist
lecturer, and since widely known in that capacity.
Next he attended a grove meeting near Eaton Rapids,
in connection with two other speakers — Rev. A. W.
Mason, of Pulaski, a progressed Universalist, and W.
F. Jamieson. The remainder of the year 1860 he
spent mostly in Michigan, the only exception being a
short trip, by way of St. Joseph, to Chicago, La Salle,
and Dixon, Ill., and Davenport, Iowa, lecturing nearly
every Sunday, and occasionally on week evenings,
though in this he was somewhat cautious, in view of
the sickness brought about by over-exertion the previous year. During this time, and more or less subsequently, he was engaged in assisting certain parties in
important business transactions, which, by the advice
of the " Old Man," were brought to a successful issue,
while many other persons received from him advice in
matters of personal moment, which was the means of
rescuing them from situations of great difficulty, and
even danger. In this connection occurred some of the
most absolute proofs of the beneficent intervention of
supramundane intelligence that can be imagined ; and
if the seal of private confidence did not forbid, I could,
in these facts alone, spread upon these pages an ample
answer to the question, " What good has Spiritualism
done ? " — and one that ought to silence forever all the
absurd charges of "immoral tendency," "breaking up
families," and the like, that have been the staple argu-
ments of the opposing world, and too often echoed —
parrot-like — by those who *might* know better, if indeed
they *do* not.

At the time of which I write, that most wonderful of mediums, Dr. Slade, of New York, resided in Albion, and in his presence remarkable demonstrations of spirit power were obtained, which were justly considered to be conclusive, as evidence of spirit existence and communion, although the two later phases of his mediumship — independent writing and visible appearances — had not yet been developed. The marked feature of the tests given in his presence was then, as now, the circumstance that all took place in the light, whether it was the levitation of ponderable objects, or of the medium himself; or, as sometimes occurred, the bringing of articles from a distance — such as geological specimens. In one instance a ring, which had been lost in Canada, was brought to the residence of Dr. Slade, in Albion, in the presence of a large company, whom " Owasso " had invited to witness the fulfillment of his promise. My brother was often present at these seances.

Among other pleasing incidents of the time just passed over may be mentioned the dedication of Merrill Hall, Detroit, to the use of Spiritualists, where he had the pleasure of assisting Mrs. Hardinge in the exercises of the occasion, and his meeting with E. V. Wilson and Miss Ada Hoyt, in Chicago. At the latter place he met with an accident which might have proved serious had there been no power to save. Of this he says, in his journal, " In going to the depot, I slipped and fell down a flight of steps upon the stone pavement; but the 'Old Man' caught me, so I only struck lightly on one knee; and all the harm I got was a little skin bruise, instead of a broken limb, as seemed inevitable. People looked astonished to see me walk away unhurt, and, doubtless, thought it a providential escape,

as indeed it was, though *they* could not behold the
helping hand."

In January, 1861, he made his first trip to Kentucky ;
and connected with this was a striking and useful test
of the ability of spirits to transport intelligence in
advance of the mail. He had written his Louisville
correspondent that he would be there January 24, if
desired, and to write immediately. He received no
answer ; but the " Old Man " said they had written for
him to come, and would be disappointed if he did not.
On the strength of that assurance alone, he started on
a journey of three hundred miles, and found the information true to the letter. But more than this, Dr.
Slade was then in Louisville, and his Indian guide,
Owasso, told *them* that Whiting was on his way and
would arrive that night, but *had not received the letter.*

He lectured several times in Louisville with good
success, then went to Frankfort and delivered two
lectures on Spiritualism, after which a committee waited
on him with an invitation to speak before the legislature, upon the "State of the Country." This he did
to a crowded house and general satisfaction. He also
lectured several times at New Albany, Ind., on his return. Among many pleasant acquaintances at Louisville was numbered the veteran journalist, George D.
Prentice. The next noticeable event was a debate,
held at Decatur, Mich., with a Methodist clergyman, —
Rev. Joseph Jones, — upon the question, " Resolved,
That the origin of modern spiritual phenomena is entirely hypothetical, and therefore the revelations from
that source are not at all reliable." At the desire of
Mr. Jones the Bible was excluded from the discussion.
The debate continued through three days, March 12,

13, and 14, and was listened to by large audiences, and afterward published in pamphlet form, having been reported for that purpose by a competent person. The latter part of March was spent in St. Charles, Ill., and the month of April in Rockford, where he was at the breaking out of the war, which he deeply deplored in common with all who were sufficiently thoughtful to realize its nature and foresee its terrible character and devastating effects. On the ensuing 4th of July he made this entry in his journal: —

"This is the gloomiest 4th of July I ever spent. There is a so-called celebration here. What a solemn mockery! We have no Union, and yet they have a farcical representation of thirty-four states, and an oration consisting of fulsome praise of Christianity, with a bloodthirsty finale. That is the present style of preaching 'peace on earth, good will to men.' . . . I hope the present Congress, convened to-day, will do something for peace. I wish to see the Union preserved. If it is, it will be through the Union element at the South. If there is no such element they can never be subjugated. I regret to see the disposition, on the part of a large body of extremists, to accumulate power in the hands of the central government to an extent incompatible with the genius of free institutions, — to rule by the sword; a scheme which, if successful, can not fail to work the subversion of all civil liberty. Would that all might feel a true love for their country at this terrible and gloomy hour!"

In the ensuing September, having leisure time, he resolved to visit the scene of hostilities in Kentucky, and see for himself the aspect of affairs of which so many contradictory reports were received. He found all excitement in Louisville, in expectation of the approach of General Buckner with his army, to take possession of the city; but the cars ran off the track, and left them sixty miles away, and they were obliged to retreat. As soon as this news was received, comparative quiet was restored to Louisville, though war regulations were enforced to a certain extent, and troops were pressed forward with all possible dispatch. He found much division in public sentiment, extending even to families — parent arrayed against child, and brother against brother, — a state of things that brought home to the heart most forcibly the horrors of civil war. General Sherman showed him every attention, both there and at the federal camp at Nolin, where there were, at that time, forty thousand troops; and as his railroad friends furnished him free passes over all the routes, he had ample opportunity to examine for himself the situation, in all its dreary aspect. He visited all the points of interest, including the secession camp, in Owen County. He found many friends in both armies, and he held their confidence equally inviolate, as he was laying up in his mind matter for future reference, for his own information and instruction, and not for the use or abuse of any other person or party.

After his return from this tour, he spent the rest of the fall and winter in comparative quiet, only lecturing occasionally at various points in this state and at Toledo, O. The last of March, 1862, he started on a trip to Detroit and Port Huron, which was extended to London and Sparta, C. W. Of this I shall give his own account.

Extract from Journal.

" At Detroit I heard the Rev. Father Smarius, the great Jesuit priest, lecture against Spiritualism. His lecture was able, but full of misrepresentations and ridicule, though not as abusive as the generality of Protestant lectures upon the same subject. He declined to debate the subject at my invitation, and evidently did not wish to meet a Spiritualist on a free platform, although he is willing to meet Protestants in argument. I next went to Port Huron and delivered a course of lectures. The friends at London sent out a man for me to go there and meet a Methodist minister, who was battling Spiritualism. I always like to attend to all such cases; so I went, and arrived in time to hear the Rev. James Scott lecture against Spiritualism, before a society called ' The Young Men's Christian Union.' There were but two or three persons in the house who knew of my presence. When the reverend gentleman had concluded, it was announced that the subject was open to debate in ten minute speeches, and a member arose and said that there was a stranger present who would, if invited, make a few remarks. The president assented; so I gave them ten minutes' worth of Spiritualism. Then another reverend got up and said a few words, and the meeting adjourned in a hurry. Thereupon my friends blackguarded them so for showing the white feather, that Scott finally agreed to meet me in debate, the platform, rules, &c., to be decided upon by a joint committee of three of my friends and three of his. They met, but could not agree. Then several letters passed between us, but to no purpose. I went to Sparta and gave three lectures, and on my return Scott sent in a proposition as follows : ' Resolved, That modern Spiritualism is a delusion, and contrary to, and not in accordance with, the Scriptures.' My friends immediately accepted in my name, and called the joint committee to arrange rules of debate, when they backed square down on their own proposition. Before I left London I sent Mr. Scott a letter, in which I told him I would debate with him any time when he got ready, if that time ever came. I had an excellent time; gave three lectures to full houses. The mayor of the city presided at my meetings, and took an active interest in all the proceedings. I had a good time also at Sparta, where Messrs. Harvey, Reynolds, and Pace are active members, not to forget old General McCleod, whose stories of his campaigns under Wellington, and during the patent war in Canada, were to me full of interest. On my return home, I paid Dr. Slade a visit at Jackson; found him well located and doing a thriving business."

The July following, he received from the Religio-Philosophical Society of St. Charles, Ill., a certificate of ordination as a minister of the gospel, with authority to solemnize marriages, &c., which placed him upon terms of legal equality with the clergy of all denominations.

I believe his was among the earliest regular ordinations made by a Spiritualist society, though not many years later many lecturers were recipients of similar certificates. But the legally organized societies were then very few compared to the present number, and hence few had authority to confer ordination.

CHAPTER X.

AS A COMPOSER OF MUSIC. — PUBLICATION OF THE
FIRST EIGHT OF HIS SONGS. — DEBATE WITH AN
ADVENTIST AT GRAND RAPIDS, MICH. — EASTWARD
AGAIN (MARCH, 1864). — SPIRIT PICTURES.

THE remainder of the year 1862 was marked by no
event of especial importance to this narrative. The war
absorbed the attention of the people to the exclusion of
all other interests, so that the demand for lectures upon
any other theme was greatly decreased, and many speakers in the spiritualistic ranks were driven temporarily,
and some permanently, to other pursuits.

My brother became interested with a friend in the
boot and shoe business in Albion, — a branch of trade
of which he had some knowledge, from our father having formerly been engaged in it, — but he never abandoned the lecture field, and during the most of this time
and the ensuing year had regular Sunday appointments
at places where he could go on Saturday and return on
Monday, spending the rest of the week in the store in
the busy season, unless called away to attend funerals,
as was often the case. This was a summons which he
always dreaded, but never refused. His leisure time
he devoted to music, which was always, to him, recrea-
tion and delight. He had composed some previously,
but had taken no pains to write out and preserve his
pieces. Now he gave more attention in that direction,

7

and in 1863 were composed several of the songs afterward published ; among them " Lena De Lorme," and
" The Land of the so-called Dead." His method of
composing was somewhat peculiar. He almost always
composed words and music simultaneously, playing and
singing the piece until complete, then writing out the
words ; while the music was not, perhaps, written until
required for publication. Then it became my task to
write out and prepare it for the press. He never in but
two instances adapted music to words already prepared,
but occasionally composed music first, and words afterward. In the summer of 1863, he had built expressly
for him, at the manufactory at Kalamazoo, a large piano-
cased, six octave melodeon, which instrument he always
preferred to a piano as an accompaniment to the voice.
The melodeon was sent home in September, and so perfect was its construction and toning that it remains in
perfect order and tune after a lapse of nearly nine
years.

In October, he again visited Kentucky, but did not
lecture, his business being to bring me home from Louisville, — where I had been spending some time with
friends, — and to take an observation of things in general.

He next filled a month's engagement at Grand Rapids,
Michigan, and during the following month, December,
held a debate at that place with an Adventist preacher
of some note, Rev. J. M. Stephenson. The question
discussed was that, " The Bible, reason, and philosophy
teach the complete and entire cessation of all consciousness at death," Mr. Stephenson arguing in the affirmative, according to the received belief of his sect. The
press and people of Grand Rapids were much interested

in the discussion, as appears from the following brief quotations from the city papers : —

THE IMMORTALITY OF THE SOUL, OR CONSCIOUS EXISTENCE AFTER DEATH.

A debate on the above question will be held at Mills and Clancy's Hall, commencing on Wednesday evening next, between Rev. J. M. Stephenson, a clergyman of the sect known as Adventists, and A. B. Whiting, the well-known advocate of the Spiritual Philosophy.

Mr. Stephenson will argue that " The Bible, reason, and philosophy teach the complete and entire cessation of all consciousness at death." Mr. Whiting will argue the conscious existence of the soul after death.

To quite a large class of our citizens this debate will be possessed of much interest and importance, as tending, perhaps, to settle doubts or establish half-formed convictions, and, perhaps, to remove errors concerning the subject in issue. Others, having clearly-defended and well-grounded convictions as to the immortality of the soul, will be repaid for attending the debate by witnessing the novel manner in which the issue will be presented from both sides.

The debate increases in interest every night. It is as largely attended as the capacity of the hall will permit. Both disputants being talented, they are enabled to give their hearers a rich intellectual feast. Judge Robinson presides at the debate with dignity and grace. It is being conducted with the greatest propriety and courtesy, both the disputants being finished gentlemen, who seem to have an elevated view of the dignity of oral discussion of religious or kindred subjects. It is a noble thing to behold two men calmly, yet earnestly.

discussing the greatest question underlying the religions of the day. None but moral cowards and religious bigots will refuse to listen to a discussion of so important a question. For such there is no room at Mills and Clancy's Hall during the continuance of this most interesting debate.

The entire debate was phonographically reported by W. F. Jamieson, with a view to its publication in pamphlet form; but Mr. Stephenson refused his consent, and it was not published. I regret exceedingly that the report was not written out and preserved, as I believe it to have contained a rare compendium of the proofs of immortality.

The last of December he again visited Louisville on private business, one item of which was to arrange for the appearance of the first published of his songs — "Lena De Lorme." He was there the memorable cold New Year's of 1864, and the following week journeyed to Decatur, Ill., to lecture — a trip not only seriously uncomfortable under the circumstances, but also rendered somewhat dangerous by the explosion of a locomotive boiler. In the spring he transferred the copyright of his published song to the publishing house of H. M. Higgins, Chicago, and a new edition was issued, together with two other pieces, "Touch the lute gently" and "By the side of the murmuring stream," the group bearing the title "Three Heart-offerings."

The success of these was so marked and encouraging as to justify, later in the same year, the publication of another group of five songs, under the title of "Sparkling Gems." These comprised "Adieu, Leonore," "Leoline," "You well know my beloved," "Land of the so-called dead," and "Maid of Glenore," and were equally well received. The lighter pieces, particularly "Leoline," attained to considerable popularity in the parlor and concert-room, — being sung by several prominent concert troupes throughout the country, — while "The land of the so-called dead" gained a more lasting reputation in the lecture-room. But the cultivation of his musical gifts were incidental, and never allowed to interfere with the business of his life, — public speaking, — but rather added a grace to it, as he frequently sang at the close of his lectures an appropriate piece of his music.

In March, 1864, he started on an eastern tour, spoke at Cleveland, and went thence to New York to visit and transact some business relating to his books and music; was informed that a large number of the "Debate" had been sold for shipment to France and England.

He lectured during April in Providence, where, among other pleasing incidents, he was presented with a beautiful little scarf-pin, made from an antique gold chain, in the form of a crescent surmounted by a star: upon these were embossed four crowns, three on the crescent and one on the star — all of which possessed an heraldic significance which augmented its value in his eyes. Any one who heard him lecture during the last seven years of his life might have noticed the glitter of this peculiar ornament upon his bosom. He attended the Spiritualist Convention held at Clinton Hall, New York, the 11th, 12th, and 13th of May, where many of the ablest workers in the cause were gathered in council, and spent the Sundays of that month at Chicopee, Mass. There he had a little experience in the then comparatively new phenomena of spirit pictures, concerning which I will give an extract from a letter written home by him at the time.

Extract from Letter.

" I was sitting for an ambrotype here the other day, and a beautiful little compass appeared on the plate, though there was nothing to take it from. I sat again another day, and the plate was covered with images, more or less perfect, and two small faces, one in profile and quite well defined, the other about the size of a gold half dollar, immediately above my head. The latter has on a turban, and is found perfect when examined through a microscope. Both of them I recognize as members of the band of Persian spirits who accompany the ' Old Man.' The artist is a young man, just married, and his wife and relatives are all opposed to Spiritualism ; but these phantom pictures have haunted him by spells for over a year, and he can't get rid of them. He says they are more apt to come for mediums than any one else. He has a beautiful one of Miss Lizzie Doten, with a spirit beside her ; and the Davenports have one, taken here, upon which the fifth hand is as plainly visible as their own."

He spoke in Springfield, Mass., the first two Sundays of June, and then returned home.

CHAPTER XI.

CHICAGO SPIRITUAL CONVENTION OF 1864. — HIS POSI-
TION THEREIN. — POLITICAL VIEWS. — LECTURES IN
CHICAGO DURING THE SESSION OF THE DEMOCRATIC
NATIONAL CONVENTION. — TRIP THROUGH CANADA.
— THE CAMPAIGN OF 1864. — FIRST APPEARANCE
IN THE POLITICAL ARENA. — KENTUCKY IN NOVEM-
BER. — NOT CAPTURED BY GUERRILLAS. — ABAN-
DONED PROJECTS.

HAVING lectured during July at Grand Rapids and
Lansing, Mich., on the 8th of August he proceeded
to Chicago to attend the first " National Convention of
Spiritualists," which had been called to convene on the
9th, " for the purpose of deciding upon some plan of
organization or associative action." His first move,
on reaching the city and taking rooms at the Sherman
House, was to have an interview with Mr. Storey, of
the " Chicago Times," and arrange for the attendance
of first-class reporters on behalf of that paper, thus
securing a full and impartial report of the proceedings.

He had not contemplated attending the convention
up to within a short time of its assembling, as other business demanded his attention, so that he could only do so
at considerable personal loss and inconvenience. But
it was foretold to him that an attempt would be made,
in view of the coming election, to throw the weight of
the convention in support of a party, by the introduc-

tion of a series of political resolutions; that a contest would ensue, and, if the resolutions passed, the object of the convention — namely, organization, — would be defeated. Deeply interested in the success and harmonious working of the convention, he resolved to leave everything, and go, and do what he could to promote that object by aiding to prevent, if possible, the introduction of extraneous and dividing topics. This he had some hope might be done from the personal assurances of many, who, though holding adverse political opinions, agreed with him in thinking it necessary that harmony should be secured, and the time of the convention devoted to the important object for which it had been called.

Unfortunately, this hope was not realized. The majority, carried away by enthusiastic loyalty and devotion to their own political views, decreed the reception of a series of resolutions on the state of the country, containing an absolute indorsal of the war, the party in power, and their candidate for the presidency. The contest being thus forced upon him, he, in common with others of different views, was left no honorable alternative but to stand up as firmly in defense of his political as he ever had of his religious principles. From this duty he did not shrink, and, although the majority outnumbered the minority nearly seven to one, and the galleries were filled by a crowd ready to hiss down the unpopular side of the question, he not only gained a respectful hearing, but won the admiration of his bitterest opponents by the determined manner with which he quelled an incipient clamor in the crowd, and compelled their attention. One, who stood opposed to him then, describes his attitude upon that occasion — when he declared that he would be heard even though he stood alone — to have been one of the finest examples of moral heroism, and personal power to command an audience, that it was ever his fortune to witness. It may be mentioned, as an incident eminently characteristic of the man, that, after the conclusion of his speech, he took occasion to make his way among that portion of the audience whence the attempted disturbance had arisen.

The resolutions were passed, — a minority of forty-four protesting, and in an ably written document setting forth their reasons for dissent, and the convention, after much discussion on organization and other matters, adjourned, as had been predicted, without having accomplished that object. He much regretted this result, although he had expected it. He saw that it was inevitable under the circumstances, and could only hope for better harmony at some future time, when the war spirit should be laid. He was deeply pained by the bitter spirit displayed by a portion of the majority; for, while he conceded to all an *absolute* right to their own opinions upon political or any other subjects, he did *not* recognize the right of any to force those opinions upon a body of persons assembled for an altogether different .purpose. This he would never do himself, and he believed such a course one that no majority could render either just or profitable. He had never taken any active part in politics, although, as was well known to his friends, he had settled convictions on those subjects as upon most others. Those views coincided, in the main, with those of the leading democratic statesmen from the time of Jefferson down. He belonged to a class of thinkers who regarded war as a blot upon our civilization, and the encroachment of military power upon individual rights as subversive of civil liberty — the very foundation of free institutions. In his travels in the different parts of the country, he had been led to observe that the differences existing between distant sections arose largely from misunderstanding of each other's character and motives; and hence he believed that, by conciliation and a better acquaintance, those differences might be reconciled, and their causes peaceably removed. Holding these views, he deplored the fatal blindness of those party leaders, who, by appeals to passion and prejudice, fomented discord, and, finally, plunged the country into the horrors of civil war. But while he condemned their action, and earnestly desired the unity of the republic, he claimed the people's constitutional right to criticise the acts of public servants in time of war, as in time of peace. He could not indorse the course of the administration, inasmuch as it seemed to him in many respects ill calculated to promote the end in view, namely, the speedy restoration of peace and union. He saw with apprehension the growing tendency to centralization in government, and regarded the suspension of the writ of *habeas corpus* in peaceful states, and the arbitrary arrest and imprisonment of their citizens, without due process of law and in violation of plain constitutional provisions, as a usurpation of power which no plea of necessity could palliate, and a precedent most dangerous to the liberties of the people. He believed that "two wrongs never could, under any circumstances, make a right;" hence the position which he assumed on this subject, and maintained by argument, not only at the Chicago Convention, but upon all suitable occasions.

Many good friends lamented that " Whiting had destroyed his influence and usefulness among Spiritualists " by advocating views supposed to be unpopular among them; but it was found to be otherwise. And I have yet to learn that a fearless defense of principle *ever* permanently injured any person or cause, even in the eyes of that so-called capricious monster, the Public. He returned to Chicago August 26, and lectured the ensuing Sunday evening, Mrs. Spence speaking in the afternoon. The audience was immense ; the hall, entrances, and even the sidewalk without, being crowded. He remained in the city the ensuing week in attendance upon the sessions of the Democratic National Convention, meeting many old friends among the delegates, and making some new ones. Among other pleasing incidents may be mentioned an interview with Hon. Clement L. Vallandigham, whom he met for the first time, and of whose integrity, ability, and sterling patriotism he formed upon that occasion a most favorable opinion.

The following month, September, he made a trip to Canada, lecturing at London, and also at a place called Mitchell, — a Scotch Presbyterian stronghold, — where, for the last time in his career as a Spiritualist lecturer, his meeting was disturbed by disorderly conduct on the part of the audience. In the early years of Spiritualism, as of all other new phases of thought, such things were common, though less so in his experience than in that of many, on account of his determined manner of meeting such demonstrations; but at this late day the experience was sufficiently novel to be somewhat amusing, as a reminder of the past. Canada was at this time thronged with refugees from the States, of various kinds and degrees of consequence, and with United States detectives employed in watching over the movements of such of these as were deemed worth the trouble, while the Dominion officials had an eye upon both ; the whole making up a drama of life under unusual and peculiar aspects, which could not fail to be highly interesting and instructive to the student of human nature. On his return, he lectured at Port Huron and St. Clair with usual success, and then, rendered uneasy by the non-receipt of his letters, hastened home. But of this more hereafter.

I have said that he had never taken any part in politics before the public, as his time and talents were absorbed in another direction, and I will here add that he never — then or afterward — took any part in working party machinery, further than as a delegate in convention ; nor was he ever, though frequently solicited, a candidate for any office whatever. Until the campaign of 1864 he had never made a political speech, and under circumstances less extraordinary it is quite possible that his voice might never have been heard in the political arena. He cared little for names, or candidates personally ; but he could not decline, when called upon, to expound the principles of constitutional liberty as he understood them, and warn the people of the dangers attending their violation. Nor did he hesitate to arraign the party, or persons, however powerful, whom he deemed guilty of such violation, and denounce in the most scathing terms that sham loyalty and bogus patriotism which, while arrogating to itself a monopoly of the virtues, could yet prefer schemes of partisan aggrandisement to the peace and prosperity of the nation.

During the two weeks last preceding the election, he delivered addresses in this and other towns in Central Michigan, which added much to his already established reputation as an eloquent and able orator. He preserved, in this new field of labor, his own characteristic style of reasoning from present facts to their inevitable sequences, as illustrated by historical parallels, showing how, by the operation of immutable law, similar combinations of circumstances invariably produce similar results ; that, in fact, history repeats itself, and that we can not hope that a course of action which resulted disastrously in the past can, in the same relations, fail to result disastrously in the future.

Immediately after the election he set out for Louisville, to officiate at the marriage of a friend, I being his companion. The trip was far from being in all respects a pleasurable one, — on account of certain circumstances to be spoken of elsewhere, — although everything possible was done for our comfort and enjoyment by our friends in that city. The wedding was properly achieved, including the dinner, which I remember to have been a triumph of culinary skill and artistic embellishment. We remained only two weeks, including a trip to Lexington, when we came near being captured by guerrillas, — the succeeding train meeting the fate which we escaped by what we then supposed was a fortunate chance ; but years after, on a subsequent visit to Kentucky, when the war was over, he was informed that *his* being on board saved the train that day. And this is the story as told to him : —

The guerrillas lay concealed in the· bushes near a small station, where one of their number, in the garb of a peaceful citizen, was detailed to inspect the train,

see if it was provided with a guard, and, if not, to give
the signal for attack. This man had, before the war,
met A. B. Whiting, and not only was indebted to him
for some kindness, but cherished an almost superstitious reverence for his character and mediumistic
powers. He saw him standing upon the platform of
the car, recognized him, and fearing he might be
harmed in an indiscriminate fire, *failed to give the signal,* and the train passed by in safety. We reached
Lexington, and returned to Louisville without detention, and came home December 1.

The ensuing months up to May, 1865, he spent
mostly in this state, speaking at Lansing, Dewitt, St.
Johns, Ann Arbor, and several other points during that
time. In the month of February he was called upon
to stand by the death-bed of Emma, wife of Dr. Slade,
to perform the last services over her earthly remains,
and to comfort and sustain his friend under a double
burden of bereavement, — an only sister having passed
on but a few months previously. To this office of
friendship he gave up his lecture engagements for the
time, and partially on this account cancelled an engagement at Cincinnati for the month of March.

During this year, he was in correspondence with
parties at various points in Colorado and the western
territories, in contemplation of a tour in that direction
in the spring and summer of 1865, but finally decided
to postpone it until some future time, as he then somewhat expected to visit Europe the ensuing fall. The
latter project he was also compelled reluctantly to
abandon, for personal reasons, with the hope of being
able to carry it out at some other time. This he certainly would have done had his life upon earth extended over a few more years.

CHAPTER XII.

AN UNWELCOME THEME. — ENEMIES, AND HOW THEY
WERE BAFFLED. — A GLIMPSE BEHIND THE SCENES.
— SNARES THAT COULD NOT ENTRAP, AND POISON
THAT COULD NOT SLAY. — POWERS MUNDANE AND
SUPRAMUNDANE.

I MUST now revert to a subject which I would gladly
pass over in silence, did the duty of a faithful historian
permit ; but it is necessary that it be referred to, as
having an important bearing upon succeeding events,
as furnishing remarkable instances of spirit power, and
as throwing light and glory upon a character at once
inflexible and magnanimous. I allude to the political
persecution to which he was subjected during the war,
and particularly during 1864–5. The extent to which
this was carried was known to few of his friends, and,
as we charitably believe, to few of his enemies. I have
no desire to recall past bitterness by any personal allusions. Several of those principally involved have passed
from the earthly stage, and by this time understand
something of the power that could so signally thwart
their purposes. Many who took minor parts in the
drama were actuated by a misapprehension of facts,
mistaken sense of duty, or excess of partisan feeling,
and had no idea that the farce in which they were
assisting might have become a tragedy. Therefore,
bearing malice toward none, and desiring ever to give

the most charitable construction to human motives, I shall state merely a few leading facts in this connection, omitting names and exact dates for the reasons above hinted at, and not from inability to give both if I thought best to do so; for though much that follows was first made known to us from spiritual sources, in the way of warnings of danger, ample mundane testimony was subsequently furnished, and some of the facts, as will be seen, were within my personal knowledge.

At even this short distance of time, it seems almost incredible that a state of things should have existed in this country, which could render it possible for personal or party spite to conspire against the liberty and lives of unoffending citizens, under color of public necessity; but that such things *were*, we, who saw them, know.

From the outbreak of the war, he, in common with many others, who, amid the general rage, dared to speak for peace, was exposed to the hatred of a set of persons who had but one word for all opinions differing from their own, and that word *treason*. He was frequently threatened, either openly or covertly, with the tender mercies of Fort Warren; but neither threats, nor the puny efforts of those who exerted their utmost power to compass their execution, troubled him much. Relying not only upon firm friends here, but upon the powerful protection and guidance of dwellers in the upper realms, he went about his business unmoved, and seemingly unconscious. Though he was well aware that he was shadowed by spies, and his most innocent action liable to be distorted by their officious zeal, yet, as he had nothing to conceal, he could afford to laugh at their waste of time and travel, and even occasionally indulge in a little harmless fun at their expense, — which he could easily do, as they, of course, did not suspect that he was acquainted with their character or business. He considered this mode of retaliation legitimate, since no serious redress was possible in the premises, and I think he troubled some of them about as much as they did him. His trips to Canada and Kentucky were watched with especial eagerness by these gentry, in the hope — as we guessed then, and afterward ascertained — of finding a mare's nest that might be construed into the carrying of rebel correspondence. That their industry went unrewarded by discovery, was not their fault; for his circumspectness refused to give them as much as a Pickwickian warming-pan to found a supposition on.

Another thing, which annoyed him far more than this personal surveillance, was the frequent detention of his mail matter, and — as he had every reason to believe — its overhauling by parties to whom he had never delegated that responsibility. His foreign correspondence and his own letters home seemed to be especial objects of curiosity to some seekers after knowledge. He noticed that whatever intelligence he imparted in his letters, regarding his future movements, quickly became known to his followers. To still further satisfy himself of the truth of his suspicions, by agreement with me, he tried the experiment of writing home a programme entirely at variance with his real intentions, and amusing himself with their consequent bewilderment. But a still more direct proof was obtained by the sending of decoy letters, marked, — I being instructed not to open them until his return, when he could determine, by examination, whether they had been tampered with since they left his hand. Of course this state of things was not particularly pleasant, or well calculated to win the affection of the recipient of such peculiar attentions ; hence it is not strange that the sense of personal outrage confirmed and strengthened his opposition to the party which he held responsible for introducing into free America the machinery of despotism.

This was the state of things which existed up to the fall of 1864, and which, doubtless, accented the determined stand taken by him at the Chicago Convention, and during the ensuing campaign. His denunciations of political spies and informers, as tools of a tyranny whose existence was incompatible with the first principles of free government, came with the force gained from knowledge of that whereof he spoke, and struck home so tellingly that he was privately offered an appointment to a lucrative office if he would " allow himself to be converted from his political errors," while disastrous personal consequences were hinted at in case of his persistence therein.

To some minds such a proposition might have brought temptation ; but a man who had stood for years in the front ranks of an unpopular cause, and, even when scarce emerging from boyhood, spurned repeated offers of church preferment at the price of his *religious* principles, was little likely, in mature manhood, to make a sale of his *political* convictions. Of course the agents, who had thus placed themselves to some degree in his power, could not forgive his obduracy, and thus the number and virulence of his enemies was increased. Had he apprehended the most disastrous results that malevolence could devise, it would not have shaken his firmness. But one who never deceived had said that his life and liberty should be held sacred even in the midst of danger. So, with firm reliance upon his spirit guards, he went calmly and fearlessly on, taking from time to time such precautions as his own reason, or their superior knowledge, suggested as tending to insure his safety. Nor were earthly friends wanting, as will be seen; and thus, though perils gathered thick about his way, each was successively evaded, and with so little apparent effort, that those whose schemes were brought to naught were fain to ascribe their defeat to chance. I will not particularize at length. Suffice it to say, that from representations made at Washington, an order was issued for his arrest, which, however, after being delayed at first because it was not deemed prudent to attempt to execute it in the State of Michigan, where he then was, was finally destroyed by the interposition of a lady friend, who afterward related the circumstance to him, and was somewhat surprised when he told her he knew the *fact* before, though not the *person* to whose kindness he was indebted.

A similar order was issued from the military headquarters at St. Louis, and embodied in a secret circular to the several chief detectives, offering a reward of five thousand dollars for his capture and delivery at one of the principal posts in that department, *or for satisfactory proof of his death.* Then followed a description of his person and dress, including a peculiar scarf which he wore at that time. All that could be construed into an accusation in this singular document was comprised in the phrase, "suspected of being a rebel mail agent," which was appended to his name; but no accusation was needed where martial law was in force; hence the choice of locality.

Men were not wanting who were eager to earn five thousand dollars, even as the price of blood; and when it was ascertained that he was about to visit Louisville, there was great rejoicing at the pleasing prospect of seeing their prey walk directly into the trap. So confident were they, that they quarreled beforehand over the division of the spoils — a quarrel which nearly proved fatal to him; for one zealous youth determined to forestall the rest, and in pursuance of that determination, dogged him on his journey southward, intending to have him seized in the city of Indianapolis, and spirited away with all possible secrecy and dispatch. My being with him, and certain circumstances which had not been counted on, defeated this brilliant plan. The auspicious moment passed. But the prize was not to be surrendered so easily. The second clause of the order flashed upon the mind of the ambitious detective; he procured a quantity of strychnine, and, watching his opportunity, at a little station where we stopped for refreshments, poisoned the coffee which had been ordered by his intended victim. My brother, with a traveler's haste, swallowed a portion of the coffee before the warning hand of the spirit guide restrained him; the warning voice whispered, " It is drugged." He disposed of the balance, so that it might be supposed that he had drank the whole, and resumed his place in the car, expecting to be very sick, — as he was for a short time; but his powerful spirit guide said, " We will soon neutralize the poison." And, sure enough, the sickness passed away, and he suffered no further immediate inconvenience, thus verifying the Scripture promise to them that believe, "If they drink any deadly thing it shall not hurt them."

Persons skeptical in spiritual things may desire to know what were our mundane sources of knowledge as to the nature of the drug administered. These I am at liberty to state in part to have been, first, medical knowledge and recognition of the symptoms induced; and, second, — a proof which has convicted many a murderer, — an examination of the residuum of the cup; while the anxious and bewildered looks of the would-be assassin confirmed the information as to his identity beyond a doubt. I think I hear some innocent person inquire, indignantly, why the perpetrator of such a crime was not brought to the tribunal of justice. Ah, my friend, you little know the state of things which existed then and there, or the immense power wielded by the secret service, backed by the army, if you believe such a course to have been possible. But, had it been possible, it would only have been striking at the instrument of an effect, whose cause would have still eluded the grasp of mortal retribution. For this poor, tempted man our natural feeling of condemnation was not unmixed with pity. We never saw him more on earth; but about six years after, when these circumstances had in some degree passed from our minds, one day he appeared to my brother in spirit, related these incidents in proof of his identity, expressed sorrow for the wrong done, and was forgiven.

But to resume: On our arrival in Louisville, the members of the detective force who had been detailed to watch for his coming were by some means thrown off the track, mistaking the object of their search for the expected

bridegroom, who, as it happened, was stopping in another
part of the city ; and the mistake was connived at by an
employee in the secret service, who, for reasons of family friendship, was disposed to be *his* friend, though personally a stranger.   This individual still further diverted
their attention by false information, until, warned by
the " Old Man " that he must remain no longer, A. B.
Whiting had left the city.   The very day of our departure the enemy made a reconnoissance upon the place
where we had been stopping, finding no one at home
but a colored woman, who told them we had all
gone to Cincinnati (which she supposed to be true,
as her mistress had really gone thither).   So to Cincinnati they posted, while we were speeding northward by
the most direct route, via Indianapolis.   From the
friendly detective, whose good offices are acknowledged
above, the confirmation of these facts was obtained,
together with many details not here set down.   Nor
was this the only unexpected friend that was raised up
for us upon this extraordinary trip.   Soon after we left
Indianapolis northward, a man called him one side and
said, " My friend, you are in danger.   There are men
on the train who have instructions to look for you ; but
they rather expect you have gone another route, and, I
think, do not know your person. · Keep quiet, and they
may not recognize you, though they have a good description.   But, if worst comes to worst, you have friends
at hand who will stand by you and see you safe through."
This was the substance of this abrupt address, though
not, of course, the whole, nor the exact words used.
He was a tall, powerfully-built man, somewhat rough
in speech, and had several companions, armed, like himself, to the teeth, and intimated that there was a much

greater number on the train upon whom he could rely in case of an emergency. Who and what he was, and wherefore his interest in our behalf; how he gained his information; whence he came with his band of armed men and whither he was going, — are questions which he did not see fit to answer, and our conjectures are not relevant to this history. Certain it is that he fulfilled his promise, and guarded us faithfully and effectually, and only bade us good by when we had left behind the regions where any overt act was to be apprehended. Whatever may have been the motive for this singular service, it *was* appreciated and *is* gratefully remembered.

After this experience, and warned that it would be hazardous to do so, my brother did not again venture his safety within the boundaries of that department while it remained under military rule, but cancelled an engagement at Cincinnati on information that its fulfillment would be the signal for still more desperate attempts to earn the coveted reward. There was little danger of his being openly interfered with in the North, as any such proceeding would not only have been liable to defeat and punishment at the hands of the law, but would have aroused a storm of popular indignation which it was not thought politic to brave. His movements were still closely scanned, however, in the hope of some favorable chance occurring, and during the winter more than one shrewd plot was hatched only to be defeated. But to recapitulate details would be, not only useless, but tedious. After a while it began to be whispered among "professionals" that to shadow Whiting was, not only a difficult, but an unlucky job; that whoever attempted it always came to grief; that he not only bore a charmed life, but could divine the inmost thoughts of his enemies ; and other superstitious interpretations of the real facts.

The nuisance gradually abated, and, though revived temporarily during the excitement consequent upon the death of President Lincoln, was chiefly maintained by amateurs, to baffle whose schemes was child's play to one who had successfully coped with some of the most skillful plotters in the secret service.

One word more before I leave this unwelcome subject finally : Many will doubtless read this chapter with astonishment, and wonder how he could have gone on so calmly, allowing no sign of disquietude to appear upon the surface ; how *we* could have borne in silence the fearful uncertainty that his frequent absence must have brought. It is, in one sense, an instance going to prove what I believe to be true, that the human mind can endure, and become in some degree accustomed to, any state of things which exists around it, and to which it can devise no remedy. But in our case it should perhaps be added, that the gift of silence is our natural heritage, and our reliance upon angel guardianship was a rock of strength, to sustain and uphold which, was not possessed by many who needed it as sorely. For *he* was not the only one subject to similar annoyances, with as little righteous cause. In times of public commotion, personal and party hatred always seeks opportunities to gratify itself under cover of the general confusion. The extent and long continuance of the persecution in his case were due to several reasons, one of which was the fact that it sprang, primarily, from two separate and distinct sources ; and another may be found in the natural disinclination of the human mind to submit to defeat, particularly when caused by forces whose existence is scarcely realized, and whose opposition, however powerful, is silent, and raises no banner of victory. But while, as I said, many will peruse with wonder, and some, perhaps, with incredulity, the narrative briefly sketched in the preceding pages, others, who, from glimpses behind the scenes, know that the half is not told, will be disappointed that I do not further elucidate the secret workings of that detective system with which he became so thoroughly acquainted, and hold up to public obloquy those responsible for its abuses, as well as the persons who instigated the turning of its machinery against him. The first I consider beyond the proper scope of a work which is *not* a "Secret History of the War," but the biography of an individual; therefore, all other reasons being laid aside, I should not enter upon it here. Nor do I feel that I could do the subject justice. For the second, we are not a vindictive race. *He* could so far forgive his enemies as to refrain from retorting injury when they were in his power, or even rejoicing when misfortunes came upon them. His magnanimity changed many foes to friends, and enabled him to aid them in the path of spiritual progress. Therefore would I throw the mantle of charity over their deeds, and, though I cannot forget, let their names sink peacefully into oblivion, knowing that the guilty will inevitably, here or hereafter, suffer the penalty of their misdeeds, and rise purified to a nobler life.

CHAPTER XIII.

NEW SUCCESSES IN THE EAST. — WASHINGTON AND THE
SOUTH AFTER THE WAR. — LECTURES IN CINCINNATI
AND LOUISVILLE. — PERSONS MET WITH AND THINGS
SEEN. — J. M. PEEBLES AND THE " WESTERN DE-
PARTMENT OF THE BANNER OF LIGHT." — CONTEM-
PLATED DEBATE AT ST. JOHNS, MICH. — HISTORY
THEREOF.

IN May, 1865, he again took his way eastward, lecturing during that month in Providence, where the hall
was too small to hold the people, though the largest in
the city, and during the following month in Charlestown, Mass. His marked success at this time was peculiarly pleasing to his friends, from the fact that many
thought that his political views would have destroyed
his prestige, as a Spiritualist lecturer, in New England.
But the result proved the contrary; for, though a few individuals were found fanatical and intolerant enough to
inveigh against him on that account, and advise people
not to go to hear him, to the credit of Spiritualism be it
spoken, they were comparatively rare; and their denunciations, far from producing any ill effect, induced many
to attend "just to see what the terrible 'Secesh' speaker *would* say," who were thus treated to a dose of un-
adulterated Spiritualism, to their lasting benefit. His
popularity, so far from being diminished, was greatly
increased, and extended to a wider circle of minds; for

the multitude instinctively admire and honor independent thought, and fearless speech. He took not the
slightest notice of the efforts of detractors, nor did he
ever upon the spiritual rostrum stoop to vindicate his
political opinions or defend his unquestionable right to
hold them. This course, which he facetiously described
as the maintenance of "calm dignity and solemn
silence," redounded greatly to his credit, and he often
recommended it to others in public life, as the best and
most effectual method of meeting personal attack and
misrepresentation.

Between his Sunday lectures at Charlestown he made
short visits to our friends in Abington and East Bridgewater, and also attended a Rhode Island clam-bake at
South Providence and a picnic at Dungeon Rock, Lynn,
where two thousand people were gathered for a good
time. These incidents, with frequent visits to Boston
and the "Banner" office, filled the time pleasantly, to
say nothing of the genial society of good friends at
Charlestown, the names of some of whom are synony-
mous with hospitality and social enjoyment wherever
known.

He returned home early in July, and during that
month remained at home a large part of the time; attended meetings at St. Johns and some other places, but
did not leave the state again until October, when he
went to Washington. There he found many changes
brought about by the rude hand of war, and, as his observations at this time may be interesting to many, I
will give some brief extracts from his letters.

"The city is changed very much since I was here.
The avenues about the Capitol look natural, except the
once beautiful yards, which are disfigured with tempo-

rary wooden buildings, some of which are, however, in process of removal. In passing the residence of Secretary Stanton one sees about six armed guards on foot and four on horseback, who keep watch over the man of sin both by day and night. I should think that his dreams would be a little disturbed sometimes.

" The dome of the Capitol is finished since I was here, and there are a number of splendidly executed paintings in the rotunda, which are the originals of the engravings on the backs of the national currency. I spent a pleasant morning in the portrait gallery connected with the Attornery General's office. It contains life-size portraits of every Attorney General from the days of Washington to the time of Johnson, inclusive. I recognized the personally well-known features of Cushing, of Massachusetts, Black, of Pennsylvania, Clifford, of Georgia, Butler, of South Carolina, Bates, of Missouri, &c., and also the historically well-known ones of Randolph, Lee, Legere, and others.

" Publicly and civilly I have every attention that heart could desire; but Washington is in rather a chaotic state socially. No foreign embassador puts on more style than Signor Romero, the minister of the defunct Republic of Mexico. I was at the White House to-day, and heard President Johnson make a speech from the steps, to the First District of Columbia Colored Volunteers. He exhorted them to be civil and law-abiding people and show by their lives that they were entitled to the freedom which the chance of war had thrust upon them.

" My old friend, Mr. Laurie, is still chief of the Bureau of Statistics, Post Office Department, a post he has occupied twenty-four years, and to which he was appointed by President Jackson. He has the walls of his office lined with pictures, many beautiful spirit drawings among the number. Yesterday I went out to his residence to attend the funeral of his little grandchild, and saw there an example of the incidental destruction caused by the war, aside from that which resulted from actual hostilities. Just before the war broke out, Mr. Laurie had moved from his former residence at Georgetown, and purchased and fitted up a beautiful place north of the city. When the first troops came on, they took possession of his property as a nice location for a hospital; for which purpose they kept it until this spring. And such a wreck! All his orchard, all the trailing vines, shrubbery, and vineyard. — not a vestige left. He has just refenced it and repaired the house so he could move back. He says they even destroyed all the windows and doors, but, by some strange fatality, the beautiful grove of oaks and maples, with the exception of a few trees, is unharmed.

" For all this he has, as yet, received not one cent. His bill of damages passed one branch of Congress last winter, but was killed by the other. He estimates his damages at ten thousand dollars, which I should think would not cover actual loss, to say nothing of rent for four years. This little item gives a faint idea of the immensity of such damages."

October 21. "I had the pleasure of seeing, at Willard's Hotel, yesterday morning, Alexander H. Stephens, late Vice-President of the Southern Confederacy. With the exception of his hair being a trifle grayer, he looks much as he did seven years ago. He wears the same, or similar, swallow-tailed coat and Byronic collar. He calls on the President to-day and starts for Georgia to-morrow.

" I find Spiritualists occupying the most prominent positions in every department; but few, comparatively, take any active part in sustaining meetings. They might, if they would combine and make themselves publicly known, give it a rank and standing equal to its claims, and wield a vast power for good.

" Many wonderful developments have occurred giving a key to the ' Old Man's ' operations last winter. If I needed anything to make my faith in him stronger, I have it here and in the culmination of those events."

The audiences steadily increased during his stay, and he was, on the whole, well satisfied with his month's work.

He went thence to Louisville for the month of November, where he was greeted with such crowded houses the first Sunday that he wrote home, —

" I don't know where I will put the people before I get through. Wilson has done great good here in the way of stirring up the people. The first meetings were got up by the efforts of two individuals, but the society, only formed in September, is now doing finely. Many of the old Spiritualists, who have not been before this season, came last Sunday, and gave in their names."

As, while at Washington, he visited all points within convenient access of that city which had an interest either from recent events or previous acquaintance, so he took this opportunity to traverse portions of the South which he had known as blooming gardens, but which now were strewn with sad memorials of the clash of hostile armies. He undertook this painful task in order to gain an exact knowledge upon certain subjects,

concerning which there were many conflicting state-
ments afloat through the country, and not from mere
curiosity or desire to tread in the track of notable
events.

The scenes of great acts in life's drama are, to the
thinker, full of instruction.

Let him who would seek glory in war go, stand
upon some lonely battle-field from which the tramp of
armies has died away, and see how time and nature
strive to heal and cover up the unsightly wounds and scars
that tell the sad tale of strife and bloodshed. Mark yonder
trees, seamed and shattered by shell and ball; how gal-
lantly they have endeavored to deck their disfigured
limbs with foliage, though, to some of them, it was the
last effort of expiring life. See how the grass has crept
over and softened the rude outlines of the trenches
where the deadly charge was made, while flowers and
trailing vines wrap in tender embrace the moldering
relics of the half-buried dead. Then turn and view
the change and desolation wrought in happy homes, and
apply the lesson — that war, so far from being a subject of boasting, is a misfortune to be deplored; and instead of tearing open the half-closed wounds, seek
rather to bring the healing balm of peace and forgetful-
ness to the many stricken hearts that are everywhere
amongst us.

He found, literally, a land of mourning, where the
story of loved ones slain and fortunes swept away was
the rule, and not the exception; where cities were in
ashes, and fields overgrown with weeds; yet whose
people were striving bravely to cover up the scars, and,
by a renewal of their industries, to open a way out of
their present state of poverty and exhaustion. Many

whom he had known when they stood on the top rounds of fortune's ladder, were beginning again at the bottom, reduced to till the bare land which was the only remnant of vast wealth, and even that held by an uncertain tenure. He saw, indeed, with pleasure, a disposition on the part of capitalists of more favored sections to come to the aid of reviving trade and commerce, and could not resist the thought, that such kindly policy — the hand outstretched to help in the hour of need — would do more to bind together and perpetuate the Union, than all the elaborate schemes of reconstruction that the most ingenious mind could devise.

His friend Dr. Ferguson had returned from Europe, where he had been with the Davenport brothers, and was in Nashville, but he missed seeing him, to his great regret. He spoke at Salem, Ind., four evenings the last of November, and at Evansville a portion of December; of which place he says, —

" This is one of the dirtiest towns I ever saw, and its theology is about as bad; but there are a few whole-souled friends here to save the city."

With only a short visit home he returned to Louisville, January 1, 1866, where, as before, crowded houses greeted him, especially on Sunday evenings. He also gave a course of Friday evening lectures on subjects of a literary character, the proceeds of which he donated to the society to aid them in purchasing an organ, and spoke one evening at Jeffersonville, Ind., and three evenings at Alton, a little place seventy miles down the river, on the Indiana side. He remained at Louisville until April, with the exception of a week's visit home in February. During a portion of the time E. V. Wilson was lecturing at New Albany. Dr. Slade spent a week in the city, examining the sick and holding circles; and quite a number of other noted mediums were spending more or less time there or in the vicinity. Among them were Dr. Warren, the healer, Mr. and Mrs. Ferris, of Toledo, and the famous Colchester; also a lady medium from Richmond, Ind., of whom he wrote home as follows: —

"Her manifestations consist in giving names and communications from individual spirits. The first time I saw her she gave the names of about fifteen of our ancestors: Sir Thomas Gardner, Benjamin Gardner, and Leah Gardner among the number; also brother Willie; but, the most wonderful of all, she remarked ' there is a spirit here who says he is your grandfather French, and husband to the Leah Gardner, but has another wife in the spirit world.' She then described him correctly, long nose and all."

The gentleman spoken of was our mother's stepfather, and always called by us "grandfather French," and was a person of rather marked appearance; hence the peculiar force of the test.

He was also much interested in listening again to the musical prodigy "Blind Tom," whom he had heard some years previously, soon after his power was first developed, and when it was little known beyond the immediate circle of his master's family and friends. With regard to him and the medium Colchester, I will give brief extracts from letters.

March 12. "Blind Tom is to be here this week, so I shall hear him once more. Colchester, the great medium of Buffalo-persecution notoriety, appeared with him at Cincinnati, or rather gave a seance at the close of Tom's concert. Colonel Oliver, Tom's master,

shocked the Orthodox people by telling them he believed that Tom was influenced by the spirit of Bee-
thoven."

March 26. "I closed my labors here last night.
Crowded don't begin to express the condition of the
hall. Fortunately it was a cool night. A gentleman
was here last week from Memphis, commissioned to
take me back with him to speak the next two months;
but previous engagements prevent. Colchester is creating a great interest here. I have seen his manifestations, — writing on the arm, &c., — and they are very
wonderful. He is one of the best test mediums I ever
saw, but very negative, and subject to every influence
that comes along, — earthly as well as spiritual."

The month of April had been designated to fill the
long deferred engagement at Cincinnati; so thither he
went direct from Louisville. He found the society
there progressing finely.

Under date of April 9, he wrote, "Yesterday we
held services in the beautiful new Academy of Music,
which the society have engaged for the coming year.
We had a large audience. Dr. Ferguson, of Nashville, was here, and spoke after me last night. I had a
very pleasant visit with him. They have a good choir,
which adds much to the meetings, and last Sunday we
organized a Progressive Lyceum."

The western department of the "Banner of Light"
was then located at Cincinnati, under the charge of
J. M. Peebles, with whom he spent such time as the
engagements of both would permit — a pleasure the
more fully appreciated and enjoyed on account of its
rarity. It is a misfortune common in some degree to
all our public speakers, that they can have but few

opportunities for unrestricted converse with each other. This deprivation he, in common with others, greatly regretted, not only because it came between him and friends whom he held especially dear, but because he believed that better acquaintance and harmony among the workers would be to the interest of the cause equally dear to all, as well as conducive to individual progress. He gave no week evening lectures during this month, with the exception of three at Muncie, Ind., as his physical strength did not warrant him in any extra effort, and remained at and near home through the summer for the same reason. In the mean while he busied himself composing new music and seeing to its publication. In addition to the eight pieces mentioned, as published in 1864, he had already given to the public five during 1865, and before the close of 1866 six more were added to the number. Those issued in 1865, under the general title of " Flowers from the West," were " O, Hear my parting Sigh," " Medora," " O, tell me not of Fields of Glory," " The Wind is in the Chestnut Bough," and " Pride of Elsinore," and were published by Whittemore, Detroit. From this house were also issued the next three, in 1866, which, under the heading of " Golden Memories," included " Whene'er in Sleep the Eyelids close," " Sweet be thy Dreams, Allida," and " She was a Rose." During the same year three others, " Spirit of Light, Love, and Beauty," " Aminta Mia," and " Lela Trefaine," were published by Whitney, of Detroit. The last of these was delivered to the publisher previous to his return to Cincinnati in September. There he found the society not so pleasantly situated as in April, — they having sustained a heavy loss in the burning of their hall, with

their organ and Lyceum equipments, — but still resolved
not to be daunted even by the elements. He comments
on their bravery as follows : —

" The society lost considerably by the fire, but, with
commendable energy, have got their Lyceum newly
equipped, and are making arrangements for a new organ.
In the mean time they have a very good melodeon,
which they rent. The great disadvantage they labor
under now is, their place of meeting is not nearly as
large or as centrally located as the Academy of Music.
The latter place will not be finished before January."

The third week of the month he spent at Muncie,
Ind., delivering a course of lectures, and had a narrow
chance of getting back to Cincinnati the following Sunday, as travel was interrupted, owing to heavy floods.
He went down on the first train for several days.
Indianapolis was seemingly all afloat, and there was a
foot of water in the great depot still. With regard to
the aspect of the country along the route he said,
" It is a sorry sight to see the thousands of acres of as
fine corn as ever stood up on the river bottom lands,
covered with water, in some fields, even to the tops of
the stalks. The loss to Ohio and Indiana from these
rains will be millions."

When brought face to face with such calamities, the
thinking mind instinctively asks, why such things are
permitted in the economy of nature ; what their necessity and use ; why fire and flood should thus waste property ; why war and pestilence should destroy the lives
and blast the hopes of men. And the universality of
the question is the surest guarantee that it will eventu-
ally be answered ; that, though our present ignorance
struggles with the problem vainly or with imperfect

success, future enlightenment will furnish the solution, and dissipate the seeming mystery.

After spending the month of October in Michigan, and at home, with the exception of two Sundays at Grand Rapids, he again returned to Louisville, for the last two months of the year. His health was not very good, but improved toward the last of his stay, and, as usual there, he spoke to large audiences; or, to use his own expression, it often happened that seats "were not nearly as numerous as people, at the hall."

He had the good luck to fall in with good company, on leaving home, in the person of N. Frank White, with whom he spent most agreeably the time, until their ways divided; and he also met quite a number of old friends during his stay in Louisville. He says, —

"I have met, among the rest, several persons whom I used to know in the South. One of these, Colonel S. D. Hay, of Texas, you have heard me speak of years ago. He is one of the oldest Spiritualists in that state, and was United States Attorney for Texas under Buchanan. He used to write for the 'Banner' a good deal, seven or eight years ago. He would like to have me go down through that country this winter; but I can not."

That travel, and the study of human nature in all classes and under numerous phases, had not diminished his keen appreciation of the humorous, will be readily seen by the following anecdote and description, which he wrote home at this time, and often repeated afterwards : —

"I think I omitted to mention, in my enumeration of our family here, two important personages of the colored persuasion, whose respective cognomens are

'Judge' Carter and 'General' Lee, and who take care of team, buildings, fires, black boots, &c. The 'Judge' is an old negro, very black and garrulous, and profoundly superstitious, — claims to be something of a 'Houdoo,' cures diseases by charms, and is greatly respected and feared by many of the colored people hereabout. When he don't want a person to come here any more, he strews salt on the pavement after they have gone, and 'says over some words,' as he calls it, and has unbounded faith in the efficacy of the proceeding. Like many white men of the same title, he is inclined tò steal if he gets a good chance. I keep everything locked up, but I find I have a better protection. The other day, when he brought in some coal, he asked me very confidentially if it was a 'fack dat eberyting in dis yar room' was *bewitched*. I assured him very solemnly that it was so, with the exception of the stove and coal-hod. I had left them all right, so he could attend to the fire."

Early in December he met with quite a serious accident, the effects of which troubled him several weeks, though he made light of it at the time in the following fashion : —

December 10. " The other night I had an unexpected fit of devotion, and knelt down in the street. Cause — a break in the sidewalk and ice thereon. Result — torn garments and a knee quite badly cut with a sharp stone. A Dutch tailor — who, I think, must have been born with a needle in his hand — mended the ugly tear in the cloth so it can scarcely be seen even on close inspection. I only wish he could mend the flesh likewise. The pavements are all glare ice. The boys skate anywhere, and enjoy it hugely, and a scared-looking cutter is occasionally seen on the street. I have received some nice birthday presents, to remind me that I am growing venerable."

December 25. "A merry Christmas for you all, though I feel anything but merry, having been kept awake all night by every species of noise from musical to infernal. You know they raise a regular *hillaballoo* here Christmas, — make a sort of ' 4th of July of it.' My wounds are nearly healed, and I am feeling quite well, in anticipation of reaching home in a few days now."

During his stay at Louisville he had considerable correspondence with regard to holding a debate at St. Johns, Mich., under the following circumstances: —

In the month of October, the notorious S. P. Leland visited St. Johns, delivering his usual series of slanders against Spiritualism and Spiritualists, besides bringing forward the cheapest imitations of physical spirit manifestations, and declaring them to be the same, and the only manifestations produced through mediums. His boastful promises to "expose the humbug" created quite an excitement, especially among those who longed to have something of that kind done, but as yet knew not how to do it; and the committee appointed by the opposers made haste to proclaim to the public, through the press, that Spiritualism had been exposed.

The opponents challenged the Spiritualists to a public investigation of their philosophy and its phenomena. The society of Spiritualists promptly called a special meeting, and passed the following preamble and resolution: —

"*Whereas*, The opponents of Spiritualism in this village have declared their willingness to investigate the phenomena and philosophy of Spiritualism, and have challenged such investigation either publicly or before private committees, or both ; therefore,

Resolved, That the St. Johns Society of Spiritualists do accept such challenge, and that a committee be appointed by the society, to consult with a like committee of opponents, to settle the necessary preliminaries, and to secure the attendance of such persons as may be thought best to represent the cause of Spiritualism in such investigation."

The committee, in discharge of their duty, invited A. B. Whiting to defend their cause in debate, which invitation he accepted in the following letter : —

LOUISVILLE, KY., November 10, 1866.

A. A. WHEELOCK.

Dear Sir : Agreeable to your request that I would forward you the terms on which I would debate with some one of the public opponents of Spiritualism, I enclose you the within propositions and rules of debate for submission to said public opponent or his representatives. I will debate one or both of the propositions with any respectable clergyman in the world, — I affirming the first and denying the second proposition.

And, being informed by you that the Anti-Spiritualists of St. Johns have challenged the Spiritualists of that place to bring some advocate of our cause to meet them or a representative of their claims against Spiritualism, I take this method of signifying my acceptance of said challenge, under the within rules of debate and the conditions hereinafter specified. The wording of my affirmative proposition embodies what I am willing to affirm as Spiritualism, and if I am called upon to take an affirmative position, should insist upon it, or one similarly worded. The negative proposition may be changed in any way to suit the special theory or desire of my opponent; provided, of course, that it shall embody a denial of the claims of Spiritualism, and not conflict with the rules of debate.

I give you full liberty to use my name at any time and place as an advocate of our religion, against all honorable opposers by fair and open argument. For dishonest cavilers all argument is unavailing; and, my friend, I have yet to learn that any libelous slanderer, reviler of Spiritualists, renegade medium, or strolling mountebank of any description, — not to mention honorable opponents, — has ever dared openly to assail the moral character or private reputation of the undersigned. Then, without pedantry, I may further say, that there is not a city or town in America where our philosophy is known, but what the Spiritualists would cheerfully indorse me as an able advocate of Spiritualism. Can the opposers bring a public disputant as fully indorsed by his denomination? I do not ask that much; but, under the circumstances, in justice to the cause of Spiritualism and my reputation as a public speaker, I can not be satisfied with an opponent unless he is indorsed by the religious denomination to which he belongs, or those whose cause he represents.

I remain, very truly,

A. B. WHITING.

The last paragraph of this letter was called out by the circumstance that the Anti-Spiritualists claimed the privilege of reserving the *name* of their proposed champion until the time of the debate, and was written with a view to make them fully responsible for the champion whom they should select under this somewhat unusual stretch of privilege.

The result of this negotiation — or rather its non-result — I quote from the report of the committee of Spiritualists, as published in the St. Johns "Republican," two months later.

"Early in November our opponents were notified of our readiness to enter upon the investigation, and a copy of the resolutions and rules of debate, submitted by A. B. Whiting, was served upon their committee, they promising that, if possible, they would find some scientific, talented man to represent their side, and have the discussion commence. More than two months have passed by, and, notwithstanding this little village has *five resident clergymen*, with a Catholic priest now and then, to represent old theology and modern Christianity, the committee appointed by the opposers of Spiritualism report their *inability*, thus far, to find any one to engage in the investigation to which the Spiritualists were challenged by them."

The resolutions alluded to in the letter were substantially the same that he had often debated, and always stood ready to debate, though in the later years of his life the challenge was seldom accepted, viz. : —

1. "*Resolved*, That the Scriptures, history, philosophy, and the spiritual demonstrations of the present day, prove that the spirits of the departed dead have communicated in the past, and can, and do, in the present age, communicate with the inhabitants of earth." And,

2. "*Resolved*, That modern Spiritualism is a delusion, and the so-called spiritual manifestations can be

satisfactorily accounted for, without admitting their spiritual origin."

The three rules of debate upon which he invariably insisted were as follows : —

1. " That any reflection upon the moral character of either of the respective parties to which the disputants belong shall be considered a breach of courtesy.

2. " That any offensive personality on the part of either disputant shall be considered a breach of courtesy.

3. " There shall be no decision, by vote or otherwise, as to the merits of the debate, by chairman, committee, or audience ; but each person shall be left free to form his or her opinion, individually and unbiassed."

Other rules were left to a joint committee.

CHAPTER XIV.

1867–8, WASHINGTON AGAIN. — DISSOLUTION OF THE "THIRTY-NINTH CONGRESS." — DR. FERGUSON AND OTHER SPIRITUAL CELEBRITIES. — BUFFALO, N. Y. ROCHESTER AND ELDER MILES GRANT. — LOUISVILLE, KY. — SUN-STROKE. — IN THE SICKROOM. — J. O. BARRETT AND THE " SPIRITUAL HARP." — STATE SPIRITUALIST ASSOCIATION AT JACKSON, JANUARY, 1868. — ALCINDA WILHELM SLADE.

THE first two months of 1867 he spent at home, speaking at Albion a portion of that time, and being further detained by sickness in the family. During this

time he assisted the Albion Society in getting up a
" Grand Festival." A proposition to publish a newspaper in honor of the occasion aroused the fun-loving
propensities of his school days, and he readily assumed
the position of editor-in-chief, " with a numerous and
able corps of assistants and contributors," comprising,
by actual count, two persons — myself and a cousin (a
gentleman a little his junior, who was a member of our
family from 1866 to 1870, now a rising member of the
bar in this county, but whose keen perception of the
humorous has not been obscured by his legal attainments). I think I can safely say, that the result of the
combined labors of these amateur Bohemians literally
fulfilled the declared intention of the " chief scribe," to
produce " a paper that should be a burlesque upon
everything in the shape of a newspaper." Less than
two days was allotted us to get the copy ready, but, as
telegrams, foreign correspondence, and thrilling items,
were all alike manufactured within the same local office,
as, it is said, often happens in the history of more pre-
tentious sheets, we progressed rapidly, and had a merry
time withal. I mention this little incident, not only
because it holds for me a pleasant memory, but as an
instance of the zeal with which my brother was wont
to devote himself to the business in hand, however
trivial it might be. This promptness and thoroughness
in the execution of any design formed, or charge
assumed, was eminently characteristic of his nature.
He was scrupulously punctual on all occasions, and
nothing annoyed him more than lack of punctuality
in others. In all his travels he was never late for a
train, unless detained by the delay or negligence of
some other person.

The last of February he again left home for Washington, calling by the way on Warren Chase, at the New York office of the "Banner of Light," and arriving at the capital in time to open his engagement the first Sunday of March. He found many prominent Spiritualists gathered together in the city, from various accidental causes, a condensed account of whom, together with one or two other notes that may be of interest, I will transcribe from his letters.

March 6. "There are a great many Spiritualist celebrities in Washington at present, though I regret to say, that the greatest man among them all is very ill at present. I allude to Dr. Ferguson. He is suffering terribly with necrosis of the bone of the leg, and seems to get no permanent relief from anything. He was at the President's, but about a week ago Major Chorpenning had him brought down to his residence, where he could be more quiet. John M. Spear and wife — just from London — are stopping at the same place. Dr. John Mayhew, from Minnesota, Mrs. Morrell, a test medium, from Baltimore, and a number of others are, like myself, here temporarily, besides Thomas Gales Forster and others who reside here, making quite a phalanx altogether.

"Mrs. Spear has a beautiful photograph album, presented her by Lady Henrietta Vance, which contains portraits of the principal spiritual notables of England, and some from other countries.

"About the finest looking old gentleman in the crowd is William Howitt. Among the number are Lord Bury, Sir Thomas Brevier, Bulwer, Professor De Morgan, Dr. Ashburner, Robert Cooper — editor "Spiritual Times," — Benjamin Coleman — editor "Spiritual Magazine," — Allen Kardec — President Spiritual Bureau of France, Count Constantine Wittig, of Breslau, Prussia, who has translated Davis' and Edmunds' works into German, and the Russian Prince, Demidorf, who has translated many spiritual documents into the Russian language. I was very much interested in looking over this album, and reviewing the history of the originals of the pictures, with several of whom I have, as you know, corresponded.

" I witnessed the expiring groans of the Thirty-ninth Congress on Monday, also the incoming of that terrible Fortieth Congress, which, everybody thinks, will attempt to depose the President. It may please you to know that, in my opinion, John Morrissey, late of the P. R., is one of the finest looking men in the new Congress. He would be called a fine looking man anywhere. Butler is, of course, the ugliest, and, I think, is rather proud of the distinction. The political atmosphere is in a very feverish and excited condition, and the general opinion seems to be that we are on the eve of a tremendous smashing up. All we can do is to wait and see."

March 11, " Dr. Ferguson is much better ; was able to come down to the parlor, and make a short speech at the reception at Major C——'s last Friday. There were about one hundred present, some from nearly every State in the Union. Among the late arrivals are Dr. Rose and Mr. Merriman, of Memphis."

After his return from Washington, in the first week of April, he spent two idle, yet busy, months at home, superintending some repairs and improvements, which he had long contemplated, and lightening for me the suffering and inconvenience occasioned by a disabled right arm. I count it among the curious compensations which time brings for sorrow and suffering, that the halo of love and sympathy, which illumined for us some darkened day, grows ever brighter with the gathering years, until the pain and gloom become glorified to our mental vision, and dwell with us only as a dear and tender memory. Thus do the tendrils of my thought cling to that time when he, "from whom death can divide me never," lent to my weakness, literally, a strong right hand.

In the month of June following, he revisited Buffalo, N. Y., after a lapse of eleven years. He found that there, as elsewhere, time had wrought many changes. Few of the old Spiritualists were left, while many had passed on to the higher life. He remained through the month, and had the pleasure of seeing the society enabled to establish itself in a more commodious hall, and in a fair way to future prosperity.

After a short visit home, including a brief lecturing trip to Almont, Mich., he returned eastward again to Rochester, where his engagement extended to the last of August, the lectures being given on Sunday and Thursday evenings, instead of, as usual, two on Sunday. This arrangement was found a very good one, both for speaker and society, it being easier for the former, and giving the latter the Sunday afternoons for the use of the Lyceum, without the fatigue of three sessions in the day. He was much pleased with the Lyceum children, not only for their proficiency in the various exercises, but still more for the spirit of harmony which seemed to prevail among them.

The last Saturday and Sunday of July he participated in the exercises of the "Medium and Speakers' Convention," held there, being appointed chairman of the committee on resolutions, and also delivering the closing address of the convention. He took for his subject on that occasion "Spiritualism in the Middle Ages."

During the latter part of his engagement in Rochester, the Adventists, under the lead of Elder Miles Grant, of Boston, had pitched their tent in a vacant lot in the city, and were holding forth nightly on the "Sleep of the Dead," "Resurrection," "Devilism," "Conflagration of the World," and kindred themes. Efforts were made to bring about a discussion with Elder Grant, who had only a short time previously been engaged in a debate with J. G. Fish; a question was agreed upon, substantially the same as that discussed with Elder Stephenson at Grand Rapids, and my brother offered to devote to the debate the only time remaining before he was obliged to leave to fulfill engagements in the west. The society even volunteered to give up their regular Sunday evening lecture, in order to allow more time; but Elder Grant signified his inability to attend to it at that time "on account of the tent meeting," and hence it was unavoidably postponed to some more convenient season. I may as well state here that that auspicious period never arrived.

His engagement at Louisville, Ky., for the ensuing month (September) passed without especial incident, as far as his public labors were concerned, but was marked by one fraught with great physical discomfort, and some danger. He was induced by the solicitations of friends, and his own love of fine horses and equestrian skill, to visit the State Fair grounds one day during the annual exhibition. The day was excessively warm, so much so that many cases of sunstroke occurred. He had always been in the habit of considering himself almost proof against heat, and his cool manner of declaring himself "just comfortable," in a temperature which was to ordinary people barely endurable, had often gained him the appellation of "Salamander;" but on this occasion he was so overcome by the heat as to be very sick for several days; nor was he ever again able to endure the heat as formerly. He had to be especially careful about riding in the hot sun, as it was extremely liable to induce the old symptoms of dizziness and nausea. This susceptibility, however, lessened each year, and would probably, in time, have passed away entirely.

He came home in October, and with the exception of a few lectures given in Battle Creek and other neighboring towns, did not leave again until the following February, being compelled to cancel his engagements for the intermediate months on account of the long and dangerous illness of our mother.

Many precious memories cluster round the days of anxiety and nights of watching, which we shared through long weeks, while our combined magnetic strength, re-enforced by angel helpers, held in suspense the trembling balances wherein life and death contended for the mastery. At length, after passing so near the shining shore that she was able to catch a vivid glimpse of its realities, the life-bark, which had drifted almost beyond our reach, was again moored to the hither side.

During our mother's convalescence, he had the pleasure of entertaining at our home Rev. J. O. Barrett, then acting as missionary agent for the Michigan Association of Spiritualists, and who was also engaged, with Messrs. Peebles and Bailey, in collecting material for

the "Spiritual Harp," which was published the ensuing summer. My brother furnished two pieces of
music for the book, entitled, respectively, "Strike the
Harp in Nature's Praise," and "Waiting, only waiting."

One of the pieces contributed by me was, by mistake, credited to him in the index of the work, and
never corrected, as it made no difference to either of us ;
and I only mention it now from the fact that the query
might arise, why I had omitted this from the list of his
compositions, and I might, perhaps, be accused of negligence in so doing.

In January, 1868, he attended the meeting of the
State Spiritual Association, at Jackson, it being the
third session of that body. He had been a prominent
worker in behalf of business organization among Spiritualists from the first, and on this occasion delivered the
opening speech of the convention upon that subject.
The following extract, from the report of a correspondent of the secular press, gives but a faint idea of the
address, but embodies his main positions upon that
question, and is included here for that reason.

"Mr. A. B. Whiting, of Albion, then delivered the
opening speech substantially as follows : —

" 'I take it not as a personal compliment to myself
that I am called upon to address you this evening, but
rather as a recognition of the number of years I have
labored in this cause. I stand, to-night, within a short
distance of the place where I emerged into the light of
this great philosophy. We have met for the purpose
of forming an organization, to the end that we may pro-
mulgate that gospel of truth which we all so love.
Spiritualism has grown up around and about us, until
it has arrived from a feeble band, few in numbers, to a

great community, comprising a large and intelligent part of society. This is cheering to all who love this glorious philosophy. . . . The truth embodied in this philosophy shows us the future of those we love — opens to our mortal vision a glimpse of that futurity toward which we are all merging. It becomes necessary to consider, not the facts of Spiritualism, for these are proven beyond cavil. There are thousands whose testimony is proof of the truth of spiritual manifestations. We can only say to scoffers, as we have a right to say, until they can account for little raps, the A in the alphabet of Spiritualism, they have no right to deprecate our philosophy, or even to look deeper into its mysteries. We are all indebted to this philosophy for our redemption from the creeds and fallacies through which we have so long groped our mazy way. We are not here to overthrow the doctrines of inspiration, but rather to build them up ; for there can be no true Spiritualism until revelation is acceded to. We claim, however, that creeds and religions are transient and progressive. Systems and creeds are like garments, to be worn for a season, then to be exchanged for something newer and better. As we cast our eye over the page of history, we there see how all earthly things fade ; how churches, like governments, have risen and fallen. The central idea of all religions, in times past and present, was *Spiritualism.* The mysteries of the inner temple of the priests of Isis, the Indian mythologies, the appearance of Moses and Elias on the mount, the visions of John at Patmos, all prove the universality and grandeur of the spiritualistic idea. The early fathers of the church, until the time of the Nicene Council, taught and recognized spirit communion.

Krome says, " You can not wall up the saints in their graves ; will ye wall up the souls of the dead ? They are everywhere present and always with you."

" ' The Catholic, more consistent than the Protestant, has never yet relinquished the spiritualistic idea, and the revelations to, and inspiration of, their saints. In times past the state exercised great tyranny over the church ; but the time is drawing near when church and state will be divorced. America, where religious freedom has been so happily planted, has taken the lead in this divorcement.'

" He then presented Spiritualism under three forms, viz. : external manifestations, philosophy, and religion, and treated of these at some length. He then impressed upon his hearers the great importance of organizing, appealing to them to throw aside their party prejudices, and aid in gathering together the millions of Spiritualists, scattered and disbanded for want of such organization. The Spiritualists of America have hitherto acted in an individual capacity, but now the time has come for building up an outward temple. For this purpose it is necessary that there be local, state, and grand associations, not for the purpose of propagating creeds or articles of faith, but to send missionaries to enlighten the ignorant and break down the prejudices that exist against us, and to draw together our scattered bands into a solid phalanx.

" He then gave some statistics, which, he said, he regretted must be taken from their enemies, for the want of proper data among themselves. From the Catholic Convention, held at Baltimore, the following statistics are taken : ' There are from ten million to eleven million Spiritualists in the United States, a num-

ber which exceeds the combined communicants of all
other churches.' Upon one half of this number as a
basis, the speaker said that this convention represented
one hundred thousand in Michigan. And from these
numbers did they not see that, had they an organization, they would bring in thousands, who, hearing their
lectures and seeing their manifestations, were inquiring,
Where is your organization? What do you propose to
do? They would then be enabled to support our missionaries and mediums, and give our doctrines free to the
people. This organization would also repel the persecution which hitherto, as individuals, they had received.
Ten millions of people were not to be persecuted.

"He then made a fervid appeal to all free thinkers,
saying that what was good in the Catholic church, the
Protestant denominations, and all religions and creeds
whatsoever, was to be found in the spiritualistic
philosophy. He remembered well the time when the
Methodists were derided and persecuted worse than the
Spiritualists had ever been ; but by their energy and
persistence, they had grown to be at once powerful
and respectable. The Jesuits had for ages kept up
the crumbling foundations of the Catholic church by
the force of their secret workings. He commended
the persistence and energy of the one and the unity of
the other, as elements which would make Spiritualism
more powerful than both combined. The spirits would
aid them in doing the work, and doing it faithfully ; but
they could not build a temple or perfect an organization
without earthly aid and co-operation.

"The speech throughout was of the most vigorous
and eloquent character, and was listened to with close
attention."

He spoke again, the last evening of the convention, from the text, " To what do all these things tend ? " At this convention were gathered an unusual number of the public advocates of Spiritualism, among whom was another who has since passed on to the higher life, — Mrs. Alcinda W. Slade, — who then, for the first time, assumed her place in the front rank of the Spiritualists of Michigan. Not many months later, the subject of this memoir was called on to speak the last farewell over the earthly remains of this efficient co-laborer. Her body was laid to rest in the cemetery at Albion, where his own has since been deposited.

CHAPTER XV.

BUFFALO. —ABRAHAM JAMES.— GENESEE CONFERENCE. — HOME. — THE "NEW CONSTITUTION." — ITS DE-FEAT. — A PLEASURE TRIP, WITH VARIATIONS. — CAPE COD SPIRITUALIST CAMP-MEETING. — MUSICAL DATA. — PRESIDENTIAL CAMPAIGN OF 1868. — HIS PARTICIPATION AND POPULARITY THEREIN. — AT THE GREAT MASS MEETINGS OF THIS STATE. — FINAL TRIUMPH AT JACKSON. — LAST GREAT EFFORT UPON THE POLITICAL ROSTRUM. — PHYSICAL EXHAUSTION. — ANOTHER DEBATE WHICH DID NOT COME OFF.

IN the month of February, 1868, he lectured again for the Spiritualist Society of Buffalo, N. Y. — with what success may be inferred from the fact that, although the first two Sundays were very stormy, he spoke to crowded houses, causing him to make the remark that he did not know what they would do if it should come a pleasant Sunday.

Dr. Slade visited Buffalo during his stay, and another well-known medium, Abraham James, was also there over one Sunday. Of the latter he wrote home the following facts, under date of February 17 : —

" You remember hearing and reading of Abraham James, the medium who discovered the Chicago Artesian wells. He has been, for the last six months, engaged in an oil well near Titusville, Pa. Last summer he made a public prophecy about it at the convention at Rochester, and desired it put on record. February 1, they struck oil at precisely the depth foretold, and the well is now flowing one hundred barrels and upward of oil a day. He was here last night, and gave a little history of the matter to the audience after lecture."

The Genesee Conference of Spiritualists met in convention at Buffalo the 18th and 19th. He participated in the exercises, and delivered two addresses during the sessions, and also sang, by particular request, one or two pieces of his composition. In his closing lecture — as reported in the proceedings of the convention — he concluded with an exhortation to fidelity to the trust committed to our times, which was characterized as " searching, pungent, and persuasive," the following being the final paragraph : —

" If we prove recreant, the future historic page must bear for us a most ignoble record. Our times are more highly favored than any preceding, and more fully fraught with all the resources of wealth, talent, and all

the elements of successful conquest. Shall the people
of the twenty-second and twenty-third centuries have
to say of those of the nineteenth, ' They had the most
glorious, angelic advent and auxiliaries of any preceding age, but by reason of their apathy and neglect the
clouds of religious bigotry again enshrouded the nations
in a night of gloom.' How much better if they are
able to say, ' Those highly-favored people comprehended their epoch, welcomed gratefully and appreciated
the truths taught in the "ministry of angels," and in
a spirit of self-denial put forth opportune efforts, by
means of which superstition was banished, and the mil-
lennium of spiritual liberty was ushered in — a price-
less heritage to all nations and generations.' "

He was detained in Buffalo some days, after the close
of his engagement, by the "great snow-storm" of
March 1st; had a very disagreeable time in getting
through at last, and was laid up with a severe cold in
consequence. This was his last long journey for the
season. He spoke a number of times during the month,
however, upon political and governmental questions, in
this and various other places in the state, in opposition
to a proposed new constitution for the state, which was
to be submitted to the people at the spring elections.

He founded his objections to the instrument presented for adoption on the general ground that it was
by no means an improvement on the old, and also on
several special grounds, one of which was, that the
provisions for religious liberty were not as well defined
as in the existing constitution, but were so framed as to
admit of their being warped to suit the plans of a party
who were even then working for the now well-known
object of incorporating into the constitutions of the land

a recognition of God, Jesus, and religion, as seen through *their* theologic spectacles. Their design in this instance was so hidden under the appearance of liberality, that many, at the first glance, failed to notice how adroitly the doorway had been left open for encroachments upon the people's rights. He also opposed the clause conferring suffrage upon negroes, as an insult to the intelligent white women of the state, and for other reasons which he set forth at length, and disapproved of certain sumptuary provisions, which, though introduced ostensibly to promote temperance, he deemed rather calculated to foster an odious system of espionage than to promote the end sought. A strong opposition was aroused, and the " New Constitution " was defeated, to the astonishment of many who had expected to see it· adopted as a matter of course, because it was framed by the representatives of a party holding a large majority in the state. It was noticed as a fact highly complimentary both to him and to the capacity of the people to appreciate principles when clearly presented to their minds, that in those localities where he gave his exposition of the peculiar beauties (?) of the proposed instrument, particularly as regarded the religious view of the matter, its defeat on the popular vote was the most complete and overwhelming. Thus it appears that, though the fame of an orator may be to some extent ephemeral, as is often remarked, yet it is not always unrewarded by practical results which endure, the fittest guerdon of well-directed effort.

The three ensuing months he spent mostly at home, lecturing Sundays a portion of the time at Marshall, and attending also several county conventions in the state.

In July, feeling the need of rest, he determined upon a trip to the sea-shore, and, accompanied by mother and myself, set out with the intention of spending two months at the shore, and in visiting our numerous relatives and friends in the vicinity of Boston. This programme was carried out, with a few unexpected additions. He desired to abstain entirely from speaking, and hence had given the spiritual press no notice of his movements, but one July morning walked into the " Banner " office, surprising not only the urbane editor thereof, but also J. O. Barrett, whom he exhumed from a heap of " copy," where he was working at the Index of the " Spiritual Harp." A few weeks later we had the pleasure of obtaining one of the first copies of that valuable work. In August, being in the vicinity of the " Cape Cod Camp Meeting," he rashly ventured to hope that he might attend as a simple spectator, and, as he was an entire stranger in that region, mingle with the crowd unnoticed. He often laughingly referred to the result afterward, saying that the next time he tried to travel *incognito* he should not go to Cape Cod when all Massachusetts was there holding a Spiritual Camp Meeting. On entering the grounds, about every third person saluted him by name, and, before he had hardly time to look around, he was captured by a Boston friend,— George A. Bacon, I think it was,— and conducted to the speaker's stand where he was warmly welcomed. He remained until the close of the meeting, and then only escaped from the whole-souled friends at Harwich by promising to return and lecture the ensuing Sunday, which he did. He was pressed by numerous other invitations, but the time was drawing near when he had promised to return to Michigan, and therefore he was obliged to decline. He was also repeatedly requested to deliver political addresses at various places, as a presidential campaign was in progress, but consented only in one instance, which was on the occasion of a flag-raising at East Bridgewater — the scene of his last school days and the residence of several of our near relatives. This was the only political speech ever made by him in the State of Massachusetts. He enjoyed the time spent in visiting more than I ever knew him to at any previous time, and particularly on account of the array of musical talent with which he was brought in contact. He had published another new composition the preceding spring, — " Evyrr Alynn, or the Outcast," — a solo and chorus in chant style, which is considered by many as one of his happiest efforts in the musical line. In sharp contrast to this, he had also just composed a semi-comic campaign song, entitled, " Old Dr. Bonds," which was issued by J. S. White & Co., Marshall, Mich., and extensively sung during the canvass, particularly in this state.

These were his last musical publications, and on this, his last extended visit among his relatives, though he called on some of them again the following year, he spent much time in singing his various compositions with me, and sometimes with a full quartet of voices harmonized by the strong tie of kindred, and in listening to such singers as the well-known " Columbian Glee Club " and other gifted amateurs. Truly the "nights were filled with music," whether in town or at the shore, and, if " the cares that invest the day " did *not* " fold their tents like the Arabs," and steal away forever, their shadows were lifted for the time, that, while the senses were steeped in melodious sound, the soul might perceive something of the innate beauty and grandeur of harmony.

We returned home the first week in September, in time to attend the Yearly Grove Meeting of the Albion Society and Friends, where he spoke as usual. The balance of the month was consumed in filling similar engagements in different parts of the state. In the month of October, he gave himself to the political field, addressing the people of the principal towns and villages of Central Michigan, and also taking part at several of the largest mass meetings ever held in the state, among which, those held at Ann Arbor, Port Huron, and Jackson are especially worthy of mention. His speeches — in which he never descended to personal invective or abuse of opposing candidates — were everywhere received with the utmost enthusiasm, and are to-day mentioned, not only among the Democracy, but by persons of all parties who had opportunities of judging, as a most remarkable display of the power of eloquence to sway the people. This magnetic quality, which enabled him, as it were, to carry his audience along with him, and the remarkable vocal power which he possessed, made him a great favorite. Crowds so large that the majority of speakers could not be heard by one half those assembled, and hence could not hope for quiet, would listen to him for two hours in silence, only interrupted by applause. Thus it happened that, at the large meetings, though many speakers might be present, much of the hardest work fell upon him, particularly toward the close, when some were exhausted by excessive speaking in the open air. This was noticeably the case at Jackson, at the last rally, the week preceding the election, when, out of six speakers, he was the only one able to make himself heard for any length of time; in consequence of which he was obliged to address both the immense concourse at the Fair Grounds in the afternoon and the crowd at the wigwam in the evening. Although he did this with apparent ease, and, it is said, surpassed on this occasion all previous efforts, the strain upon his strength was too great, and outraged Nature did not fail to vindicate her rights, and exact rest, as the atonement for over-exertion. He spoke no more in that campaign, being obliged to recall the remainder of his appointments; nor did he ever again put forth any elaborate effort in the political field.

In the month of December, having partially recovered from the illness induced by physical exhaustion, he went to South Bend, Ind., to deliver a course of lectures. Just as he was leaving the place he received a communication from the pastor of the Christian Church, Rev. W. B. Hendryx, taking exceptions to the idea, as broached by him in the course of his lectures, that the teachings and phenomena of Spiritualism were in many respects identical with those of Jesus and the apostles, and signifying a readiness to debate that proposition. To this he replied that he would willingly discuss, not only that point, but the entire subject as contained in the following resolution, which is substantially the same that he had declared himself willing to defend upon on all occasions.

"*Resolved*, That the Scriptures, history, and the testimony of reliable living witnesses, prove that the spirits of departed human beings have communicated in the past, and do still hold intercourse with the inhabitants of earth."

To this proposition Mr. Hendryx demurred as too

broad, and, in response to a request that he should affirm a proposition as opposed to Spiritualism, sent this, viz.: "That Modern Spiritism is anti-Christian, and subversive of the peace, happiness, and perpetuity of moral and religious society."

˙ This Mr. Whiting agreed to accept, overlooking the implied slur upon ten millions of Spiritualists, provided Mr. Hendryx would also accept *his* affirmation, and discuss each in succession. He also empowered the friends who were acting in his behalf to offer the reverend gentleman a more restricted affirmation, if they saw fit, in this form: —

"*Resolved*, That the Bible sustains Modern Spiritualism in all of its phases, both as to spirit communion and the state of the dead."

With these liberal concessions upon his part Mr. Hendryx was not satisfied; and, as the Spiritualists of South Bend refused to concur in any further limitations, even if *he* were willing to submit to them, the arrangement was not consummated.

CHAPTER XVI.

1869, 1870.

LAST VISITS TO NEW ENGLAND, PHILADELPHIA, AND
LOUISVILLE. — THE LAST BIRTHDAY. — A NEW YEAR'S
GIFT, AND ITS USEFULNESS. — DAYS OF SUFFERING.

THE early part of the year 1869 he spent mostly at
home, on account of impaired health, but, the last of
April, was sufficiently recovered to venture on a long
journey, and went to fill the desk of the Portland (Me.)
Society during the month of May. He was unfortunate
in having bad weather the first two Sundays, and, as
the city was too godly to permit the running of street
cars on that day, people could not get to meeting very
conveniently. He says, concerning this matter, —

" My first Sunday here was marked by the awfulest
rain-storm possible. About two inches of snow had
fallen in the morning, and the wind blew a gale, which
continued with rain all day. This being a very *pious*
city (in its own estimation), the street cars don't run
Sunday ; so I had the pleasure of walking a mile to the
hall, and got somewhat wet, but, wonderful to relate,
I am not sick, — except of the weather, — and that is
enough to disgust a respectable dog.

" The Lyceum is large and well disciplined. The
brothers Davenport and William Fay are here. Their

demonstrations are just as reported in the "Banner,"
going ahead of the descriptions rather, of the two.
The latter part of his stay was more pleasant in an
external point of view, and he left with some regret,
having just begun to feel at home again in this city,
where he had formerly spent many happy days. The
status of things spiritual in Portland, as they appeared
to him at this time, may be gathered from the following
extract from a characteristic letter, written by him to
the "Present Age," and published in that paper: —

"The Portland Spiritual Association was organized
in 1854, and has retained its organization intact to the
present time, being one of the oldest organized spiritual
societies in the country. The venerable James Furbish
is still its president. They have a nice hall, which they
control, central in its location and easy of access. A
Children's Progressive Lyceum was organized in 1865,
and numbers at present one hundred and fifty members.
Last Sunday was convention day, and devoted principally to reading, singing, and declamation. The Portland Lyceum is particularly fortunate in possessing a
large amount of musical talent, which, under the direction of an accomplished musical director, has been
well developed. Is it not wonderful what an amount
of musical and dramatic talent these Lyceums are
bringing out, wherever once established?

"There have been many changes since I was here last
(ten years); some old and tried friends have passed over
the river of death, others have changed location in this
world, and doubtless some have switched off the track
of open advocacy of Spiritualism to a *quasi* indorse-
ment of some of the forms of old theology; but I trust
this class numbers but few, for certain it is that no

person once a Spiritualist can ever *honestly deny* the truth of our beautiful philosophy.

" Puritan theology is very powerful in Portland, and the 'Christian Young Men' have their reading and praying rooms as elsewhere, and, I presume, advocate the same doctrines of Evangelism, and a union of church and state to regulate the religion of the people. There are a great many earnest, whole-souled workers in the cause of Spiritualism here, some of whom have been connected with the society ever since its formation, and everything now looks favorable for greater progress in the future."

He spoke, the first Sunday of June, at Charlestown, Mass., having the pleasure of a short visit with brother Peebles in Boston, *en passant*, the second in East Abington, and the third in East Bridgewater, spending the intervening week in visiting, and attending the Great Peace Jubilee, in Boston, in company with a joyous bridal party. This was his last farewell to New England, — his last two lectures within its borders being given in the town of his birth, and that which was the scene of his last school days. He reached home the first of July, and during that month filled the desk of the Battle Creek Society. The balance of the summer was given mostly to attending grove and county meetings in this state.

In October he revisited Philadelphia, to speak, after an interval of twelve years. He was fortunate in reaching the city just before the great floods, which in the early part of that month spread such devastation over a large portion of Pennsylvania, interrupting railroad communications for some days. Of these he wrote, under date of October 5, —

11

"I suppose you have read of the terrible floods in this region. All the railroads are more or less flooded, bridges washed away, &c. The Schuylkill and Delaware rivers are both running mad this morning, and great damage has been done along the banks above the city, and many mills inundated and bridges swept away in the city. The Spiritualists here have good grit to turn out, for I had a very good audience Sunday evening, though it rained 'prodigious.'"

October 22. "Last Thursday, by invitation, I visited a very fine gallery of paintings, by eminent foreign and native artists. I was especially delighted with two little gems by Rosa Bonheur, though some of the larger pictures would win more admiration from the majority of people, no doubt."

"Friday, 15, I went to hear Emma Hardinge. She is speaking in this city Sundays, and goes to New York every Monday, and remains until Friday, reading proof of her book — 'The History of American Spiritualism.' Last evening I went up to Kensington, four miles from here, but still in the city, to attend the exhibition of their Lyceum. If the spirit of mother's uncle, Caswell Gardner, ever hovers around his former home, he will see a very great change from his once country estate to a crowded part of the city."

This was his last visit to Philadelphia, where he had a few dear and tried friends of many years standing, and many newer ones.

The ensuing month he spoke in Detroit, and also, during that time, was called upon to conduct funeral services over all that was mortal of a faithful worker in the spiritual vineyard, Mrs. Alcinda Wilhelm Slade, who, less than a year previously, had adopted this state as her home, under the most flattering auspices.

The remainder of this year, together with the first half of 1870, he spent mostly in this state. In February, in addition to his Sunday lectures in Coldwater, which called forth especial mention from the local press, he accepted an invitation to deliver a literary lecture before the Young Men's Association of Marshall, following Henry Vincent in the course. His subject was "The Ideal and the Real," and he spoke entirely without notes, as was his invariable custom on all occasions. An abstract of this lecture, written by me at the time, and published in the "Present Age" and other papers, will be found in the second part of this volume. It, of course, can convey but a mere skeleton of the address, as it fell from his lips at the Academy of Music, Marshall, February 25, 1870.

Early in the following autumn, he gave his last lectures in Chicago, and at Kalamazoo, Mich., attending, in the mean while, the yearly picnic of the Albion Society, as usual, and speaking in many places in the vicinity of home. In October he spoke at Farmington and Milford, and, the very last of that month, gave his last address at Battle Creek, the occasion being the funeral of an aged Spiritualist — Mrs. Merritt. From there he went to Louisville, Ky., to fill an engagement for the two following months — November and December. Of his first Sunday there he wrote, "It was the largest audience I ever had in this city. The hall is large, theater-shaped, and consequently easy to speak in." I will insert a few extracts from his letters, mentioning incidents of this his latest visit to Louisville.

November 20. "Last Sunday morning, by invitation

of some of the prominent Jew Spiritualists, — of whom there are a good many, — I attended the synagogue. They have the best organ and choir I have heard in a long time, and have instituted quite an innovation in allowing the men and women to sit together — a thing I never saw before in a Jewish meeting. The services were the same as I have witnessed before many times, and the sermon, I was informed, was very good, but, being in German, I was obligèd like brother ——, on a like occasion, to take the word of a reliable gentleman as to that matter. I was introduced to the Rabbi, who seems to be a very liberal man. He reciprocated by attending my lecture in the evening, and, as he understands English, he is so much ahead."

November 29. "Last Sunday night, after lecture, I spent about half an hour at a circle, where the principal medium was a young lawyer, of Jewish birth, named Dinkelspiel. The manifestations were very wonderful, — spirits talking audibly, and other feats of like character. I have also been to see Mrs. Hollis — a medium who has writing on the slate, same as Dr. Slade."

The evangelical clergy of the city became very much exercised over the great interest which was being aroused in the subject of Spiritualism, and several of them preached especial sermons of warning to their flocks. Among the number was Rev. Mr. Hopson, whom my brother reviewed in a discourse on "The Varieties of Faith," an abstract of which was published in the "Courier-Journal." He afterward sent to that paper the following challenge to the clergy of the city : —

"Inasmuch as there has been, during the last few weeks in this city, much controversy upon the subject of Spiritualism, and the opponents thereof and myself have been compelled to reply to each other through reportorial notes, — which in my own case must necessarily be very meagre, as I speak entirely extempore, and about two hundred and twenty words a minute, — I would suggest the propriety of holding a public debate upon the subject, to continue three or more evenings during the week. In reply to reports second hand, there must necessarily be more· or less unintentional misrepresentation. Now, in order that the citizens of this city may hear on equal terms both sides of this important subject, I propose to Elder Hopson, or any other clergyman of this city who represents his denomination, a public discussion of either of ·the subjoined questions, under parliamentary rules : —

1. "*Resolved*, That the Scriptures, history, and present demonstrations prove that the spirits of departed human beings have communicated in the past, and can, and do, in the present, communicate with the people of earth.

2. "*Resolved*, That the Bible (King James' translation) sustains modern Spiritualism in all its phases.

"My object in interpolating the phrase — King James' translation — is to avoid any loss of time disputing regarding Hebrew, Greek, or Latin idioms, and bring the subject on its own merits directly before the people. In addition, I am ready to receive and consider any proposition from Elder Hopson, or any other clergyman, which they will be willing to affirm, and upon which there is between us a point of difference." . . .

Then followed provision for rules, committee, &c., the same in substance as elsewhere stated in correspond-

ence with other clergymen. This communication, however, met with no response from the Louisville evan-
gelists.

The second week in Decemher he went to Paris,
Bourbon County, to deliver a course of week evening
lectures, — passing there his thirty-fifth birthday,
upon which occasion he wrote as follows : —

December 14. " Thirty-five years old to-day, and I
don't know as I feel any older than I did yesterday.
It is a lovely, sunshiny day, cool, but not uncomfortable.
This is one of the oldest towns in this part of Kentucky,
and the place where was first made the celebrated
Bourbon whisky, which has since had more thousands
of barrels named for it than ever there were gallons made
in this county. There are a great many old style in-
fidels here, but a few Spiritualists. My lecture last
night was the first ever given here on the subject, and
was listened to by a large audience with apparent
interest."

Soon after his return to Louisville, a soreness of the
throat, which he had considered of little consequence,
becamê serious, and developed into a large abscess, which
obliged him to disappoint his audience upon the last
Sunday of his engagement. Indeed, he came very
near passing over the river at that time, as the surgeon
who lanced his throat said that, if it had broken while
he was lying down, strangulation would have been almost certain. As it was, he came near starving on account of the swelling preventing the taking of any food
but perfect liquid for some time. This and the severe
pain reduced him very much, and inflicted a shock upon
his system from which it never fully recovered. As

soon as able he came home, having been presented by his Louisville friends with a very handsome cane to lean upon in his weakness, which proved of great service to him, not only then, but during the remainder of his life on earth. He arrived in time to spend New Year's with us, and, though still very feeble, entertained a few friends on that day, to whom he gave a whimsical account of the way he had "been starved, had his throat cut, and been caned," in explaining to them his altered looks.

CHAPTER XVII.

FEEBLENESS OF BODY AND STRENGTH OF SPIRIT. — LAST LECTURES AT CINCINNATI, OHIO, AND AT PORT HURON, FARMINGTON, AND MILFORD, MICH. — HOME AND REST. — ON THE THRESHOLD OF ETERNITY. — FAREWELL ADDRESS. — THE GREAT TRANSITION. — FUNERAL SERVICES AT ALBION, AND HONORS TO HIS MEMORY ELSEWHERE.

ON the 10th of January he considered himself recovered sufficiently to speak at the county convention of Spiritualists, at Albion, which he did, delivering the closing address of the convention on the subject of " The Hand writing on the Wall." The following week he attended the Quarterly Meeting of the Eaton County Circle at Charlotte, and the last of January went to speak at Farmington and Milford, Mich. He filled

this engagement, however, at the expense of considerable physical suffering, writing home as follows: —

FARMINGTON, February 11, 1871.

I have been sick for the past week; had a severe chill
Sunday morning. Mrs. McCain (a clairvoyant physician
of fifteen years' practice at Milford) doctored me up, so
that I went through with my public duties in a manner
satisfactory to them, but very exhausting to me. My
old friend, Dr. Irish, controlled her, and told me I ought
to stop speaking and get recruited up. He says I have
overtasked the brain and nervous fluids. I shall try to
take his advice after I have fulfilled my present engagements; hope I will not be compelled to before. One
queer idea he advanced, viz.: that it is very injurious
for me to attend so many funerals; but I don't see how
I can help it: people will die.

I guess I have written enough of the doleful; as I
told J. M., the day I had the chill, I could play the
part of the " Hypochondriac " with the natural expression.

He came home soon after, but his disposition would
not allow him to rest longer than absolutely compelled by
weakness, and in March he went to Port Huron to fill
an engagement of long standing. Not being able to fix
the exact date of this visit, on account of the loss of one
or two letters, I wrote recently to his friend, Dr.
Pace, of Port Huron, for the required data, receiving in reply a letter from which I take the following
extracts: —

UNITED STATES CONSULATE AT SARNIA,
ONTARIO, March 29, 1872.

MISS R. AUGUSTA WHITING, Albion, Mich.

Dear Madam : Your letter of 21st instant, in reference to your brother's last visit to Port Huron, was duly received. . . .

Your brother's last engagement with the Spiritualists of Port Huron was for the two last Sundays of March, 1871. He was in very feeble health at the time, and on the last Sunday of his stay with us he leaned upon my arm on his way to the lecture-room. He walked very slowly, and was evidently very much exhausted. I expressed some fear that he would not be able to speak that day ; but said he, " Don't be alarmed ; the spirits will take care of that. I shall speak *to-day*, but I can't promise you much for the future. My labors on earth are nearly finished."

When we arrived at the hall, I assisted him on to the platform, and gave him a glass of water ; and as the choir commenced to sing, the angels commenced to baptize him with their magnetic strength. He arose firmly to his feet, and in a loud, unfaltering tone of voice gave us a lecture which occupied over an hour in its delivery, and *such* a lecture as could only fall from the inspired lips of A. B. Whiting. . . .

I am, very truly, yours,

S. D. PACE.

On his return from Port Huron, we urged him very strongly to throw up his engagement at Cincinnati the next two months ; but so great was his dislike for disappointing people, that he could not feel that it would be right to do so if it could be avoided. When the time came for him to go, however, he was not able to travel, and sent a dispatch to that effect; also wrote, explaining the reason and asking to be released from the engagement, but stating that he might perhaps be able to come in a week or two. He received an answer desiring him to come as soon as he was able, and they would keep up the meetings as best they could until his arrival.

Being somewhat recruited by another week at home, he accordingly went, and remained seven Sundays, though at what expense of physical suffering was known only to him and the angels who attended and sustained. I *felt* it all by virtue of the mystic tie, but it was not until afterward that I *knew* that chapter of heroic endurance from outward sources. He complained little in his letters, except of being tired and homesick.

After the first Sunday there he wrote, —

"I was terribly exhausted with the noise and jar of the cars, but got through Sunday better than I expected. Miss Keyser gave some wonderful tests, in describing spirits and giving their names, after lecture. It is warm weather, and fruit trees are in bloom forty miles north of here."

Later. "I could not read the papers you sent me on account of my eyes, which are very bad, caused partly, I think, by my going over to Covington in the wind a few days ago. I have tried to get them to let me off with this month, but they don't seem disposed to; so, if I keep as well as now, I shall probably have to stay the two months out."

May 8. "No particular change in my health. I don't know that I am any worse for being here. I have no engagement except the one at Farmington and Milford, — the two last Sundays of June, — and shall make no more. I have had an invitation to go to Paris, Ky., and spend three weeks, but shall not accept. I want to get home. My friends urge me to come to Louisville, but I am afraid the fatigue of travel would overbalance the benefit derived from the pleasant company of friends."

May 11. "I think I shall be able to weather it through. The Executive Board met last night and I told them I would be glad to be let off after next Sunday, but they wouldn't hear to it at all; so, unless I lose my voice, I shall stay the month out. I sometimes think it don't make much difference, as I average about as well as when I left home; but when I feel as I did last Monday I want to be home."

May 21. " One Sunday more and this is over. Yesterday was a terribly hot day. I believe an egg on the desk would have cooked enough for my dinner. My cane has come very handy, as I have scarcely been able to walk a block since I have been here. I ride to the hall, and get up stairs with the help of my cane. The reason is, that my ankles seem to give way, and they pain me nights terribly sometimes. I write this that you may not be alarmed to see me looking rather worse than you perhaps expect."

He came home in this condition, and continued to suffer exquisitely with his ankles for several days longer; but home care and the medical aid obtained from a clairvoyant physician, Dr. Rowe, of Mason, relieved him, so that he determined to fulfill his "one more engagement" at Farmington and Milford, the last two Sundays of June. He got through the first Sunday very well, but the second he became so exhausted that

he fainted immediately after concluding his evening's
lecture, and lay in a state of prostration for several days,
too weak to attempt the journey home. Fortunately
for him, he was staying at the home of the clairvoyant
physician, Mrs. McCain, of Milford, mentioned in connection with his visit to the same place the previous
winter. The prompt action of this lady, under control
of her spirit guides, and the tender care bestowed upon
him, doubtless saved his life at this time. Before leaving
for home he received a peculiar test of spirit foresight.
An old physician, whom he had known in earth life, and
whose funeral he had attended many years previously,
conversed with him through the mediumship of Mrs.
McCain, and, after giving him other advice with regard
to his health, said, " You must give up speaking entirely for at least six months, or you can not possibly re-
gain your health. You ought not to address an audience
again ; but you will be called upon soon to attend the
funeral of an old friend, which you will feel compelled
to do, though at great peril to yourself."

He had been at home but a few days when a messenger
came to announce the death of Mrs. Hiram Hammond,
of Onondaga, Mich., she having left the especial request
that her funeral sermon should be preached by A. B.
Whiting. Twelve years before, she had asked and received his promise to perform for her that service should
he survive her, and he felt that he must redeem that
promise if it were possible. He resolved to go, but,
though the distance was short, he did not dare attempt
to go alone ; so I went with him. The distance was
about thirty-five miles by rail, and we went the evening
before the day appointed for the funeral, the first Sunday of July. The little journey fatigued him very much,

and he passed a dreadful night, a night of terrible anxiety to me then, but of blissful remembrance now — of thankfulness that I was privileged to sustain him through that sharp struggle for life; that mine was the hand to which he clung in those fearful paroxysms of pain. The morning found him so exhausted as scarcely to be able to raise himself from the bed, his stomach refusing to retain a particle of anything either solid or liquid. Yet, when the time came for the services, he arose and dressed with my help, though with considerable difficulty; was assisted into the carriage, and rode two miles to the church, where he delivered a most beautiful address, of about forty minutes' length, in his usual clear and powerful tones, giving no outward sign of weakness after the first few sentences. Probably no person present suspected that he was suffering from more than a slight temporary illness. Not daring to trust himself on the cars again, we returned home in an easy carriage the same afternoon. He never left Albion again. For three weeks and more he was confined to the house; then he seemed to gain strength, and began to ride out, and then to walk a short distance every pleasant day. This he continued to do through August, and we had strong hopes that, when the cool days came, he would improve more rapidly.

On Saturday and Sunday, the 2d and 3d of September, the Albion Society of Spiritualists held the usual Yearly Grove Meeting, at Spectacle Lake. Miss Susie Johnson was the speaker engaged. Mrs. Lois Waisbroker was also present, and by invitation addressed the audience on Sunday morning. It had been announced upon the notices of the meeting that A. B. Whiting (health permitting) would be present. He told the friends, however, that he would not be able to speak, even if he were present, so that he might not feel under any obligation to go, if he did not feel well enough.

On Saturday he walked out as usual, but did not go to the meeting that day. Sunday afternoon, however, he rode to the grove, — a distance of two miles, — though with no intention of speaking.

Of course he was eagerly welcomed, and requested most urgently to say " just a few words " to the friends assembled. To our surprise, he consented, and impelled, as it seemed, by an irresistible impulse, extended his remarks to an eloquent and comprehensive address, occupying about twenty minutes in rapid delivery, and closing with an improvisation upon the subject, " 'Tis only a Question of Time." The power and pathos of that last address, that farewell poem, will never be forgotten by those who listened to his voice that day. Many were moved to tears ; for his words were pervaded by a prophetic undertone, touched by the shadow of the coming change. Had he stood up with the deliberate intent of taking thus his farewell of the spiritual rostrum, he could not have chosen better the words or the occasion. He was much exhausted by the effort, though he spoke with all the vigor and apparent ease which were so eminently characteristic of him as a public speaker. He remained and listened to Miss Johnson's lecture, and then rode home and entertained several guests at tea with his usual pleasant hospitality. The following morning he complained somewhat of weariness and nausea, but kept up, and spent the time in conversation with us and Mrs. Bailey, of Battle Creek, who was our guest. He had, the evening previous, expressly desired Miss Johnson

to take dinner with him that day, and exacted her promise to that effect with such peculiar earnestness that
she felt compelled to accede to the request, although
at considerable inconvenience. He sat at dinner with
us, and dispensed the hospitality of his table for the last
time, referring, in a laughing way, to his inability to partake of the same dishes as the rest, his diet being confined to soup and oatmeal gruel on account of the
stomach refusing to retain other food.

After dinner he bade a cheerful good by to Mrs.
Bailey, who left for home, conversed with Miss Johnson a few minutes, and then went to lie down, as was
his custom. Less than an hour later he called me, and
asked for a glass of water, complaining of nausea and
faintness, but desiring me not to disturb Miss Johnson
(who had gone to lie down), or let mother know he was
sick. This I was accustomed to, as, throughout his
sickness, he had always chosen to conceal his sufferings
as much as possible. I therefore stood by him until he
seemed somewhat relieved, and then, as his hand still
clasped mine, sat down upon the side of the bed, to wait
until he should require my assistance to rise. He lay
quietly a few minutes, then moved uneasily, as if in
pain; said, in answer to my inquiry, "It seems to me
I never felt so badly in my life!" and, as I raised him
from the pillow, breathed his last in my arms, with a
struggle so brief that it had passed almost before any
other person could reach the room. The arms that had
clasped me convulsively relaxed their hold, and he lay
sleeping, apparently, as peacefully as a tired child.

We could scarce believe that the change had indeed
come; for his slight improvement had greatly strengthened our hopes of his final recovery. It is true, the

"Old Man" had told us that he would be "worse before he was better," and that his life would be in the most imminent danger until after the fateful month of November should be passed; but there are some calamities which the mind refuses to conceive as possible, until compelled by stern necessity. Those who have read the preceding pages will not wonder that we relied much upon those angelic guardians, who in so many situations of doubt and difficulty had *demonstrated* their power to protect and save; or that we dared hope that in this case, as in many others, they would be able to do for us *more* than they ventured to promise.

To the public the shock was even more sudden and unexpected; for, except to a very small circle of friends, many of the circumstances that rendered his condition especially perilous were entirely unknown, particularly the presence in his system of the lurking remnants of the deadly drug administered seven years previously, which to a certain extent defeated the action of remedies that might otherwise have availed for his relief. Had the malice of enemies survived the lapse of time, it might be gratified to know that it had been even a distant and indirect cause of his premature death; but he had, for the most part, outlived either his foes or their malignity, so that some, who might *then* have rejoiced at seeing him laid low, are sincere mourners *now*.

What his loss was to the world can be in some measure realized by those who thoroughly canvass the story of his life, — better by those who, through personal acquaintance, are qualified to fill up and round the outlines which alone are possible to a work of this kind. What the removal of his visible presence was to *his own*, can only be understood by those who have had removed from them the support of an earthly arm upon which they relied with perfect trust and confidence, the sight of an earthly face that was to them the mirror of heaven. What it would have been without the *knowledge* of his immortal life, his continued love and presence, his ever-watchful care, I do not dare imagine. Faith is beautiful and holy ; but thrice blessed is knowledge, through life and in the hour of death.

Funeral services were held at his home in Albion, September 6, at three P. M., and his mortal remains deposited in the cemetery at the same place. Miss Susie Johnson delivered the address, taking for text, " He has fought a good fight; he has finished his course; he has kept the faith." She was listened to by a large concourse of people, of all shades of belief and opinion religiously, but who all agreed in their esteem for the arisen one, and in deeming her remarks a fitting tribute to his memory. Rev. Parker Pillsbury was also present, and said a few words. Two of his own musical compositions — " O, hear my Parting Sigh ! " and " Land of the so-called Dead " — were sung by a chosen quartet to the accompaniment of his own instrument, — that melodeon upon which he composed the most of his songs, — and the simple, unpretentious ceremonies were ended.

Not only the spiritual papers, but the secular press generally, offered tributes of respect to his memory, and letters of condolence poured in upon us from individuals and societies all over the country ; all of which tokens of sympathy were deeply appreciated, although the multitude of similar favors received made it impossible to reply to each in detail.

A few of the press notices, chosen almost at random,

are appended, together with an abstract of the memorial sermon preached by Mr. Peebles at Louisville, and a poem written expressly for this work, and dedicated to his memory, by Mrs. L. E. Bailey, of Battle Creek, Mich.

SELECTIONS FROM PRESS OBITUARIES.

From the Banner of Light, September 30.

THE LATE A. B. WHITING.

AGAIN has the Angel of Deliverance swept suddenly down from the upper hights, and loosed from earthly bonds the spirit of one of our oldest and ablest lecturers.

From his home in Albion, Mich., on Monday, September 4, A. B. Whiting passed to spirit life. He had been out of health, but not considered dangerously ill, for several months. Only the day before, he had spoken a short time at the annual Spiritualists' picnic of his towns-people, in a beautiful grove about two miles from his home; and I thought, while he was speaking, I had never heard him talk more forcibly and eloquently in defense of our common cause, and the general principles of progress. He closed his remarks with a soul-stirring poem, which, as we afterward reverted to it, seemed almost prophetic of the events which followed. The subject of the poem was, " Only a Question of Time." I dined with him on Monday, and he remarked that he was usually well. Between two and three P. M. he left us without even a "good by." The struggle of separation was but momentary with *him*, at least, and as a peaceful composure settled over his features, we felt that "our loss was his gain." The physicians pronounced the immediate cause of his change to have been congestion of the heart.

His funeral was attended by Parker Pillsbury and myself. No words of mine will add anything to Mr. Whiting's public record; it is humanity's inheritance, and *his* most fitting eulogy. As a friend remarked to us at the funeral, "he died at his post." And as we folded the lid over the beautiful blue eyes and draped the body for the grave, the words of Paul seemed appropriate: "He has fought a good fight; he has finished his course; he has kept the faith; henceforth is laid up for him a crown of righteousness."

Thus the *old* workers cotemporary with myself take their departure one by one to the higher schools of experience, and but a few are left to struggle and counsel together here. But O, how inexpressibly comforting is the consciousness that it is "only a question of time," and we shall rejoin them, and together carry forward the grand purposes of being!

And while we listen with expectant ears to catch the words of wisdom dropping like refreshing dews from loving lips in the other and higher life, let us not forget to repay their watchful care by our ministries of sympathy and assistance to those they have left behind. We hope Mr. Whiting's numerous friends throughout the country will send words of friendly appreciation and comfort to his mother and sister, who are lonely, though *not alone.*

SUSIE M. JOHNSON.

DETROIT, September 7, 1871.

From the Banner of Light, October 14.

The Society of Spiritualists at Port Huron, Mich., passed the following resolutions September 10, in respect to the memory of A. B. Whiting: —

Whereas, The physical body of A. B. Whiting has yielded to the ravages of disease, and the beautiful soul that once animated it has taken its flight to a purer clime and a higher life, be it therefore,

Resolved, That this Society have always entertained the highest regard for his talent and appreciation of his labors, and realize that, in his transition, the cause of Spiritualism has sustained an irreparable loss.

Resolved, That the Spiritual Society of Port Huron, Mich., do hereby tender to his bereaved mother and sister an expression of our sympathy and heartfelt regret.

Resolved, That a copy of these resolutions be forwarded to his mother and sister, and that the spiritual press be requested to publish the same.

J. S. NEWELL, *Pres.*

S. D. PACE, *Sec. pro tem.*

From the Albion Recorder, September 8.

DEATH OF A. B. WHITING.

The people of Albion were surprised and pained to learn of the sudden death, by rupture of a blood-vessel, or of the heart itself, on Monday afternoon, of A. B. Whiting. Mr. W. had been in feeble health for some time, but was able to be about, and attended the spiritualist picnic a day or two before, on which occasion he spoke briefly, but not in any labored effort. He was a man of strict integrity, and fine intellectual attainments. As a lecturer and advocate of the faith of the Spiritualists he was widely known, and exerted a great influence. His funeral was attended by citizens generally, and by friends from other places. Remarks were made by Miss S. Johnson and Parker Pillsbury. The following sketch of the life of Mr. Whiting has been furnished us: —

He was born, December 14, 1835, in Plymouth County, Mass., where he received his education, graduating at East Bridgewater Academy. He was carefully educated, but never entered upon a classical course. As a boy at school he was remarkable for his facility in mastering his studies. Endowed with a wonderful memory, he seemed to acquire by intuition, and, what is singular in one who learns so readily, he seldom forgot anything. His delicate health never permitted him to indulge in the rude sports of boys, for which he manifested no inclination. He rather sought the society of those older than himself, in whose conversation he appeared to delight, but seldom took part. He seemed always to live in the world of thought, and not of action.

He came to Brooklyn in this state, with his parents and sister, in 1853, where he lived, doing what labor his health would permit, upon the farm of his father. In 1860 he removed to Albion with his mother and sister, his father having died, which place he made his residence up to the time of his death.

He began his career as a public speaker at the early age of eighteen, advocating the cause of Spiritualism, to which he devoted the best energies of seventeen years of his life. His energy and perseverance were untiring, and he died with "harness on his back." Notwithstanding the unpopularity of his faith, he won "golden opinions from all sorts of people," and commanded the respect and esteem of all who knew him. Amidst the fierce assaults of vituperation and calumny he was never known to swerve from the right or falter in his course.

His death has left a deep void in the ranks of those with whom he was identified, which can not be easily filled.   ·

His memory will be ever loved and respected by those whose privilege it was to know him. He was widely known; having delivered addresses in nearly every large city in the Union. And many there are throughout the land who will be sincere mourners at the sad news of his death.

In the private walks of life he was an exemplary man. His honesty and integrity were the common remark of all. " He was the stainless, spotless man," one who would "speak no slander — no, nor listen to it."

> " We have lost him; he is gone.
> We know him now; all narrow jealousies
> Are silent, and we see him as he moved, —
> How modest, kindly, all-accomplished, wise,
> With what sublime repression of himself,
> And in what limits, and how tenderly.
> . . . And through all this tract of years
> Wearing the white flower of a blameless life,
> Before a thousand peering littlenesses."

From the Port Huron Commercial, September 13, 1871.

IN MEMORIAM. — A. B. WHITING.

The many friends and admirers of A. B. Whiting will deeply regret to learn that he departed this life at his home in Albion, in this state, on Monday, the 4th inst., at the age of thirty-six years. Although he had long been in delicate health, his decease at this time was totally unexpected. Only the day previous, to the surprise of many to whom his weak state of health was known, he had taken part in a grove meeting of Spiritualists, at Spectacle Lake, where he delivered an address which is described as one of the most eloquent efforts of his life. The unwonted exertion upon this occasion probably hastened his departure, and was, we may say, his last act upon earth. He went home apparently more than usually prostrated, although he complained but little. On Monday about noon, complaining of feeling "very strange," he lay down, and shortly after, a member of his family, hearing him make some unusual noise, went to his side, and found him just breathing his last. He passed away easily, not seeming to realize the nearness of the summoning angel till the final warning came. His remains were followed to the grave on Wednesday by a large number of sorrowing friends, the burial services being conducted by Miss Susie Johnson, assisted by Rev. Parker Pillsbury.

In this city, last Sunday, a memorial address was given in the evening by Mrs. Smith, at the close of which Dr. Pace, after some brief and feeling remarks, offered a series of resolutions of respect, which were unanimously adopted by the society. We may also

incidentally state that Dr. Pace, in his official capacity
as American consul at Sarnia, caused his flag to be suspended at half mast during the day after the reception
of the news of Mr. Whiting's decease.

So closed a useful and a busy life. For seventeen
years, or since he was eighteen years of age, Mr. Whiting has been in the lecture field advocating the cause
of Spiritualism. To this cause he gave without stint
the treasures of his rich young existence, and crowded
into a few short, busy years the work of a lifetime.
Many who read this will remember him when, a mere
boy, he appeared in our midst, and spoke with the
same fervor, the same tone of conviction, which glorified the efforts of his riper years. He was a remarkable man, with a gift of burning eloquence which took
all hearts by storm.

He was, with his other gifts, a natural musician and
a musical composer of no ordinary merit. His songs
are popular wherever the English language is spoken,
and in such surpassingly sweet and tender creations as
"Lena de l'Orme," "Leoline," "Touch the Lute
gently," "The Wind is in the Chestnut Bough," &c.,
he has called forth such touches of sweet harmony as
will live in the hearts of people who will come after us,
long beyond the time when, in the busy whirl of the
world, the gifted composer would else have been forgotten.

We do not wish to close our tribute without some
slight reference to Mr. Whiting's political labors. He
was all his life an ardent Democrat, and during the canvass of 1868 took the stump in favor of the principles
he cherished. Those who have heard him will bear us
witness that he carried with him into the political

arena the same brilliant and captivating style of argument which characterized him upon the religious platform, only intensified by the exigencies of the calling. Those who listened to him with such rapt delight upon the occasion of his visit to this place, in his political capacity, whatever may be their religious differences with him, will, we are certain, think of him kindly.

He always appeared to have a preference for Port Huron and her people, and to visit here always appeared to give him especial pleasure. His circle of warm friends was not limited to those of his own belief, but numbered those of all beliefs and all parties. With his music and his attractive conversational powers, he was a charming addition to the social circle; and even when his bodily sufferings pressed heavily upon him, as they often did in his later years, he never relaxed his efforts to be agreeable. He was never married, and rarely referred to the subject in his conversation; but from the fact that the burden of his songs was principally the " tender passion," we have often fancied that perhaps, in his early youth, there was some one whom he had loved and lost, and some time hoped to meet and be happy with " over there." No word was ever said against his private reputation, and scandal was never associated with his name, which he took with him unblemished to his grave. His habits were simple and unaffected, and his life throughout exceptionally pure and blameless. He resided with his mother and sister in a pleasant home in Albion, where the family had the sincere respect of all who knew them. His friends were about him in his last moments. Loving hands laid his body to rest, and loving hearts will cherish his memory until they meet him in that fair land of promise " beyond the breakers."

MEMORIAL SERMON AT LOUISVILLE.

From the Louisville Courier-Journal, October 16, 1871.

THE DREAD FUTURE.

A very good audience gathered in the west wing of Weisiger Hall, yesterday morning, to hear Rev. Mr. J. M. Peebles. His discourse was upon the life and death of A. B. Whiting, a gentleman who was well known in this city. It will be read with interest by the many friends of Mr. Whiting. The audience last night was much larger. There was scarcely standing-room for those in attendance. Mr. Peebles is an able speaker, and charms his hearers not only with his oratory, but with a freshness and vigor of thought that is striking. The following is only a synopsis of his address in the forenoon : —

They rest from their labors, and their works do follow them.

Philosophically speaking there is no death, — only change onward and upward for ever. It is evidently impossible to find absolute rest in the universe. Motion is everywhere, and change, by methods inverse and diverse, is a fixed law, ever evolving the more etherealized forms of life. Leaves are now falling from the maple, the oak, and the elm; friends are falling; all your eyes have wept and hearts ached ere the present occasion. How true that man, the earthly man, " dieth and wasteth away " !

Winter dies in northern latitudes that spring may carpet the earth in grasses and grains; and man, the mortal of man, that his spirit, disinthralled from the physical organization, may traverse space and pass on in its path of destiny toward perfection.

Being knows no destruction. Annihilation is a meaningless term. The conservation of forces demonstrates this position. It is physically impossible for something to become nothing; all that was is, and eternally will be. Death, so called, is no enemy, but, natural and beautiful, it must precede immortal life, as must the acorn the oak, or the bud the opening flower. Stars that fade from our skies fade to illumine other portions of the sidereal heavens, and friends — our cherished friends — that pass on through the valley of shadows, go to people the love-lands of immortality. They take with them consciousness, reason, memory, and their souls' holiest affections. Pure love is immortal. This true, our dear departed loving us still, they delight to project their thoughts earth-ward; delight to impress us with the increasing beauties of their progressive existence; delight in becoming to us what the facts of the nineteenth century demonstrate — the actuality of ministering spirits.

Churchmen joining hands with deists and atheists in denying present inspirations, revelations, and communications from the spirit world, generally entertain erroneous conceptions of death, speaking of it as a " tyrant," as " the king of terrors," and picturing it as a grim, bony skeleton, with scythe mercilessly mowing down humanity. And then, to intensify the horror, they will join in this Christian hymn : —

> " Hark! from the tombs a doleful sound;
> Mine ears, attend the cry;
> Ye living men, come view the ground
> Where you must shortly lie."

Such hymns, with the accompanying theological dogmas, — the resurrection of the body, the day of judgment and future endless hell torments, — are the pitiable remnants of an imported paganism. The preaching of these and other unreasonable chimerical doctrines, is filling the country with a scoffing infidelity.

To Spiritualists death is birth — the second birth, into a higher state of existence. The body returns to earth, to reappear again only in grasses, flowers, and forests. As well ask the oak to return to its acorn, the winged bird to return to the nest and reinhabit the shell, as to ask an immortalized spirit to return to some gloomy graveyard and take on the dead material body. " Flesh and blood can not inherit the kingdom of God. " Paul further said, " We sow not the body which shall be." The body which shall be is the " spiritual body," and essential spirit is the life, the conscious intelligence of this spiritual body, connecting mortals with immortals and angels with God, who alone hath underived immortality.

All the popular religions of the day rest upon traditions. Spiritualism alone rests upon the basic foundation of present, tangible facts. It is the living witness of the future existence. Considered historically, it unites the past and present. Referring to the Bibles of all nations, and especially the Old and New Testaments, we see that immortalized beings held conscious communion with mortals for some four thousand years. Angels or spiritual beings appeared to Abraham, Hagar, Lot, Jacob, Moses, Elijah, Gideon, Ezekiel, and Zachariah. Also to Mary, the mother of Jesus; to the two Marys at the tomb; to the shepherds on Judean hills; to Peter in prison; to Peter, James, and John, on the mount; to John, on the Isle of Patmos; and nearly all

of the scriptural characters. These immortalized beings
are sometimes called "angels," "angels of the Lord,"
"men in shining garments," "men in white garments,"
"men of God;" "the man Gabriel;" "thy fellow-ser-
vant," &c., showing them to have been once men living
upon the earth. They appeared for thousands of years,
according to the Scriptures — then why not now? Has
God changed? Have God's laws changed? To ask, is
to answer the inquiry. How truly did the preacher
say (Eccl. iii. 15), "That which hath been is now;
. . . and God requireth that which is past." More-
over, Jesus said, "These signs shall follow them that
believe. . . . They shall lay hands on the sick and
heal them; make the lame to walk, blind to see, deaf to
hear," &c.' These signs do follow spiritualist media —
but churchmen have lost the spiritual gifts promised in
the New Testament. The apostate and "fallen" condition of our Christendom is a painful theme for reflection. It is Babylon, and nothing more, while Spiritualism is original Christianity — the *Christianity* of Jesus
and the apostles. The earliest of the Christian fathers
had spiritual gifts — such as trance, vision, inspiration,
and prophecy. So had the most distinguished men and
women of the ages — Constantine, Tasso, Savonarola,
Joan of Arc, Louis XVI., George Fox, Ann Lee, John
Wesley, Baron Swedenborg, and hosts of others.

Our friend and *your* friend, A. B. Whiting, who has
recently ascended to the homes of the angels, was a
most able and efficient advocate of the phenomena and
philosophy of Spiritualism. He consecrated to this
work seventeen years of his life, speaking in public the
very day previous to his translation to the world of
beatific blessedness. He had been in feeble health

nearly a year, but generally filled his lecture engagements up to the summer months.   Resting a while from
his mental labors, his most intimate friends thought him
gradually improving, and encouraged his attendance at
a grove meeting in the vicinity.   He addressed the
audience in his usual happy and eloquent style, and at
the conclusion improvised a beautiful poem.   The next
day, suddenly complaining of illness, and tenderly lean-
ing upon his sister Augusta's shoulder, he calmly
breathed his last in her arms.   Our loss is his gain.
Residing ten years in Michigan, within an hour's ride
of Albion, I frequently shared the social fellowship and
generous hospitalities of friend Whiting's home, as well
as the cheering companionship of the mother and sister, with whom we deeply sympathize in this trying
affliction.

It is but justice to say, that those who knew Mr.
Whiting best esteemed him the highest.   He was a
man of positive convictions, of keen moral perceptions,
and exalted aspirations.   In his public ministrations he
was overshadowed by angelic influence, an ancient
Egypto-Persian, a cardinal conversant with ecclesiastical history, and others, who had long summered in the
spirit world.   Touching historical matters relating to
the church, he had, as a lecturer, no equal in our ranks.
Superstition quailed and bigotry hid its hateful head
before the thrilling inspirations that dropped like pearls
from his lips.   His musical gifts were of a superior character.   In public meetings and at state conventions he
sang his own compositions, thrilling the people with
such melodies as doubtless obtain among the harpers
that the mystic John heard in heaven.   Our noble
brother, who, at the bid of the death angel, has gone up

one step higher, loved Spiritualism — loved his co-workers in the spiritual vineyard; and, be it said to his lasting praise, he never, through envy or jealousy, vilified or in any way sought to undermine the influence of his fellow-toilers, engaged in constructing the same spiritual temple. Many would do well to emulate those virtues that characterized his public life. His was a royal nature; and now, resting from his earthly "labors, his works do follow him."

Last evening, attending a very pleasant and harmonial séance, our brother announced his presence, and assured us that he should be with us to-day, while speaking of the after-life and a fadeless immortality. He then gave us this message: —

"Tell the people in your discourse that in passing to this state of existence I found that the principles and doctrines I had taught under the control of my angel guides were true, and that, if possible, I cherish deeper desires for the promulgation of the heavenly truths of Spiritualism than when in the body. Much that was faith then is fruition now. I bask in the smiles of those 'gone before,' and am supremely happy. My vision is enlarged, and the future is all radiant with the grandeur and glory of eternal progress. The work in which I was engaged must and *will* go on to complete victory. I had hoped to address my Louisville friends once more before passing to this life, but it was not so ordered. Pleasant are my memories of them and all the friends of earth. I find this world more real and beautiful than I conceived it to be, even in the moments of my loftiest inspirations. I shall speak to you again. Good night."

This message was given in an earnest, pathetic tone, touching the depths of our sympathetic natures. O, how richly are we blessed in this privilege of conversing with our loved ones in heaven! Our noble self-sacrificing workers are one by one putting off their sandals, and passing the death-rolling Jordan, where their white feet press the golden shores of immortal blessedness. The Rev. Dr. J. B. Ferguson, Mrs. Alcinda Wilhelm Slade, and more recently brother A. B. Whiting, all eloquent advocates of the spiritual philosophy, have put on their crowns of rejoicing. Angels are their companions, and Spiritualism is just as much better than any churchal system of religion as knowledge is superior to faith. "Add to your faith knowledge," said the apostle Paul. Spiritualists have done this, and have been blessed in the doing.

Spiritualism has no creed; Spiritualists can never become a sect. To crystallize is to die. Sectarisms, under the name of religion, have drenched nations in blood, and cursed this beautiful earth quite too long already. Excelsior is the divine word of the Harmonial Philosophy.

It has demonstrated a future progressive existence, converting atheists, deists, and secularists to a knowledge of immortality, and revealed the immutable law of compensation. It has unrolled before us a new geography of the heavens, and testified that no personal devil raves "over there," nor brimstone flames scent and soil the garments of the risen. Unbarring the gates of death, it has brought the loved inhabitants of the summer-land into our cities, our homes, our chambers, permitting us to clasp their shining hands, and listen to the music of their voices. It has given the world new inventions in mechanism, and laid open to view the heretofore hidden laws of magnetic reciprocity. It has not only foretold future events of vast moment to individuals and nations when aflame with the living fires of prophecy, but it has warned the more susceptible of steamer burnings and fearful railway collisions. With the wand of clairvoyance it has scanned ocean beds, described geologic strata, suggested new planets, and measured starry distances, while scientists were laggardly adjusting their instruments of observation. Under the name of psychometry, it has read by oral emanations the unwritten history of Egyptian pyramids and Assyrian ruins, of Grecian culture and Druidic worship, and can trace the life lines of mortals by the touch of ringlet or garment. Each act is photographed upon the conscious sensorium. The judgment seat is within, and memory is the recording angel.

Strengthening the weak, warning the erring, waking the dormant, unvailing the treacherous, and startling the sinful, it continues to re-thunder the wilderness words of the Baptist, "Repent — confess and forsake your sins." Only the "pure in heart" see God. To "him that overcometh" is the promise of access to the tree of life. Kindling in all believing souls the loftiest endeavor, Spiritualism is the sweetest answer to prayer, and the inspiring genius of every reform movement of the times. Meaning science and progress, morality and pure religion, it is God's living word to humanity through angels and ministering spirits. "O, come, let us worship in its temple."

13

MEMORIAL POEM.

MY BROTHER STILL LIVES.

DEDICATED TO THE MEMORY OF A. B. WHITING.

My brother lives ! O, joy to know,
Although we mourn him here,
He lives again, freed from all pain,
In yonder heavenly sphere.

Yes, he still lives ! my noble friend,
Although on earth no more
We listen to the joyous songs
He sang in days of yore.

Others his music oft will chant ;
His words be often sung :
While his familiar voice we miss,
Our lips with grief are dumb.

How much we miss him none can tell,
Save those who knew his worth ;
Yet never we one moment doubt
The soul's immortal birth.

Thy son still lives ! a spirit bright,
O, mother, pure and true,
And often sends fond words of love,
Sweet messages, to you.

Our brother lives! dear sister, kind,
  In whom we gladly trace
Resemblance to that noble form
  And well-remembered face.

And he has left to you a trust,
  Which you have well begun —
The work which he so suddenly
  Was called to leave undone.

But we shall miss his earnest words —
  The pulpit, too, and press,
Have lost in him an advocate,
  Their ablest and their best.

His memory lives in noble deeds;
  For truly it is said,
No words of slander ever passed
  The lips now cold and dead.

He lives in name from east to west;
  The north and south proclaim,
His eloquence has justly earned
  An eminence to fame.

              L. E. BAILEY.

BATTLE CREEK, MICHIGAN.

CHAPTER XVIII.

CONCLUDING WORDS. — HIS LECTURES AND IMPROVISA-
TION. — FAVORITE SUBJECTS.

IN conclusion, I have but few words to offer. Properly speaking, my task is already done; since to trace
the pathway of the ascended soul is not within the
scope of my intent, and on the hither shore its wander-
ings are ended. Yet it may be that a brief backward
glance at the life so short, and yet so long, will not
seem inappropriate.

First, with regard to his spiritual sight, manner of
speaking, &c., I will give his own statement as embodied in a paper prepared by him at the request of
Mrs. Hardinge, in 1867. After speaking of his early
possession of the open vision, its temporary withdrawal,
and final return, he says, —

"From that day to this, — over thirteen years, — I
have not been twenty-four hours at once without this
opened vision; and I am assured that this gift will never
wholly leave me again, and that the changes through
which I was passing, mentally and physically, made it
necessary that it should be taken from me for the six
years. Generally speaking, the possession of this gift
is productive of far more pleasure than pain, but there
are times when I see so many, and they come in such
crowds, that it produces a temporary annoyance — a
sort of pressure upon the sight: then my kind guardian will draw something like a vail between me and

them, and they are shut from my sight for the time being.

"Since I have been a public lecturer I rarely get any communication direct from any, except my own circle and personal friends. The mass of spirits that I see make no more impression upon me than the crowds I would meet in Broadway, New York, at mid-day. I recognize my friends, and pass on. I see, not only the dead, but the living also, in places where their bodies are not. This, however, is not a constant gift; nor do I see these as clearly as those who have left the earthly mold. I used sometimes to get the two con-founded, and mistake the living for the dead, and *vice versa*. I think such mistakes on the part of mediums lead to many cases of mistaken identity and miscalled falsehood on the part of spirits. Now I rarely mistake the double for a departed spirit. . . .

"It is now thirteen years since I have followed this changing life, under the guidance of true and faithful guides, who have never deceived or misled me in the slightest degree. During these thirteen years I have seen all phases of spirit control and demonstration of which I have ever heard, and recognize each as filling its appropriate sphere. I am not one of those who would wish to pull up the ladder on which I have as-cended, or decry any form of mediumship, however humble; nor do I, like some, hold to the vain belief that I have reached, or ever shall reach, a condition so exalted as to be above or beyond the assistance and inspiration of my spirit friends.

"My manner of speaking is wholly inspirational. I rarely know beforehand what I am to say, or even the particular theme upon which I am to treat, but am fully conscious of what I say at the time it is spoken, and my remembrance thereof is about the same that I would have of another's discourse to which I had listened. Under whatever circumstances, or upon whatever theme I may speak, I recognize the same support. It has never failed me in a single instance. It has been to me an educator, bringing forward historical facts unknown to me previous to their utterance, but, when sought out, found uniformly correct in substance, and sometimes verbatim — philosophy of which in my youth I was ignorant, and language that, of myself, I was incapable of using. These were among the — to me — strange things of my early experience. Now they are part of myself in mind, and matters of every-day life in reality, as well as form and expression.

"I have thus obtained a good, thorough education without the routine of study or the prestige of collegiate honor. Connected with my speaking has been the gift of improvisation upon almost any given subject. Probably in my lecturing career I have composed extemporaneous poems upon more than two thousand occasions. Last winter I kept account of the number of different themes improvised upon in a space including November and December, 1866, and the result was forty-two; which, I think, would be a fair average for the last twelve years."

In later years the aid and support of which he speaks continued with him, and became even more intimately blended with his consciousness, as he grew nearer allied to the spiritual realm. It was only at rare intervals, when physical weakness bore heavily upon him, that he passed into the utter rest of unconscious trance.

His favorite themes were of an historical character,

particularly such as related to the rise and fall of nations, civilizations, and religious institutions, with the lessons to be drawn therefrom. With this class of subjects he became especially conversant, but by no means confined himself to those. As I have before observed, he had well-defined opinions upon most subjects, and was always willing to state and defend those opinions upon all suitable occasions.

He affirmed the existence in some form of the spiritual ideas of immortality and spirit communion, or revelation, as basic principles in all religions of which we have authentic record, and in the progress of religious ideas in the past saw the type of the greater progress possible in the future.

He declared, that to assert a finality in religious belief and attainment was as absurd as to assert a finality in scientific research, and that there was no more danger to true religion from that fact, on the one hand, than there was to science, on the other. He asserted the supremacy of reason, knowledge, and demonstration over mere faith and belief.

He often chose subjects of a scientific cast, as the " Antiquity of Man " and " Origin of the Races," and, especially in addressing literary societies, a still more extended variety of topics — " The Philosophy of Life," " Happiness the Desire and Destiny of Man," " The Ideal and the Real," " Mission of the Beautiful," and many others.

His political addresses were always devoted to the discussion of principles, with their logical tendencies when carried out in the administration of government, and not of mere personal issues. Perhaps his most famous efforts in the political field were those of 1868,

wherein he treated of "The three Corner-stones of
Despotism." These he defined to be — first, war
with its consequence — a standing army; second, a
large and increasing public debt; and third, a union
of church and state.

His line of argument consisted in proving by historical parallels that, wherever these three requisites had
been secured, the result was always and inevitably the
same, namely, despotic rule, under whatever name of
courtesy it might be called; and in pointing out the
danger that in his view seemed to threaten to lay open
the possibility of such a combination, and the method
of defeating that possibility, and thereby averting the
danger.

I might add incident after incident illustrative of his
habits of mind, his readiness of resource and promptness in action, his unswerving integrity and utter fear-
lessness in defense of principle, his constancy in friendship, and, more than all, the chivalric devotion to his
own that made his watchful care a shield and a defense
ever round about them; — but of what avail?

The fullest and frankest biography must be to some
extent superficial. Every human soul lives two lives —
the inner and real, only shining dimly through the
outer, the seemingly more actual existence. Yet the
latter is all that we can grasp sufficiently to embody
in words and give it to the world. The richness of
the inner life can not be thus revealed, but stands — a
sacred mystery, only to be comprehended by the quick-
ened sense of kindred souls. Therefore it is that the
sternest conflicts of life can never be recorded; that
through the darkest paths of our spiritual pilgrimage
we must walk alone — absolutely alone, so far as the

outer senses reach; while much from which we suffer most acutely could never be revealed to others; still more, could never be understood, if it were revealed; and still more, ought never to be repeated, if it could be understood.

It is customary, as I am aware, to conclude a work like this with an estimate of the life and character of the subject. This I shall not attempt, lest, in the endeavor to restrain eulogy within the bounds of modesty, I should fail in justice. His life and labors, with their present and possible results, speak for him more eloquently than words, and rear unto his memory the surest, most enduring monument.

PART II.

POEMS.

BY

A. B. WHITING.

EARLY POEMS.

MUSIC.

Music, sweet Music, thou wondrous theme,
Of which poets write and lovers dream;
Sorrow and pain are forgotten in thee,
And sadness gives place to laughter and glee.

Music, sweet Music, thy charms all admire,
The blithesome youth and the gray-haired sire;
In lowliest hovel or gilded saloon,
Alike they call thee a precious boon.

Dear to the laborer, hastening away
To his welcome rest at close of day,
Dear to the noble, the prince, and the queen,
Gift of the Most High where'er thou art seen.

Music, blest Music, all men name thee fair,
Pride of the earth and gem of the air;
No other enchantment like thine doth allure
The care-burdened mind unto all that is pure.

205

PRO LIBERTATE.

GLIDE on, majestic, rolling river!
Give thanks unto the mighty Giver
    That thou art free!
No chains can ever stop thy course;
Thou canst not be subdued by force;
    Flow on in glee.

O lofty mountain, towering high,
Thy summit seems to reach the sky;
    Thou, too, art free:
Still thou wilt catch the sun's first ray,
The moon's pale light; a tyrant's prey
    Thou canst not be.

Ah, no! 'Tis not the lofty mount,
Flowing river or silvery fount,
    That is not free.
'Tis man — O, cruel thought! A slave?
O God, who life unto us gave,
    Can such things be?

Yes, e'en in freedom's boasted land
Man is deprived by might's strong hand
    Of liberty;
Man by his fellow-man is sold
For filthy gain — "for paltry gold."
    What mockery!

Then let the tears for Freedom shed
Draw vengeance on the hoary head
    Of Tyranny!
And let us strike one mighty blow,
Give one strong effort to o'erthrow
    All slavery!

Yes, strike! Let tyrant custom die,
Its advocates for quarter fly
    To liberty.
Strike! for the flag of freedom waves
O'er freedom's land and freemen's slaves;
    Let them be free.

IN MEMORIAM.

APRIL 1, 1853.

I HAD a brother once,
  A mild and beauteous boy,
A pleasant, young companion,
  My boyhood's pride and joy;
Time's unwearied footsteps
  Still onward swiftly glide;
Eight long, long years have passed
      Since Willie died.

But thought still turneth back,
  With fond recollection,
To him, the object of
  My youth's strong affection.

No tear-drop glistened in my eye ;
I neither sobbed nor sighed ;
They told me that I cared not,
            When Willie died.

O, could they but have known,
What none may ever know,
How deep the inward wound,
The heart's unspoken woe;
For, though I showed no grief,
Although I never cried,
My child-heart sobbed and moaned
            When Willie died.

O, THINK OF ME!

O, THINK of me when fortune's flowers
Are round thy pathway strewn;
O, think of me in pleasure's hours,
Wherever thou mayst roam.

O, think of me in adversity,
When fortune frowns on thee;
When sorrow checks thy buoyancy,
Then think, — O, think of me!

O, think, then, how in former years
We roamed o'er field and glade,
And gave no thought to fashion's gear,
To money or parade.

O, think of me, although I go
   In other climes to roam,
Where other flowers may blow
   Than deck my childhood's home.

O, think of me! Our paths may blend
   Nor meet on earth again,
But years may pass, and still your friend
   I ever shall remain.
     14

WRITTEN IMPROVISATIONS.

1855–1857.

FLOAT ON.

FLOAT on, float on, my heavenly bark,
  Above the earthly tide ;
Bear swiftly o'er earth's trials dark
  The joys that with thee glide.

Float on, and truth's serene starlight
  Shall guide thee swiftly o'er
Earth's breaking waves and gloomy night,
  To heaven's happy shore.

Float on, my graceful moving bark,
  And ever be my guide ;
I'll ever to thy whisperings hark,
  And by them will abide.

Float on, and in the silent night
  Thine aid I will invoke
To bear me to a land of light,
  Released from error's yoke.

'Tis done ; on wisdom's plain I stand,
Free as the truth I breathe, in heaven's happy land ;
Float on, blest messenger of hope,
And minds of earth to wisdom ope.

I LOVED.

I LOVED a song-bird of the spring,
  That sung his wild songs of glee;
I loved him for his notes of joy;
  They sounded sweet to me.

I loved a little violet peeping
  Above the mossy ground,
And the ivy wild a creeping
  Upon the rocky mound.

I loved the white-capped waves,
  Dashing wildly and free;
The sunny shores they lave
  Were beautiful to me.

I loved the deep, blue sea,
  And the sea-bird's shrill cry,
The proud ship beneath me,
  And the cloudlets on high.

I loved the genial clime
  Of my own sweet Italy;
I loved the gentle chime
  Of love's sweet minstrelsy.

I loved its clear, blue sky;
  I loved its fertile shore;
I said, "My own sweet Italy,
  I ne'er will leave thee more."

I loved a beauteous maiden,
Radiant, rare, and beauty-laden;
When she was near me
Heaven was around me,
The sweet spell with magic bound me.

I love heaven's glories now;
  I've passed from earth's dark sphere;
With love's own crown upon my brow
  I come, your life to cheer.

I love all things that God hath made, —
  The flower, the tree, and singing-bird;
The murmuring stream, the leafy glade,
  Are all to me as God's own word.

God's word is found in everything:
  Go, then, and wisdom learn
From flowers in bloom, and birds that sing;
  Learn error to detect and truth discern.

'Tis holy love, — O, heavenly word! —
  That calls us from our home
To tell the tales that we have heard
  In heaven's celestial dome, —

Where song-birds ever warble free,
  And fairer roses bloom
Than earth can e'er afford to thee,
  In cypress wreaths of gloom.

Riches that never fade away,
  Love-joys that never die,

Roses that bloom not to decay,
　Truth ever hovering nigh, —

These are the gems of heaven, my home,
　Peace, harmony, and love ; —
That little word thrills every soul,
　From earth to spheres above.

O, love ! sweet theme ! on thee I dwell ;
For thee I tune my silvery harp,
　And touch my light guitar ;
For thee my notes in rapture swell,
For thee I tune the golden shell,
　And sing of worlds afar.

———

THE FOUNT OF LIGHT.

O, COME to the fount of living light,
And drink of waters pure and bright,
Which come from God, divine above,
Whose attributes are truth and love.
O, come, and pluck the fairest flowers,
That bloom in heaven's Elysian bowers ;
We'll weave them in a garland bright,
And fill thy soul with calm delight.

O, come to us when trials grieve ;
For we thy side will never leave.
We'll drive dark sorrows all away,
By kindling truth's immortal ray ;

We'll make the earth with praises ring,
As we our songs of glory sing,
And bring the angels' purest joy,
Which cares of earth can not destroy.

O, come to the mount of wisdom high ;
We'll lead thy way o'er earth and sky,
O'er rock, and glade, and silvery stream,
Where'er a ray of love shall gleam.
O, come where truth fills every soul,
And heavenly strains of music roll,
To blend all joys in harmony,
In heaven's own rapt melody.

O, blend our lays, ye mortal throng,
With earthly poesie and song ;
Let earth be filled with heavenly love,
All souls in gladness ever rove.
Angels bright will guide your way
Where love and truth their charms display ;
Will guide your course from sphere to sphere,
And ever be your guardians dear.

O, come where heavenly beauty dwells,
Where mirth and song each spirit swells ;
Music which angels only know
We come to sing to you below.
Then strike again the minstrel's lyre !
Then light again heaven's holy fire,
And fill the earth with joy and glee ! —
The love-lit songs of spirits free.

THE STAR OF TRUTH.

THE star of truth shines o'er me,
  And my soul upbounds in love
To the golden orbs that shine
  In heavenly worlds above.
O, brighter far and clearer
  Than diamonds most rare
Are those gems of light on high,
  Where thought is free from care.

My soul is filled with melody,
  And thrills with blissful joy
To breathe a joyful lay again
  Of " love without alloy."
The spirits bright around me
  Are singing songs of love ;
Then join again your mortal mind
  With angel choirs above.

Then sigh no more for earthly gems,
  That glitter and decay,
Nor mourn again for earthly wealth,
  That comes to pass away ;
But lift your thoughts to brighter joys,
  That come from worlds on high,
Where wisdom guides and love responds,
  In spheres beyond the sky.

O, learn to love the beautiful,
  The holy joys of heaven ;
Improve the words of wisdom pure
  Which angels bright have given ;

O, strive to blend their good advice,
   In every walk of life,
With nature's word divine, revealed,
   And banish fear and strife.

My soul is filled with joyous glee,
   With happiness divine ;
I would that all the minds of earth
   Were free from care as mine.
I rove in heaven's resplendent light,
   Where beauties know no end,
Where all the thoughts that fill the soul
   With kindred virtues blend.

We speak, we sing, we ever breathe
   Our songs of joy to thee ;
Proclaim the truth to all mankind,
   And make their spirits free !

TRUE LOVE.

THERE is a rose in nature's garden
   Blooming wild and free,
Where no cold wind can touch its leaves
   For love its petals be.
No autumn frost, nor winter snow,
   Nor hoary-headed time,
Can blast that flower ; for truth has made its bed
   In heaven's blest clime.
Truth is its couch ; its tendrils twine
   On wisdom's holy tree,

And heaven's genial dews fall gently
    O'er the flowery lea;
While gentle winds are wafting
    Its fragrance on the air,
Sweet songs of angel tongues arise
    Its beauty to declare.
Though other roses round it bloom,
    And share its lovely bed,
Still, this one flower above them all
    In grandeur rears its head.
Around it flowers of varied hue
    In purest beauty blend,
And share the pearly dew-drops pure
    As they soft descend.
No poison weed, nor evil stalk,
    Can mar its mossy bed,
Nor deadly serpent twine its folds
    And rear its flattened head
Above the rose; nor yet a thorn
    Can ever there be found
With that fair rose that blooms on high,
    In heaven's holy ground.
That flower is love; for truth has made its bed
    In heaven's sunny land,
And in the human soul bright angels wake
    Its music bland.
'Tis nature's rose, implanted in the mind
    By God, the Source of all
No earthly fetter e'er can bind,
    In error's thrall,
This holy gem, which God has given
    To fill earth's sphere

With higher hopes than earthly gems bequeath
'Twill banish fear.
Not carnal joys which man has christened love, —
O, mockery those!
A poison yew tree might as well
Be called a rose, —
But holy love that strikes anew the harp
Of heavenly hope,
As to truth's ever glorious light
The senses ope.
That holy charm that fills all space
Below, above,
Which angels strive to wake in every soul,
Is this — true love.

―――――

WE feel its magic wand
In heaven's happy land;
We hear its music bland,
Sung by an angel band
From error free.
Its glories know no end,
Its beauties ever blend;
We're happy to descend,
In harmony to lend
Its charms to thee.

―――――

THE fount of light! what glories swell
And ripples sparkle as they glow!
A sweet tale of love they tell,
Breathe truth and wisdom as they flow

From world to world, from sphere to sphere,
   While every world in glory bright,
Guided by beauty's gondolier,
   Crowned with a garland of love's light,
Moves onward in its wonted course
   Untouched by error's fiery train.
No earthly janglings, loud and hoarse,
   Can blot with their foul, sinful stain
The starry orbs that, twinkling, move
   In heaven's vast ethereal blue ;
Guided by wisdom high, they prove
   The beauties pure of love most true.

———

ALL nature sings of thee, sweet love,
   And shall I cease
Thy ever-shining beauties to unfold,
   And joy increase
To earth's dark minds in error bound
   And sorrow dark ?
Or shall I still with rapture light
   Truth's holy spark,
Blend heaven's celestial notes
   With hope's gold fane,
And to thy charms, sweet love, still pour
   My joyful strain ?
I hear thy murmurings in my soul :
   They softly tell,
" Let strains of love and music blended
   In rapture swell."

———

O FOUNT of light, thy beauties roll,
And penetrate the mystic scroll
Of earth's dark errors ;
All doubts and terrors
Flee before thy glorious light.
Blest love, in beauty bright
Thou dwell'st, pride of the earth ;
Sweet child of heavenly birth,
Bright gem of heaven most rare,
Nurtured by truth's celestial air,
Thou art free, O love, in worlds on high,
Free as the sunny orb in yon blue sky ;
Not marred by error's dark perversion,
Nor checked by vanity's assertion.
O beauteous love, thy glories fill my soul ;
What holy strains of music roll
From thy celestial name !
Ever thou art the same,
On earth below, in heaven above,
A holy truth, a carrier dove !
Thou art the fount of light
O love ; thy radiance bright
        Shall set man free.
O love ! for thee I wander back to earth ;
For thee I leave my sunny land
Beyond the glorious birth,
And chant thy music bland.

HAPPINESS.

Sweet bird of paradise, thy pinions bend,
And to this earthly vale again descend ;
Let thy blest plumage glitter bright
O'er mundane scenes and worldly night ;
And still inspire, with thy love notes,
My spirit, as to earth it floats.
And thou, blest muse of heaven,
The gentle aid which thou hast given
Still shower upon my head in sweet profusion,
That earth's dark minds may know our mission.
Descend, I pray thee, bird of heavenly birth ;
Whisper sweet words of joy to minds of earth ;
Tell them of thy genial clime,
Where, lulled by Music's gentle chime,
Angel spirits, bright and free,
Sing their wild songs of love-lit glee.
Where darkened minds in sorrow dwell,
There tune thy voice, and let thy beauties tell
Of heavenly joys and pure delight.

But no ; thy home is heaven, sweet bird !
Still thou canst breathe a gentle word
To cheer us in our work of love,
And be our beacon-light above.
Would that earth might know, and be,
All that thou hast told to me.
('Tis Happiness that I invoke
To free mankind from error's yoke.
She is the bird of paradise that dwells above,
In the beauty of all-pervading love ;

Of her I sing; unto her charms
I tune the lay that now my spirit warms.)
Thy home of love, where showers of holy light
Deck thy pinions with their beauty bright.
We are hastening onward to thy sunny shore,
Where truth and gladness, free from earthly lore,
Reign in triumphant loveliness;
No error gross can mar thy own bright holiness.
For thou canst feast on lilies pure, —
Thy glorious beauties ever shall endure, —
And thou canst drink at Wisdom's flowing stream,
Bright heaven's sunlight o'er thy pathway gleam.
We know thy land is fair, sweet bird;
As we catch each holy, love-lit word,
Each gem of heavenly beauty rare
Breathes gentle echoes of thy home so fair.

The will is thine, sweet bird, to blend
    Love's richest gems,
  In one harmonious whole,
    With diadems
From thy delightful home,
    In joy divine,
All souls to lead, in wisdom's light,
    To thy blest shrine.
Dark minds will change to purity;
    Thy magic wand
Falls like a gentle dew of love;
    Thy music bland
Wafts gentle echoes to the sorrowing mind,
    In purest joy
Ever cheering; earthly tumults high
    Can not destroy

Thy gentle charm, sweet bird of fairy-land!
    Yet once again
Inspire the love-muse in my soul,
    And breathe a strain
Of thy rapt melody, and guide my soul to sing
    A song of home.
Chant, in thy sweet accents,
    Nenda 'lone!

SONG.

Give me my home in heaven above,
    Where bright angels warble
Their sweet songs of love;
    Where love, truth, and goodness
In harmony blend,
    And hope's purest beauties
In gladness descend.

I wist not, I grieve not
    For the dark things of earth;
My spirit has passed
    The glorious birth;
All nature is breathing
    Her sweet songs of love
To guide every spirit
    To pure joys above.

Then give me the gems
    Of heaven's blest home,
Where bright spirits happy
    So joyously roam —

And thou, lovely bird,
  Of heaven's blest clime,
Descend to this earth
  In the fullness of time,
That this world below,
  And the heavens above,
May join in one song
  Of beauty and love.

O Happiness, still breathe
  Thy notes of gladness,
And earthly minds enwreathe
  With joy, their course to bless!
Bird of the summer land,
  Thy form bedecked with beauty rare,
The bright-eyed angel band
  In heaven's celestial air
Gazes with rapturous delight
  On thy refulgent beauty ;
Thy golden pinions bright
  E'er guide to truth and duty ;
For happiness divine,
  Our being's end and aim,
Its gems of light are mine ;
  All may its charms attain ;
Its beauty can alone be found
  In love's eternal charm
Which wisdom high has bound
  To shield it from all harm.
True happiness above doth dwell,
  In quietude and calm content,
Where love's own music, magic spell,
  Its holy charm hath lent.

Not in the gilded hall alone
  Is pleasure found, and purest joy,
But in the cottage oft are blown
  Pure truths without alloy.
Not in the gorgeous palace hall
Where monarchs rule and kingly thrall
Is law and truth; where humble courtiers serve
A tyrant, from whose will they dare not swerve;
Nor in the marble festive hall,
Decked with costly gems, and robed in splendor all.
Though earth's diadems may glitter bright
By yon chandelier's brilliant light,
And beauteous forms may move to music's measure,
Or laughter's peal proclaim earth's pleasure,
Discordant minds may mingle there,
Minds bowed down with earthly care,
Or some unholy passion's stain
May lead the soul afar from truth's bright fane.
The outward form may be beauteous and fair,
The smiling face, the sparkling eye, and lustrous hair
May tell a sweet tale of truth;
While, cased within the comely youth,
Error and darkness have entwined
Their folds, and seek to bind
The little germ that God hath planted there
T'unfold in beauty in heaven's home so fair.
But when the soul by love's pure chain is bound,
And wisdom dwells with beauty, to surround
That germ which God hath given, — .
To dwell on earth and live in love in heaven, —
Then truth and goodness wreathe a chain
Of purity; love's music breathes a gentle strain
15

Of heavenly bliss ; ecstatic joy divine
All hearts shall gladden as it quickeneth mine.

True happiness alone is found
  Where heaven's beauties all combine.
The SOUL in beauty must abound,
  And purest joys entwine.

Then blow, gentle winds, from heaven's blest clime,
  And breathe pure notes of bliss !
Waft love-music's holy chime,
  And beauty's honeyed kiss !

Sing holy songs of heaven divine,
  And notes of purest joy,
Where glee and gladness both entwine
  Pure love without alloy.

Angel bands on high, in glory bright,
  Will bring pure thought to thee
From their blest home of pure delight,
  Where every soul is free.
And thou, sweet bird of heaven,
  I've tuned my muse to sing
Thy charms, which God has given ;
  I pray thee, gentle bird, to bring
Fresh garlands from thy happy home,
  And sing of wisdom evermore,
Where loved ones gone in beauty roam,
  On heaven's happy shore.

I'll tune my love-lit harp
  To thee again, sweet bird,

And tune my minstrel lyre to sing
  The love-tones I have heard.
Farewell, then, now ; and when
  In thy blest loveliness
Thou com'st to dwell, O, THEN,
  Happiness, eternal and divine,
All souls shall wreathe with beauty
  As it circleth mine.

A LEGEND OF EARTH AND AIR.

" O, LET me not die in spring-time ! "
I heard a maiden say ;
" Earth looks too bright and winsome,
Too beautiful and gay.
The grass is gently peeping
Above the damp, cold ground,
And birds are sweetly singing
In gladness all around.
" O, let me not die in spring-time !
Spring life is so joyous and free ;
I would list again to the whippoorwill's song
And the busy hum of the bee.
I would see the lakelets melting
'Neath the sunshine's genial ray,
For long has winter held them
Beneath his iron sway."
" O, let me not die in spring-time ! "
This feeble maiden said,
As she laid her slender hand
Upon her fevered head.

" O, I would like to see again
The little voilets bloom,
Before I take my long, last sleep
In the cold and darksome tomb."

The spring-time passed away ;
The gorgeous summer came ;
Night's gentle dewdrops sweetly kissed
The rose's crest, the lily's bud.
All earthly beauties seemed to blend ;
'Twas nature's nuptial season.
Angels still watched by the bedside
Of that feeble, timid maiden
Who, unconscious of their presence,
Dreamed that earth was all the love-life,
All the joyous, happy free life,
That a mortal could enjoy.
She only knew what man had taught her
Of the angel world above ;
She supposed she could not see it
Till the resurrection dawn.
She could not hear the gentle music, —
Music soft, and wafted sweetly
From those homes of bliss on high,
Where the loved, who'd gone before her,
Dwelt in beauty, pure and bright.
She knew not that the spirits sung
Songs of love, and hope, and joy.

It was a starry evening
    When she tuned her voice again ;
Still feebler was its accent,
    Sad was the mournful strain :

" O, I would not die in summer !
'Tis the blossom of the year ;
I would twine a flowery garland
For the friends I love so dear.
See ! — the roses kiss each other
As they bend beneath the dew ,
They look so free and happy,
So beautiful and true.
O, let me not die in summer !
For it is the happy season
Of bird and flower and tree ;
For the future looks dark and dismal ;
It brings not life and health to me.
If I could be a singing bird, and live,
I now would loudly sing for joy ,
Sad as I feel, I'd banish sorrow's strife,
Taste bliss without alloy.
O, could I live, and be a rose
In some romantic spot,
I could most happy be
In lonely dell or shady grot.
Life, life, is all I ask ;
I care for nothing more ;
'Tis what no power but one can give,
The power that gave before.
But, if I must die in summer,
At nature's bridal hour,
O, bury me 'neath the roses
In some sweet, lovely bower.
O, let me not die in summer !
I love it better now than ever ;
I fain would sing, but vain endeavor ;
O, life, from thee so soon to sever,

'Tis sad and dreary ; dark, sad thought
To burst asunder every tie,
Part from all I hold so dear,
And lay me down to die.
Oh, must it be ?
Summer, sweet season,
Must I part from thee ?
The morning's brightness ;
Noontide's sun,
Bright joy and lightness,
Must I go from thee forever ?
Must I every love-tie sever ? "
Then she sadly closed her eyelids,
Those bright eyes that oft had beamed
With joy and pleasure, pure and free ;
And her brow grew paler, colder ;
In the sleep of death she lay.
Her auburn hair in tangled masses
Kissed her pale and sallow cheek,
Clasped were her tiny hands, —
Those lovely jeweled hands,
That oft had plucked the blooming flower
And twined the golden band
Of summer roses — cold in death.
Yes, she died in summer,
While the birds were singing sweetly,
While the sun was shining brightly,
In nature's bridal season ;
She was buried 'neath the roses,
In a bright and lovely bower,
Where the tall green trees are waving —
Sadly waving, — o'er her grave
And the wild rose sweetly blossoms,

Nature's love birds freely sing;
At the evening, sad and plaintive,
Sings the night bird loud and long;
Birds of morning, birds of evening,
Pour their thrilling lays of love,
And the whippoorwill of spring-time
Sits upon the marble stone
In the calm and lovely twilight,
Tunes his tribute to the maiden.
She loved all of nature's beauties
That the mortal eye could see;
Beauties all combined within her;
She was love, and loved to all.
Spring's radiant verdure bright
And summer's loveliest flowers
Were her companions in earth life,
Were her playmates, were her jewels;
For affinity of soul was there —
Soul with flower and bird uniting
In the sweetest, happiest ties.
She sleeps, as mortals say,
Beneath the ground, beneath the stone;
And pine trees gently waving,
Softly waving, murmur back
A brief, low, sad response.

Months rolled away, and autumn
Came with sere and yellow leaf,
With its hoarse winds chilly blowing,
With its sheaves of golden corn,
Ripened fruit in bunches hanging
From the low and drooping boughs;
And the forest trees were scattering

Fast their leaves upon the ground,
And all beneath looked dark and drear.
Came this maiden's sister, brother,
To her grave at close of day.
'Twas a silent moonlight evening,
For the sun had gone to rest
Behind the towering mountains,
The lofty, snow-capped mountains.
The cold, pale moon shone brightly,
Gently twinkled many a star,
And the brightest star of evening,
Venus, holy queen of love,
Shed her rays upon the youth,
Youth, and happy joyous maiden
That was standing by his side.
Sister, said I? brother's loved one,
('Tis all the same to me.)
He was brother to the maiden,
To that summer-loving maiden
Who was buried 'neath the roses.
They came with tearful eyes to view
Again the spot where they saw placed,
The form of her they loved so well.
The youth knelt down upon the mound
Beside the stone, and with emotion
Deep, and quivering accents, said,
" Here sleeps the loved one, sister dear :
I weep for that bright eye and face,
Radiant with joy and loveliness.
I weep while ivy wild is creeping
Over the stone, and stars above
Their love-watch pure are keeping.

Sister, thou hast left forever,
Left me never to return, —
Left me to the cold, dark world, —
World of sorrow, care, and pain ;
Thou hast loved me ; I have loved thee ;
And I never can forget thee, sister dear · —
Thy pure young mind, thy kindness."
Then the maiden knelt beside him, —
There in silence long they knelt,
Till the cold wind pierced them, —
Chilled them. The cold and dreary wind
Mourned through the swaying branches
Of the tall and gloomy pines :
Then there came a dove and cooed
Sadly, mournfully above them ;
And the waving of the pine trees
And the cooing of the dove
Added sadness to their sorrow.
They arose, enrapt in grief,
Yet silently, to pass away
From the sad spot where lay the sleeper, —
When they heard a sweet voice singing, —
Gently, softly, sweetly singing,
With a beauty far above
All earthly music, mundane song :
Struck with surprise they stood,
Yet still the voice sang on.
It was his sister's voice ; she sang
A wild and thrilling lay ;
The sweet, pathetic music fell in strains
Melodious upon the listening air.
Then her form in angel beauty
Hovering o'er them they did see, —
With a robe of snowy whiteness,

With a face of dazzling beauty;
Her bright eye was softly resting
Upon those loved ones near and dear;
Her glossy auburn ringlets waved
O'er her brow of spotless white,
And the autumn cold and wild around
Pierced not her heavenly robe;
She softly whispered, " Brother, sister,
I am not dead; I live above."

SONG.

"From a land of fadeless beauty
    I have come,
To tell of joy and purity
    In heaven's home.
From the land where roses blossom
    Evermore,
With love's blest charm within my bosom,
    Wisdom's store;
From a home where truth entwineth
    Sweetest flowers,
And with gems of thought enshrineth
    Happy hours,—
Where stars of truth are ever shining
    Bright above,
And every beauty's interlining
    Songs of love;
Where song birds ever gayly sing,
    Blithe and free:
All to them is nature's well-spring
    Full of glee.

We dwell where all is pleasure
  Fond and fair;
Celestial beauties without measure, —
  Gems most rare, —
Fall upon each soul in heaven land
  Plenteously;
There gems of thought adorn love's band
  Gloriously;
Music's silvery, joyous strain
  Sweetly sounds;
Afar, o'er hill and plain,
  It resounds.
In the angel country thought is free, —
  Free indeed;
Its golden beauty all can see,
  All can read;
There new fields of thought are spreading
  For the mind:
O, 'tis ever good and cheering
  Truth to find.
I love my happy spirit mansion —
  Home on high;
'Tis not a flitting zephyr transient,
  In the sky,
But a land where summer's love-flowers
  Ever bloom,
In bright, unfading bowers,
  Beyond the tomb.
Earth is not the only love-life,
  As I thought,
But a land with every joy rife
  Can be sought, —
Sought and found by every mortal,

Who will live
As though he stood at heaven's portal,
    Saying, Give!
O, I love to come to earth-land,
    From my home
Of light and beauty bland,
    Free to roam.
So, when birds of spring-time warble
    I will come,
And beside the silent marble
    Gently thrum
The lute-strings of my soul,
    Breathe a strain
Of joy, let music sweetly roll
    Yet once again.
When the summer flowers are blowing,
    I will twine
A wreath of fairest roses, showing
    Love divine.
Yes, I still can whisper love songs
    Wild and gay;
Spirits pure, in heaven's love throngs,
    Softly say,
'Song is bright, and pure, and holy,
    In that clime
Where all is love, and truth, and beauty,
    Music's chime.' "

She ceased to sing; and echo,
Murmuring softly, sweetly, gently, —
Breathing strains of love divine, —
Wafted back the heavenly music
To the loving, listening pair.

And the pale moon, silvery shining,
And the twinkling, glimmering stars,
Looked mildly down on shadowy earth-land
From the clear blue sky above.
All nature seemed inspired with music ;
The cold breeze, sighing in the pine trees,
Seemed to wake an answering song,
And the leaves of autumn falling,
Moved with heavenly harmony.
Then sweet echo, sweetly singing
In love tones, gently seemed to say, —

" O, ye pine trees, tune your branches,
  Treasure beauties in each bough ;
O, ye rivers, murmur softly,
  Sing the songs of heaven now.
Roll proudly on, thou silvery night orb,
  Light earth's children through the night ;
When the day-star sinks to rest,   .
  Shed thy pale and loving light.
Ye stars, that ever brightly twinkle
  In the sky of azure blue,
Teach earth's minds in love to mingle
  With the beautiful and true.
Youth and maiden by the moonlight,
  Listening to that angel voice,
Let your souls respond with trust,
  And your hearts in love rejoice."

So ends my legend strange ;
And if by its wild strain
I touch a chord responsive
In the human soul, I will again

Awake the love-notes of my spirit,
Tell a wild and thrilling tale
To light earth minds with interest,
Waft again thought gems to assail
With truth's eternal shaft;
With arrows barbéd strike pale error's heart,
Descend from heaven's eternal spheres
The angel's love words to impart.

SHE WAS A ROSE.

SHE was a rose ; the sunbeams kissed
      Her pure white brow ;
The balmy breeze her ringlets tossed ;
      Her voice, I trow,
Was sweet as Æolian melody,
      When angels bright
Inspire the soul with joy, and sing
      Of love's delight.

She was a rose ; the moonbeams played
      Around her form,
And nature's dewdrops nourished her
      From night till morn.
'Twas in the lovely summer time,
      When all was gay,
That my loved Caradora, dear,
      First saw the day.

Where the Adriatic's waters
      Roll along in glee,

And lave the genial shores
 Of Italy, —
(Italia, once my happy home
 Of joy and love,
Where sleeps the form my spirit left,
 To dwell above), —

There lived a beauteous maiden,.
 Happy and free,
Heaven glowing charms combined
 With mirth and glee.
I loved her ; but the cold dark world
 Knew not the charms
With which pure, holy love, eternal,
 The spirit warms.

The grasp of iron-hearted priests
 Stole my fair one.
I wept with heartfelt anguish when
 The deed was done.
The convent wall loomed up between
 Me and the maid
Who first had taught my soul to love.
 I sadly laid
My hand upon my heaving bosom,
 Sought repose :
I could not sleep ; my soul could only say,
 " She was a rose."

Years rolled away : I saw the form I loved
 Laid in the ground.
I saw the hireling priest stand sanctimoniously
 Above the mound,

Blaspheme the holy name of love,
    And dare to say,
That God in wrath and vengeance dark
    Had ta'en away.
I dared not speak, although my heart
    Was full of woes ;
My soul in sorrow whispered soft,
    " She was a rose."

'Tis past and gone ; death came
    To my relief ;
I laid my earthly form aside, —
    My woe and grief.
Death came — a messenger of love —
    To lead my soul
To those blest lands of light on high,
    Where beauties roll,
And heavenly truth sits, calm-browed,
    On the shore,
Where all is joy and gladness
    Evermore.

O, life of love in heaven !
    My spirit swells
With untold wishes to return to earth,
    And ever tell
Of that bright home
    Where sorrow can not come, —
    Where all is bliss divine, —
    Where truth-stars ever shine,
    And wisdom e'er doth guide ;
    Where peace and hope abide.

But, while heaven lives and moves,
   And living beauty proves
That love's blest fount for ever flows,
I'll ever sing in accents soft
   " She was a rose."

HOPE.

SWEET flower of heaven-land, gem divine,
Hope ever doth fresh charms combine
To lift our thoughts to worlds on high,
To brighter lands beyond the sky.
She ever speaks of brighter joys,
And whispers, as with angel voice,
Of happier homes, of fairer climes,
Where love her golden charm entwines.
She tells of wisdom high, and peace,
Of heavenly joys that ne'er shall cease.
Hope is the love-flower of the soul;
When heavenly spheres their charms unroll,
She whispers, softly whispers, — " Mortal, see
The gems that angels have prepared for thee;
And look beyond the present NOW
To charms that future years shall place upon thy brow."
In gloomy earth-land, when dark sorrows come,
Hope says, " Weep not; there is a happier home
Where love shall twine a garland fair,
And blend the glittering diamonds rare
That these blest spheres above reveal,
The soul to calm, the wounded heart to heal."

16

Hope is a blooming rose within the soul,
Striving its tiny petals to unfold,
Seeking to catch the dewdrops pure that come
From that celestial fount 'neath wisdom's dome.
How oft, when trials harsh in darkness hover round,
And future life looks dreary, Hope has found
A gleam of sunlight, to inspire the mind
With trust that future years may be more kind.
When mortals o'er earth's sorrows linger,
Hope points above her jeweled finger,
To invoke sweet angels to descend,
And heaven's holy love-words blend,
To lead their minds to wisdom's mount,
To bathe in beauty's holy fount.
God placed this charm within the soul
To tell of happiness; to toll
The death knell of all human sorrow,
To sing, " There is a happier to-morrow
For every soul, for all mankind ;
A home where free shall be the mind."
Awake, then, child of earth-land ! sing
Of love and truth, and hope shall bring
Pure truth, and tell of future joy,
That error, dark, cannot destroy.

Hope lives in every soul ; she can not die,
Though nature all in ruins lie.
She lives in truth's resplendent light ;
She moves on wisdom's lofty height ;
She dwells in every flower of love
On earth, or in the spheres above ;
Her voice is heard 'bove earthly strife,
Bright prophet of a happier life.

Nourished by every star that shines,
Her orbit every planet interlines;
She sheds a gleam of heavenly light
O'er earthly scenes, o'er error's night.
When storms of anguish round the earth shall roll,
And " heaven together moveth like a scroll,"
Hope in beauty bright shall twine
A wreath of roses round the soul divine,
And lead it calmly upward to that shore,
Where wisdom reigns serene for evermore.

FRAGMENTARY POEMS.

"THE GOOD OLD DAYS."

CANTO I.

YE DECLINE OF PERSECUTION.

In the good old days a man arose,
Some eighteen centuries since,
Who made the Scribes and Pharisees wince
By precepts, words and blows.
That man, — now worshiped as a God
By many a mind of earth, —
Was scoffed and jeered at for his worth,
And chastened by the rod;
Despised by all the wise and great
(In their own estimation),
The pride of the Jewish nation,
As history doth relate;
Tried and condemned to cruel death,
Because he dared to teach,
In the synagogue dared to preach,
In spite of the Jew's vile breath.
So they nailed him to the cross,

Jesus, the good man and true,
Because he brought to human view
The truth, "to die was no loss."
He healed the sick, gave sight to the blind,
And caused the deaf to hear;
His soul divested of all fear,
He lived for all mankind.
"Away with him," all Jewry cried,
"He casteth out devils by Satan!"
Thus, with superstition's baton,
They tortured him 'till he died.
In that same age his apostles, too,
Were followed by persecution,
And bloody execution,
The fate of good men and true.

Years rolled away, and in his name
(Jesus, the holy in truth and love,
That messenger from worlds above)
Tyrant's authority claim
Under the sign of the blood red cross;
Like Constantine the Great,
Clothed with pomp and regal state,
All manner of crime to gloss.
So the early fathers — a tyrant host —
Were bound in duty to lie for the church,
Or by theft leave people in the lurch,
Or make them give up the ghost.
So, in the lapse of ages past,
In the good old days gone by,
'Twas deemed a duty for church to lie,
That the glory of God might last.

Some there are at the present time
Who are willing for church to lie,
But the day for such has gone by, —
We chant their praise in rhyme.
O, blessed Hypocrisy! thou art dead!
Or dying, which is the same;
Kings and pontiffs praise thy name;
For thee their tears are shed.
Tyranny, thou art an angel bright
That ruleth man for his good,
Controling the servile brood
By use of kingly might.
" O, for parson-power," said Taylor,
" Hypocrisy's praise to sing,
Its heavenly anthems ring."
(Priests call him a railer);
But, like him, we sing for good old days
When tyranny, rampant, ran wild,
And watched, and lovingly smiled
At autodafe's holy blaze.
O Gold, thou art mighty to-day,
But hast lost thy resolution,
And power to give absolution,
Beneath the papal sway!
Sad is the thought that man is so low
As to think he is progressing,
That freedom is a blessing,
When contrary we know.
Alas! mankind have lost respect
For all imperial station,
And by self-exaltation
Both king and priest neglect.

O, sinful Man ! when will ye learn
That bondage is a blessing,
Your every wrong redressing,
And to your chief's return.
Thrice holy is mental bondage,
And every credal chain,
To bind you again and again,
Is a godsend in this age.
O, sad it is for us to know
The world is retrograding ;
'Tis no use the truth evading
For the *church says* it is so.
Of what avail are turrets high,
Lofty cathedral, domes and walls,
If the creed no more inthralls
Each soul a votary.
What though some still bow the knee,
And kiss the chains that bind them,
Wherever they can find them,
If many minds are free ?
O, sad indeed is the story, —
But truth we must always tell, —
Belief is losing its spell,
Its lovely wand so gory;
For the wiles of wicked, sinning man
Have filled earth with confusion,
And many a sad delusion ;
For knowledge leads the van
Of all mankind, advancing
Their mission to fulfill,
In spite of kingly will,
Their happiness enhancing.

The good old times have passed away,
When kings and popes, with iron hand,
Ruled the minds of every land,
With naught their power to stay ;
When Inquisition's rack and fire,
Torturing rope and breaking wheel,
And laws that made the people feel
The strength of priestly ire.
No more are absolutions sold
To license every bloody crime,
And make men happy for all time,
By means of paltry gold.*

CANTO II.

YE TERRIBLE STRIDES OF SCIENCE.

IN good old times the earth was flat ;
Around it moved sun, moon, and star,
And every planet near and far,
By power of God's fiat.
When Galileo, wise in nature's lore,
Asserted the world turned round,
In a dungeon dark a home he found,
Where wise men had been before.
The Inquisition was brought to bear
Upon this man of science then ;
Prelates, bishops, — all holy men, —
Applied the torture there,
To make him abjure the things he knew ;

---

* See " De Cœmenin's History of the Popes " for the tariff of prices
for the absolution of all crimes, established by Pope John XXII.

The telescopic power so grand,
Bright worlds to read in starry land,
Reveal them to men's view.
At length, when brought before the pope,
Arrayed in costly robes and power,
Vicegerent of the earthly hour,
Sat Urban, God's own will to quote.
" Look through my telescope, O, man,
Sitting in solemn judgment here,"
Said the wise man, loud and clear,
 " And bring it to your ken."
" What care I though it is provable ;
Am I not Pontiff, infallible, great? "
Said Urban, in his regal state, —
" I SAY EARTH IS IMMOVABLE."
But the world moved on and moveth still,
As Galileo said it would do ; ·
The truth is now received as true,
Despite Pope Urban's will.

In former times 'twas thought by all
That in six days God made the world ;
Creation's banner then unfurled
O'er all things, great and small ;
But earth's own rocky records show
That there's a slight mistake,
And God could not his own law break, —
All must have time to grow.
In good old times it was a sin
For Science to assert her claim
In any guise, by any name,,
Or in any form begin ;
For many there were in days gone by, —

And some in the present age I ween,
As their works are often plainly seen,
Hold the same thought on the sly, —
That carnal reason must lie down
Before the shrine of faith, belief,
And never dare to give relief
When popes and prelates frown.
" Learning is useless," said Pope Paul,
" And science opposed to religion."
" Sacred is each church tradition, —
Then let it conquer all."

Holy wars were rife in the good old days
When the many were slaves to the few,
And men their fellow-mortals slew,
All for their Maker's praise.
The Saracen fought the Christian brave,
And the Christian slew the Turk ;
Blood and carnage thus set to work,
Made many a martyr's grave.
Then the lance and the shining blade
Settled the strife and disputes of man ;
Dread warfare was the only plan
By which laws were broke or made.
One thing is certain the wide world o'er,
If ever a truth was spoken,
Or ever a human skull broken,
Holy wars are a curse and bore.

Geology has proved to man
That earth is very agéd,
And we are all enragéd,
At its stupendous plan.

The Bible record is o'erthrown,
If this new science is correct;
'Twill all mythologies affect,
Man has so knowing grown.
If years on millions earth has stood,
Of what avail the Genesis account
Of ark on Ararat's tall mount,
In safety from the flood?
The earth was all in six days made
Says Scripture (that is very plain).
'Tis true or false, we here maintain,
In language plain arrayed.
Science, thou name for infidelity!
Geology, Astronomy,
And all such like economy,
Is blackest heresy.
O, 'tis lamentable to see
How these errors are gaining ground;
In every school-house they are found,
Taught openly and free.
'Tis strange that even pious souls
Fail to see the errors dark,
Shown by the electric spark
That Science's chart unrolls;
But such is their consistency,
That earth *may be* both round and flat,
Made in six days by God's fiat,
Millions in reality.
" Six days doth mean long ages vast,
The way we mortals measure time;
Thus Science doth with Bible chime,
The present with the past."
O, depth of folly, hight of crime!

Thus to distrust the scriptures old,
Written by God's own finger bold,
For every age and clime.
The world is going to ruin, sure,
For science opposes religion ;
In every land and region
Its teachings firm endure.

For years and years the world believed
All people came from one first pair ;
Such is the Bible record fair,
.That ought to be received.
But some now doubt this simple truth, —
It as a falsehood dare to brand,
Saying, that " every age and land
Produces man and youth ;
And beast and bird, and creeping thing,
All come forth by nature's laws ;
By power of one Eternal Cause
Each flower and tree doth spring ;
The white man and the Indian red,
The black man and the yellow, —
And every other fellow, —
Each in his place is bred ;
Instead of the races being one,
Of every stripe and nation,
Throughout the wide creation,
Beneath the shining sun,
They are as diverse as the birds
Or quadrupeds that walk the earth,
And every climate gives them birth
By law, not spoken words."
" Don't scripture say all are one blood ?

Then stop these ethnologies,
And other idle heresies!
The Bible long hath stood.
Should ye not believe its words and maxims,
That plainly are expressed,
By the Holy Spirit blessed, —
Its God-appointed axioms?
If it tell you black is white,
Believe it or be damned;
Consent thus to be crammed,
Or go to eternal night."

YE MILL, AND YE WHEELS.

My lay is a lay of a mill;
A mill whose grim old wheels went round,
And round, with a terrible din, —
Din that was never a moment still;
Still gloomy and dull was the sound,
Sound that took the good people in.
This dull old mill was built of stone,
Stone and mortar and brick, —
Brick, and wood, and fresco work, —
Work that was well and strongly done,
Done in a manner stout and thick, —
Thick with craft, and skill did lurk, —
Lurk around the old building there.
There were charms of life without,
Without were trees and blooming flowers;
Flowers that grew by walks so bare, —
(Bare save when the millers were out —

Out in the evening's silent hours.)
This mill had many a wheel, —
Wheel of peculiar make,
Makes noises more wonderful still.
Still every cog seems to feel, —
Feel only for its owner's sake.
Sakes alive! how it does his will.
These wheels are mysterious, too,
To many a listener's mind;
Mind, each tells a tale of its own,
Own language.   It speaketh to you;
You may curiosities find, —
Find what each wheel has seen.
These wheels are of divers sizes, —
Sizes both large and very small;
Small ones feel large as the largest,
Largest as large as the prizes, —
Prizes that, given to all,
All try to obtain the choicest.
This mill had a lofty dome, —
Dome that was roofed with slate, —
Slate without and wood within;
Within, the mill was fair to some;
Some loved its massive dome so great, —
Great dome to take the people in;
Some loved its big wheels' solemn song.—
Song in French, Italian, and Greek,
Greek and Latin, Spanish and Dutch,
Dutch and Hebrew, loud and long.
Long each wheel could sing or speak;
Speak, for each wheel could chatter much;
For know they all had tongues, —
Tongues, and hands, and feet;

Feats of mind in their estimation, —
Estimation, a song they always sung ;
Sung of themselves : each day did repeat —
Repeat their selfish exultation.
Thus for a hundred years or so,
So had the dull old wheels moved on ;
Moved on, except, when one wore out,
Out it was thrust, and another to go, —
Go in its place, — was seized upon, —
Upon the grist its work to bestow.
Many a miller had grown gray —
Gray in the battle of life, while young,
Young were the apprentices shy,
Shy or bold, morose or gay.
Gay *never*, were the wheels so glum, —
Glum for ever, forever and aye.

FROM HOPE TO KNOWLEDGE.

HOPE is the guiding star,
Onward, upward ever
On earth or in the worlds afar,
She will leave thee never.
In thy highest aspiration,
Every thought shall feel its power ;
Reaching in its exaltation,
Each pure drop of wisdom's shower ;
'Till thy soul shall feel and see,
That, from hope to knowledge free,
A fair path is shown to thee.

ALBUM LINES.

I'D rather be a written page,
To cast a sunbeam on life's stage,
Than be a monarch on his throne,
Who ruled by power and fear alone.
I'd rather be a love thought free,
Than rule the land or rule the sea
By man applauded.

May truth alone shine on each leaf,
Free from sorrow, doubt, and grief;
May wisdom guide each hand to write,
May love all hearts in joy unite,
To trace within this volume fair,
Words of truth in garlands rare
Of friendship's roses.

———

'TIS but a thought I give to thee;
One gem from friendship's holy shrine, —
A thought that tells of beauty free
Dwelling in worlds of joy divine.
Each glowing thought that plays around thee
Lifts thy soul to regions bright;
It will ever help to lead thee
Along the way to truth's blest hight.

THE FEAST OF BELSHAZZAR.

FRAGMENT OF A POEM IMPROVISED AT THE MELODEON, BOSTON,
DECEMBER 6, 1857.

[These lines were printed at the time in the "Banner of Light,"
which said concerning them, "They were furnished us by a gentleman who was appointed on the committee to select the subject for a
poem, and who suggested that on which it was given. They were
written from memory by the gentleman who was an utter skeptic; and
as he is somewhat noted for his retentive memory, we have no doubt
that they are correct."]

THE pompous King at his table sat,
With nobles and courtiers around;
He quaffed the rich wine, and with impious hand,
He swore that his kingdom for ever should stand.
The song went round, the unseemly jest,
The scoffing words, and blasphemous breath;
The haughty king, with his brazen arms,
Ruled o'er the fair city of palms.
But, lo! upon yon distant wall
Appeared the spirit hand.
The trembling King, with guilty fear,
Looked o'er the affrighted band.
But, see! the hand in words of light
Glanced glittering o'er their eyes;
Dread silence, horror, awful fright,
As moving on it flies.

17

MENE, MENE was writ on the wall,
And TEKEL, UPHARSIN, appeared to them all.
They sent for the Prophet, the King looked around,
" Thou'rt weighed in the balance, and wanting art
  found."   -

. . . . .

[The entire poem comprised about one hundred lines.]

THE BANNER OF PEACE.

WAR, with its dark and bloody hand,
For three long years has ruled the land,
And the fourth is on the wane,
Marching in the bloody train.
And our country, once so glorious,
Over every foe victorious,
Now lies bleeding, torn and broken,
By the sword's unhallowed token.

> Then raise the snow-white banner,
> The beautiful flag of peace;
> And in the name of human rights,
> Declare that wars shall cease.

Millions of men came forth at call,
Bravely resolved to rule or fall
'Mid the war-king's fiery train,
Dazzled by his lurid chain.
"Union and Freedom" was the cry, —
"We will conquer now or die!"

Thus full many a brave one fell,
Without shrive, or shroud, or bell.

Then raise the snow-white banner, &c.

Now the gauzy veil is lifted,
Now the ship of state has drifted
On the rock of "lust of power,"
While the clouds of terror lower;
Now the war-king, red with gore,
Calls "five hundred thousand more!"
While the orphan's feeble wail
Echoes in each passing gale.

Then raise the snow-white banner, &c.

Up, then! Arise, ye freemen brave,
And in your might your country save;
Hurl the usurper from his throne;
Cease orphan's sigh and widow's moan.
Conciliation's mystic charm
Must be the nation's healing balm;
"Union and Peace" our motto be;
"Freedom from all tyranny."

Then raise the snow-white banner,
The beautiful flag of peace;
And in the name of human rights,
Declare that wars shall cease.

STRIKE BOLDLY, AND FEAR NOT.

STRIKE boldly, and fear not;
Angels round thee hover;
Through the lone path of life
Their footprints we discover.
They ever watch and guide,
Fondly they caress us,
Still gently by our side
Striving aye to bless us.

What care I for power,
Earthly wealth or grandeur,
Creatures of an hour,
Ambition and splendor.
Only let good spirits bright
Smiling o'er my pathway,
Shining in spotless white,
Near me for ever stay.

Roll on, dark wave of life;
Unheeded commotion;
On with your dashing strife,
Fate-troubled ocean!
For with the angels true,
Backward turning never,
New thoughts e'er come to view,
Beauteous forever.

Strike boldly, child of earth!
For wisdom surrounds thee;

With its fair gems of worth
In love-ties hath bound thee ;
The gloom of error dark
Is gone from before thee,
Touched by the hallowed spark
Of angel truth o'er thee.

COME, BRIGHT MENONA.

COME when the morning sun is shining,
Come when the rays of light combining,
   Blend their glories rare ;
Come when the lark is gayly singing,
Come when the bells of morn are ringing,
   With their cadence pure.

Come with thy sweet and gentle voice,
It doth make my soul rejoice
   In its melody.

Come when the silvery moon is gleaming
With the stars of night that, beaming,
   Breathe hope's rhapsody ;
Come when the evening lamps are lighted,
And our hearts in love united
   Beat in harmony.

Come with thy sweet and gentle voice
It doth make my soul rejoice
   In its melody.

O come, Menona, gem of duty,
Come in thy splendor, peerless beauty,
   With thy notes of love ;
Join with the word my soul is speaking ;
Bow to the fate thy heart is seeking ;
   Onward let us rove.

Come with thy sweet and gentle voice,
It doth make my soul rejoice
   In its melody.

WELCOME TO PEACE.

WRITTEN AFTER THE CLOSE OF THE CIVIL WAR.

THE clouds of war have passed away.
   The angel of peace appears !
All hail, the dawning of the day ;
   Fill the air with gladsome cheers ;
Black were the clouds and streaked with fire,
   As they rolled athwart the sky,
While bloody waves of anguish dire
   Flowed drearily, sadly by.

Homes of the North and the South land
   Have felt the war-king's power ;
Tearful eyes have seen the death wand,
   The bullet's fatal shower.
We've heard the wail of .loved ones,
   Borne on the midnight air ;

The dying, wounded, and lost ones,
Far from home and friendly care.

Now the deadly strife is ended
Let the past forgotten be,
And our country, reconstructed,
As of yore, united, free.
By the memory of each martyr,
Let us skill and mercy show ;
Let us serve our Magna Charta
Scorn to strike a fallen foe.

Group I. Three Heart Offerings.

LENA DE L'ORME.

YES, thou art gone in the pride of thy youth,
  The fairest of all the valley ;
Gone in the light of thy beauty and truth,
  Gone where the night winds rally.

      Yes, thou art gone,
      Pride of my heart,
      Beautiful Lena de L'Orme ;
      For thee teardrops freely start,
      For thou to the angels art gone.

The ivy grows dark o'er the grassy mound,
  The brook goes murmuring by,
The night bird shrieks with its dreariest sound
  O'er the spot where thy form doth lie.

The star of thy life went down in its youth,
  And thy throbbing heart lieth still,
But thy spirit liveth in love and truth
  Beyond death's murmuring rill.

                    265

Hark! there comes a voice from out of the skies;
'Tis the voice of my angel love;
It tells of a spirit hovering nigh,
Revealing its joy from above.

The love of the soul ends not with death,
But liveth forever on high;
Thus Lena speaks in the zephyr's breath,
In the night wind's sweetest sigh.

BY THE SIDE OF THE MURMURING STREAM.

O, THE happy, happy days of my childhood,
By the side of the murmuring stream,
Where I culled the sweet flowers of the wildwood,
By the light of the first morning beam.
　　But those pleasures are fled forever
　　In the passing of life's fitful gleam,
　　And I'll gaze on those beauties never,
　　By the side of the murmuring stream.

The little white cottage, near the haunted rock,
That covered my forefathers too;
And the willow rent by the lightning's shock,
By the side of the waters so blue.

I remember the place in the old churchyard
Where I wandered in days of yore,
There sleeps my love in the earth hard,
Yet in fancy I see her once more.

O, the many, many joys of my youth's days
　Have fled like a weird fairy dream;
But I'll treasure them still in my heart lays,
　While I sing of the murmuring stream.

TOUCH THE LUTE GENTLY.

O, TOUCH the lute gently, love,
　　Gently, love, gayly,
　And wreathe a sweet garland of song;
Dulcet notes e'er they prove.
　　Truly Atheli,
　Thy spirit to mine doth belong.

　　Then touch the lute gently, love, gently,
　　　And wreathe a sweet garland of song,
　　O, touch the lute gently, love, gently,
　　　And wreathe a sweet garland of song.

Roaming now in other lands,
　　Sadly and lonely,
　Longing for joys that are fled;
Sighing now for golden bands,
　　Bound to thee only,
　Weeping for hopes that are dead.

· O, sing again those songs of yore,
　　Ever soul-thrilling,
They come to my sad, lonely mind;
Heavenly tones o'er and o'er,
　　Murmuring and trilling,
　They lead me life's treasure to find.

Far o'er the sad and lonely wave,
　　Echo shall reach me,
With its sweet murmuring voice ;
Joys of life thy presence gave,
　　Purely will teach me,
And bid my sad soul rejoice.

O, touch the lute, and o'er the sea,
　　In sweet communion,
In song then united we'll dwell ;
Heart with heart then shall be
　　In blessèd union :
Then we'll know all is well.

Group II. Sparkling Gems.

ADIEU, LEANORE !

ADIEU, adieu, Leanore !
Forever fare thee well ;
Weep not, for I adore
The charms that with thee dwell.
When I am passed away·
To that immortal shore,
My light song still will stay,
And whisper, I adore.

　　Adieu, adieu, Leanore ;
　　Forever fare thee well,
　　Till on the immortal shore,
　　We shall together dwell,

Adieu, adieu, Leanore!
'Tis broke, the golden spell;
Earthborne am I no more, —
To thee a sad farewell.
When roses round thee bloom,
And lilies o'er thee twine,
From lands beyond the tomb
My love shall purely shine.

LEOLINE.

LEOLINE, though thou art far from me,
Yet my spirit e'er doth turn to thee;
In my memory oft thy smile
Will the weary hours beguile;
I am sad and lonely waiting
For thy presence, soul-elating,
Longing still to see my fairy,
Blithesome one, so light and airy.

Leoline, Leoline, Leoline,
Though thou art far away,
Still I hear thee say,
I am thine for aye.

Leoline, the dew is on the lea,
The moon shines on the heaving sea,
The rolling waves are dancing light,
To echo back my song to-night;
Then waft me from thy lovely clime,
Some silvery tone, some music chime,
To help me wait the distant hour,
When I may claim my wildwood flower.

"YOU WELL KNOW MY BELOVED."

GOOD night, good night, my well-beloved,
    May bright angels guard you in your dreams;
You well know, you well know, my beloved,
    That my love for you for ever fondly gleams.
        You well know, you well know,
        My beloved, you well know
    That my heart beats ever fond and true,
    Ever beaming, ever gleaming is my lovelight,
    As beams the star from out yon sky's fair blue.

Good night, good night, may angels keep you,
    From every trial dark of earthly life ;
In the future, peerless beauty, may I meet you,
    Free from all sorrow, care, and warring strife.

LAND OF THE SO–CALLED DEAD.

SWEET land of the spirit, I'm pining for thee,
O, beautiful land, where the bright spirits be,
    Where the dearly loved have fled, —
        That beauteous land,
        That glorious land,
    The land of the so-called dead.
        In my dreams thou art near,
        In my dreams thou art near.

The loved of past years gladly greet me there,
Beyond error's gloom and all sorrowing care ;

To their love-encircled shore.
    To that magical land,
    That mystical land,
The home of the gone before.
    In my dreams ever near,
    In my dreams ever near.

And the boatman pale o'er the river of death,
In a sweet interlude of murmuring breath,
    Will come with his light canoe
      To bear me to rest.
      In that mansion blest,
    Where dwell the holy and true.
      In my dreams ever near,
      In my dreams ever near.

Yes, I know I shall see thee in time, sweet land,
And join with the seraph throng, hand in hand,
    When the journey on earth is o'er;
      For the radiant beams
      Of the light that gleams,
Shine bright from the further shore.
      Yes, in life ever near;
      Yes, in life ever near.

MAID OF GLENORE.

MAID of Glenore, awake from thy dreaming,
    List to my soft-sounding lay;
While bright stars above are brilliantly beaming
    Hearken to what I would say.

The south wind softly is blowing,
The air with fragrance is glowing.
Come forth in thy light,
Sweet beam of the night,
While flowers thy pathway are strewing.
Maid of Glenore,
Maid of Glenore,
Beautiful art thou, Maid of Glenore !

Maid of Glenore, the stars will grow dim
In sight of thy flashing eye ;
I implore thee heed the love-song of him
Who breathes every word with a sigh ;
The night-bird ceases its singing
To list to thy laugh's sweet ringing ;
Come forth in thy light.
Sweet beam of the night,
While moonbeams their pure light are flinging.
Maid of Glenore,
Maid of Glenore,
Beautiful art thou, Maid of Glenore.

Maid of Glenore, a love-chord is twining
Around thy spirit and mine ;
Stars from above in beauty are shining
O'er kindred souls, mine and thine ;
Fond looks are cast on the comely,
Blest, holy beam that art lonely,
One day robed in white,
Sweet star of delight,
There thou wilt shine on me only.
Maid of Glenore,
Maid of Glenore,
Beautiful art thou, Maid of Glenore.

Group III. Flowers from the West.

O, HEAR MY PARTING SIGH.

O, HEAR my parting sigh;
  O, heed my parting prayer;
Death's angel hovers nigh;
  Soon I'll be free from care.
Death cometh with relief,
  To lift the soul above,
To free the mind from grief, —
  A messenger of love.

O, hear my parting sigh,
  And watch my failing sight
'Tis nothing now to die,
  The pathway all is light.
Death comes an angel dark
  Only to those who mourn;
Still lives the immortal spark,
  By angels upward borne.

O, hear my parting sigh,
  O, see that holy throng,
That comes from worlds on high,
  To join my parting song.
Death, with his finger fair,
  Doth point to mansions blest;
Vanquished is lone despair,
  That gave the mind unrest.

18

MEDORA.

MEDORA sleeps 'neath the cold, cold stone,
And the wind harp is breathing
    Its sad, sad moan.
The ivy is creeping o'er her tomb,
And the pine trees wave darkly,
    In chilling gloom.

They parted her golden ringlets light,
O'er her marble-like forehead,
    So cold and white ;
They laid her to rest at close of day,
In the lone murmuring shades,
    Where night-winds play.

She's gone afar from dull sorrow's care,
From the false hearts that led her
    With fitful glare.
No phantoms pale of poverty's home
To her moss-covered mansion
    Ever can come.

Medora lives, a bright angel now,
And heaven's purest laurels
    Deck her fair brow ;
Gladly she sings, with a holy band,
Happy songs of rejoicing,
    In spirit land.

O, TELL ME NOT OF FIELDS OF GLORY.

O, TELL me not of fields of glory,
  Where foemen meet, and fight, and fall.
Alas! the splendor of the story
  Is draped with deep funereal pall;
For vivid then arise before us
  The horrors of the battle plain,
And victory's loud, exulting chorus
  Sinks burdened by the shrieks of pain.

They say that fame, with trump immortal,
  Of those who bravely fought shall tell;
Within her temple's loftiest portal
  Shall twine the wreath for those who fell.
But O, a manly form reposes
  Full lowly on the bloody plain,
And death's dark evening shadow closes
  O'er eyes that ne'er shall wake again.

Then tell me not that glory liveth;
  It ne'er restores the fallen brave;
Nor is there aught that glory giveth,
  Can light the darkness of the grave.
For what can fame avail the lonely,
  Who weep above a loved one slain?
It maddens grief to anguish only;
  The sad heart knows 'tis all in vain.

But there are angels gently hovering
  Around us, in the hour of need;
Their mission to console the suffering,
  To heal the hearts that inly bleed.

They tell us, too, of fields of glory,
· Beyond the realms of death's domain ;
Nor woe, nor warfare dim the story ;
There joy and peace forever reign.

THE WIND IS IN THE CHESTNUT BOUGH.

THE wind is in the chestnut bough,
The wind is in the pine ;
Come nearer, nearer to me now,
Dear spirit friend of mine ;
Come nearer, nearer to me now,
· Dear spirit friend of mine.
Howl on, ye surging blasts, howl on !
Nor heed the prayers of mortal men,
If thou, bright spirit, will but breathe
Thy thoughts to mortal ken.

The wind goes moaning o'er the deep,
And whistles in each sail,
It lulls the mariner to sleep,
Or wakes him to the gale ;

The wind is restless in his wrath ;
He rushes o'er the plain ;
And on the gloomy desert path
His echo moans again.

Roll on, ye wrathful, restless blast,
Nor heed earth's fleeting joy ;
The day on earth will soon be past ;
'Tis but a passing toy.

PRIDE OF ELSINORE.

Sweet pride of Elsinore, for thee
   Love's purest incense e'er shall rise,
For thou art all the world to me,
   Blithe maiden that I prize.
Another face may be more fair,
   Another form more light,
But thou dost blend the virtues rare, —
   More precious in my sight.

Fair maid of Elsinore, O be
   My own bright shining star to guide,
For with my song's pure melody
   I'd woo thee for my bride.
Another eye, with flashing gleam,
   May thrill the changing heart,
But love that from the soul doth beam,
   Can play a nobler part.

Lone pride of Elsinore, so fair,
   A mind like mine you ne'er may view,
Then listen while I here declare
   My vows of friendship true.
Another mind may only love
   With earth's wild flickering glare;
But angel pens record above
   My promised watchful care.

Group IV. Golden Memories.

WHENE'ER IN SLEEP THE EYELIDS CLOSE.

WHENE'ER in sleep the eyelids close,
Kind angels aye their vigils keep,
The weary heart can find repose,
And joy return to those who weep.
Fell disappointment's arrow-dart
The quiet dreamer glances by;
The form at rest, the saddened heart.
Knows not the anguish often nigh.

Whene'er in sleep the eyelids close
The weary heart can find repose;
When still in death the eyes shall close,
The weary heart will find repose.

Some fairy dream may cheer the soul,
Made sad and careworn all the day;
Some vision bright may purely roll,
To light the darkness of the way.
Sleep, fair one, sleep, while fancies glide;
Dreams that while waking ne'er may be;
Fond hopes and pure thy visions guide;
Waking thou'rt sad, asleep made free.

When still in death the eyes shall close,
And sorrowing friends so lonely weep,
Some weary heart has found repose,
While pitying angels love-watch keep.

There is a life that knows no end,
    Not all a dream, a fancy wild, —
There, too, are joys that sweetly blend,
    And thrill the soul with accents mild.

When still in death the eyelids close,
    The weary heart can find repose ;
When still in death the eyes shall close,
    The weary heart will find repose.

SWEET BE THY DREAMS, ALIDA.

SWEET be thy dreams, Alida ;
    Soft memories o'er thee glide :
May happy thoughts for ever
    Gayly shine thy steps to guide.
When love-lit eyes are beaming,
    In fanciful vision free,
May hearts with more than seeming,
    Most truly confide in thee ;
May hearts with more than seeming
    Most truly confide in thee.

    Sweet be thy dreams
    Sweet be thy dreams,
And gentle memories o'er thee glide,
    Sweet be thy dreams
    Sweet be thy dreams
And gentle memories o'er thee glide.

When thou shalt wake, Alida,
    To find that the dream has fled,
May sorrow's thorn crown never
    Rest heavily on thy head.

` May all thy days be happy,
    As the dreams of night foretell;
Then more than joy can rally
    To the sound of memory's bell.
Then more than joy can rally
    To the sound of memory's bell.

Group V.

SPIRIT OF LIGHT, LOVE, AND BEAUTY.

SPIRIT of light, love, and beauty,
    Bind for me thy golden band,
Teach my heart to know its duty,
    Guide me to your glorious land.
    Spirit of light, love, and beauty,
        I implore thee, smile on me.

Spirit of bright joy and gladness,
    Twine for all thy silvery lay;
Banish error, fear, and sadness;
    Lead us to the wisdom way.

Soul of song, we hail thee gladly,
    Coming with thy holy calm;
Healing every mind that sadly
    Wanders from thy blessèd charm.

Spirit of light, love, and beauty,
    Chant for all thy lovely song,
Lead us aye in paths of duty,
    Till we join the angel throng.

AMINTA MIA.

ALTHOUGH we never met before,
  Light in thy pathway shone;
In beauty wrapt thee o'er and o'er,
In beauty wrapt thee o'er and o'er.
Calm was the soul that gleamed from 'neath
  Each eyebrow's penciled throne,
Soft smiles thy face in gladness wreathe,
  Aminta, *mia ora belle.*
  Aminta, *mia ora belle.*

Thine be the holy mission pure,
  Enveloped in life's care,
With those to dwell whose loves endure,
With those to dwell whose loves endure.
And while on earth thy love shall glow,
  Radiant, bright and rare,
Trust, angels watch thy path below,
  Aminta, *mia ora belle.*
  Aminta, *mia ora belle.*

LELA TREFAINE.

LELA TREFAINE, the month of October is near,
The mocking birds sing in the palm tree,
The grosbeck's shrill whistle you hear
  Echo sweetly and clear.

Friendship of yore, thy harmonies never can cease,
Bringing back happy joys to me,
Bright joys that life's treasures increase,
  Joy of freedom and peace.

Come once again, happy days,
Blessed days of fortune and peace,
Come once again, blessed days,
Life treasures that ever increase.

Lela Trefaine, the river rolls sluggishly by,
The cypress and willow bend low;
O'er graves of the parted they sigh;
  " They fought but to die."
Answer me back, ye night birds, that warble
    free;
Tell again of the days long ago,
And friends that were cherished by me,
  Ere I crossed the blue sea.

Lela Trefaine, in the land of strangers I roam,
Far from my own native south-land
From thee and my dearly loved home;
  Yet in fancy I come.
Never forgot; for, treasured in memory's shrine,
As touched by affection's love-wand,
Blessed remembrance ever will twine;
  Early friends, love divine.

Lela Trefaine, the mignonettes bloom as of old,
When we gathered them side by side;
The night-jasmine petals unfold;
  Dewy petals of gold.

Joy to the soul ! in spirit I cross the dark sea ;
Once more o'er the waters I glide :
There's hope in the future for me ; —
Home, freedom, and thee.

Group VI.

EVYRR ALLYNN ; OR, THE OUTCAST.

THE cold snow is falling, the bleak hills are dreary,
    Wild is the way, and the daylight is past,
Night shades fast falling, dark, lonely and cheerless,
    O, when will my weary limbs find rest at last ?
I will sleep on the hillside, among the white snowdrifts,
    Nor cover my face from the rain and the sleet,
For when I awake some good angel may find me
    A haven of rest for my wandering feet.

        Evyrr Allynn,
    The wild flowers now bloom o'er thy grave,
        By the side of the silent river ;
    The frost-king has fled from the hillside ;
        Rest in peace with the heavenly giver !
        Evyrr Allynn !   Evyrr Allynn !

In all the wide world there is no one to cheer me ;
    Friendless and sad I wander alone ;
I will turn from the world that has left me in sorrow,
    To the path that leads up to a happier home.

Far, far in the distance, above the bleak tree-tops,
　The white wings of angels gleam through the dark sky;
How kindly and sweetly they gaze on the outcast;
　Their soft eyes will smile on the heath as I lie.

Yes, this night with my child I will rest on the hillside,
　Nor shelter my form from the pitiless blast;
For an angel hath whispered, " Thy sins are forgiven,
　And thou shalt awaken in heaven at last."
Thus, when the gray morning stole over the tree-tops,
　And o'er the dark mountains a ghastly light shed,
It fell on two faces, that looked up to heaven;
　Two forms from which the spirit had fled.　　-

OLD DOCTOR BONDS.

My name is Doctor Bonds, — who are you?
They say I'm a leech; that is true;
I've bled the country well since sixty-two;
I'm bound to have my gold, spite of you.

So sings old Doctor Bonds, in his glee,
And quaffs his brandy tod, taxes free,
And bleeds the working-men, don't you see?
Takes two for one, and more, taxes free.

Asleep fell Doctor Bonds in his chair,
One Sunday summer day, sultry air;
He had a frightful dream — a nightmare, —
As he slept, that summer day, in his chair.

He dreamed he was afloat on the sea,
In a vessel made of bonds, taxes free ;
Strange voices filled the air, wild with glee,
Sang, " Sink old Doctor Bonds in the sea."

'Tis voices of the poor who pay tax ;
We've worked for you too long, now "make tracks,"
We'll make you take your pay with a tax,
The same you paid to us in greenbacks.

We'll wake old Doctor Bonds with a song
Of white men and their rights — mighty throng ;
We'll shout, in Freedom's name, Right the wrong !
Make hill and vale resound, loud and long.

  Hark ! the echoes ring ;
  High the banner fling ;
 The banner of equal taxation ;
  Ten thousand garlands bring ;
  Myriad voices sing ;
 Columbia sees hope for the nation.

Group VII.

STRIKE THE HARP IN NATURE'S PRAISE.

O, THE budding leaves of spring-time,
 With their lovely verdure bright
Are filling the earth with beauty,
 And the soul with calm delight.
Are filling the earth with beauty,
 And the soul with calm delight,

Then strike the harp in nature's praise,
 For all things bright and gay,
For soon the autumn days will come,
 And the flowerets pass away.

O, the roses come in summer,
 With their fragrance, sweet and rare,
A glorious, bright new comer,
 Whose brilliance fills the air ;
A glorious, bright new comer,
 Whose brilliance fills the air.

Now the autumn days are near us,
 With the sere and yellow leaf ;
But golden grains shall cheer us,
 And promise earth relief ;
But golden grains shall cheer us,
 And promise earth relief.

It is thus with fleeting hours,
 In the life of man on earth ;
He comes like the spring-time flowers,
 And falls in autumn's dearth ;
He comes like the spring-time flowers,
 And falls in autumn's dearth.

But there is a land of beauty,
 Of wisdom, love, and truth,
Where, in the path of duty,
 We shall live in endless youth ;
Where in the path of duty,
 We shall live in endless youth.

Then strike the harp in nature's praise,
  For all things bright and gay!
For, though the flowers of earth-land fade,
  We shall live in endless day;
For though the flowers of earth-land fade,
  We shall live in endless day.

WAITING, ONLY WAITING.

I AM waiting, only waiting,
  For the dawning of the day,
When the joys of life relating,
  I shall walk the heavenly way;
    Then no longer sadly waiting,
      I shall sound the joyful lay;
    Then no longer sadly waiting,
      I shall sound the joyful lay.

I am waiting, hoping, trusting,
  That the future fair and bright,
Every wrong and ill adjusting,
  Shall announce the rule of right;
    Then no longer sadly waiting,
      I shall see the joyful sight;
    Then no longer sadly waiting,
      I shall see the joyful sight.

I am waiting in the twilight
  Of a morning yet to be,
When upon my fading eyesight
  Angel forms shall come to me;

Then no longer sadly waiting,
Heavenly glories I shall see ;
Then no longer sadly waiting,
Heavenly glories I shall see.

Thus we all through life are waiting
For the coming of the morn,
When, life's pleasure reinstating,
We shall be as angels born ;
Then no longer sadly waiting,
We shall hail the glorious dawn ;
Then, no longer sadly waiting,
We shall hail the glorious dawn.

THE IDEAL AND THE REAL.

AN ABSTRACT OF A LECTURE DELIVERED BEFORE THE
MARSHALL (MICHIGAN) LECTURE ASSOCIATION, BY
A. B. WHITING, FEBRUARY 25, 1870.

WEBSTER defines the Ideal to be a conception of the mind proposed for imitation, realization, or attainment, while the Real is that which actually exists.

It is the nature of man to aspire, to hope and strive for something better in the future for himself, and for those who come after him. He forms an ideal of that good which he desires, and labors earnestly to attain it. All improvements and inventions first exist in the human mind, in the mind of an idealist.

The speaker referred at length to the ideal in art and mechanism, and drew a graphic picture of the idealist Galileo, as he bowed before the throne of the Sovereign Pontiff and tendered him the wonderful telescope he had invented, asking not honors, but mercy, and was hurried away to a dungeon; while the Pope declared, by virtue of his infallibility, that the world was *immovable.*

The railway and the steam engine are very real to us, but a few years ago they had no existence, save as an ideal in the mind of man; and when Stephenson first proposed to build a steam carriage to run on rails, and claimed that he could attain a speed of twenty miles

19

an hour, his friends said, "Don't! nobody will believe it *possible;* just say *nine* or *ten* miles an hour and we will try and help you." But when the engine was built it *did* run twenty miles an hour, to their great astonishment; and now it seems very strange to us that its success should have been doubted.

. Franklin was an idealist, and his theories laughed at by the intensely practical men of his day, until he drew the lightning from the clouds to testify for him. After him came another idealist, Morse. . His mind had conceived the possibility of making electricity the servant of man for the conveyance of thought. He asked Congress for aid to enable him to demonstrate his theory, but was met with sneers and gibes by the wiseacres of only twenty years ago; and an honorable member, thinking to kill the wild scheme at once and forever by turning it into ridicule, proposed that one third of the sum appropriated be given to Father Miller, to aid in demonstrating his theory of the end of the world, and another third to the investigation of the claims of the Book of Mormon. The name of this sapient legislator is preserved only in the columns of the *Congressional Globe* of that date, while that of Morse is known and honored wherever the *click* of the telegraph is heard.

All men are, in some sense, idealists. We divide them into three classes, which we call the retrospective, the taciturn, and the progressive. The Retrospective Idealist looks continually to the past, and is always mourning for the *good old days* that will never return, and lamenting the degeneracy of the present. He looks at the past through a rose-colored lens, and sees only its beauties, while its evils are forgotten. This class of idealists has always existed. Macaulay tells us that the ancient Saxons were wont to mourn the good old days of their fathers; and Ossian sings of the heroes and bards of former times, and laments the decline of valor and of song. The province of this class of idealists is to preserve the records of the past, which might otherwise be lost. The Taciturn Idealist sees only the present, and if he said anything, it would be like this: "Life is, has been, and will be always the same." There is really neither advancement nor retrogression; that which seems so is only the ebbing and flowing of waves, which exactly balance each other, and so the equilibrium is maintained. On the other hand, the Progressive Idealist says, Life, indeed, is a sea; it has its ebb tides and its flood tides; but every flood tide raises us a little higher than the preceding, while the ebb tide sinks *not quite so low;* and so goes on the grand march of ideas realized in the progress of civilization.

The speaker then sketched, in brief, the progress of civilization from its birthplace in the far east until now, having swept over this continent, it is breaking down the barriers with which the inhabitants of the celestial empire were wont to exclude all outside barbarians. Having paid, in passing, an eloquent tribute to the great idealists who were the founders of our government, Mr. Whiting then proceeded to speak of the wild fancies of fanatics, or idealists run mad, classing among these those men who expected to reform the world in a day by the adoption of *their* pet hobby or belief; those who thought they could invent perpetual motion; and the man who said he could lift himself in a bushel basket, and excused his failure by the remark that he *had* done it a great many times, but was not as strong as he used to be.

An idealist becomes a fanatic when he proposes to contravene natural law, known and capable of mathematical demonstration; but outside the domain of pure mathematics it is not wise to pronounce the word impossible; for that which seems to us so to-day may in the light of to-morrow appear the most natural of events. When Stephenson told the British Parliament that a steam-engine could be made to travel twenty miles an hour, the wiseacres of his day, all the world, said, " It is impossible." When Morse proposed the telegraph, an enlightened American people said, " It is impossible." Even when it was first proposed to build a railroad from Boston to Albany, a member of the Massachusetts legislature, in a speech opposing the bill, said, " If it *could* be done it would never pay expenses, *but* it is a *natural impossibility.*"

Nevertheless, railroads and telegraphs span the world with their network of power and intelligence, and, in the light of history, it behooves us to be careful how we pronounce anything impossible; but when a new theory presents itself, we should investigate its claims, and give it a chance to demonstrate its truth.

In conclusion, the speaker urged the necessity of a noble ideal as an incentive to the acquirement of knowledge and the practice of virtue. " We should not," said he, " become mere imitators, or try to make all think alike, to cast all minds in the same mold, as has been the dream of some ; this is as absurd as the idea of Procrustes' making all men fit his iron bedstead. It is not exact similitude, but unity in diversity, which is the plan of nature. As the diverse portions of country, so widely different in soil, climate, and productions, go to make up our great composite nationality, and as we do not strive to make all similar, and yield similar products, but rather to develop the resources peculiar to each, so should we strive, not to move all minds in the same channel, but to each develop his own individuality by the culture of all that is noblest and best in himself. So shall each fill his own place, and so, in the great nationality of mind, shall be preserved that unity in diversity which is the gage of harmony and progress.